ALSO BY

DEBBIE URBANSKI

After World

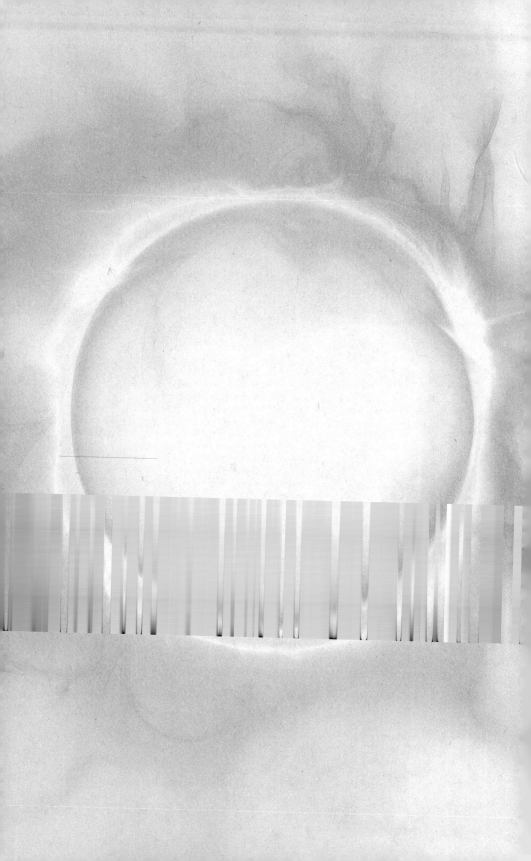

Portal mania

STORIES

Debbie Urbanski

SIMON & SCHUSTER
New York Amsterdam/Antwerp London Toronto Sydney New Delhi

An Imprint of Simon & Schuster, LLC
1230 Avenue of the Americas
New York, NY 10020

This book is a work of fiction. Any references to historical events, real people, or real places are used fictitiously. Other names, characters, places, and events are products of the author's imagination, and any resemblance to actual events or places or persons, living or dead, is entirely coincidental.

The stories in this collection were originally published in slightly different form by *Alaska Quarterly Review*, *Fantasy & Science Fiction*, *The Kenyon Review*, *Lightspeed*, *New England Review*, *The Southern Review*, *Strange Horizons*, and *The Sun* magazine.

First Simon & Schuster trade paperback edition May 2025

SIMON & SCHUSTER PAPERBACKS and colophon are registered trademarks of Simon & Schuster, LLC

For information about special discounts for bulk purchases,
please contact Simon & Schuster Special Sales at 1-866-506-1949
or business@simonandschuster.com.

The Simon & Schuster Speakers Bureau can bring authors to your live event.
For more information or to book an event, contact the Simon & Schuster Speakers
Bureau at 1-866-248-3049 or visit our website at www.simonspeakers.com.

Interior design by Lewelin Polanco

Manufactured in the United States of America

10 9 8 7 6 5 4 3 2 1

Library of Congress Cataloging-in-Publication Data has been applied for.

ISBN 978-1-6680-6111-4
ISBN 978-1-6680-6113-8 (ebook)

To anyone who has needed a portal

You'd go?

Yes.

You don't know what's out there.

That's why I would go.

—ANOTHER EARTH

Contents

Portal mania

THE PROMISE OF A PORTAL

I remember as children we were warned about the women who drove the unmarked white vans that circled around our neighborhood during those long hot summers, in particular creeping slowly down the boulevard that ran alongside the park, where if you positioned yourself at the right angle, I suppose in front of the swings, you might be able to see a flash of a child's private yellow underwear as they pumped their legs upward.

"Where'd you get that stupid idea? These women aren't interested in anybody's underwear," my mom snapped at me.

"But you said—"

"Are you ever listening? That was something else. These women are different." *The portal creepers*, my mother and the other mothers called such women. I don't know why the vans were always white and always dirty, as if they had driven through trenches of mud, or why the drivers of the vans were always female, or what they received for doing what they did. "Irrelevant," my mother told me sharply when she was describing the women to me again after the weather turned warmer one particular March, and it was only a matter of time before the daffodils sprouted up and I would be spending my afternoons at the park, on the swings. I was ordered to stay away from those vans, especially if the driver rolled her window down and looked me over in a familiar way, like a great-auntie might, beckoning with her hand, which usually held some kind of otherworldly sweet, a sticky crystalline globe, or what looked to be a salted lemon drop. I was told to avoid the globes, crystalline or not, as well as any salted drops that they might offer me. Or not me, exactly. I mean, what was offered to the other children. No one had ever told me, *You're the one I was looking for.*

I dreamed about those vans. In certain dreams, a white van paused—finally!—in front of me. The passenger window lowered. A moist and yeasty scent poured forth from the inside. Time slowed down. The driver of the van leaned out of her window and shook a piece of candy. Each movement of her arm took an hour. I stood there, uncertain of what to do, hoping the decision would [illegible] the van would drive away or the hand [illegible]

[illegible]

home for kids who didn't feel at home here. A place that turned you into something better than—"Don't be ridiculous!" my mother shouted at me. "If, one day, you forget everything I've told you, and you get into a van, and that van takes you to a portal, and that portal opens its jaws up—you need to close your eyes and run." She turned to glare out of the kitchen window. I turned too. What I saw out there was the dark. Or, rather, our reflections on top of the dark. My mother's voice quieted. "Or else you'll lose yourself. Are you listening to me? Those glittery worlds will eat you up."

The children who were taken that summer I didn't know very well, except for a girl named Leslie, who was my friend. Not my best friend. I didn't have one of those. But Leslie would let me tag along with her most afternoons to the park. We were on the swings when that particular white van pulled up and its window lowered down. I thought the driver pointed to me. She wore a pair of mirrored sunglasses so I couldn't see her eyes. It was like my dream in a way, only without the indecision. I jumped off the swing at its fullest height. I wouldn't have been surprised had I stayed suspended in the air. Anything could have happened. "Bye! I'll miss you!" I shouted to Leslie. What happened was the portal woman shook her head before I could run even a dozen paces across the grass. She pointed again, this time clearly singling out my friend. "I'll miss you too!" Leslie shouted back as she hurried past me toward the boulevard.

I hurried after her. Around us, or, rather, around Leslie, I could almost feel a new world assembling. It almost felt like a source of heat. I would have given up a lot, everything really, including my current or future family, for entry into that new world. The woman shook her head again, more sternly this time. She looked about to drive off if I continued to approach. Leslie, my friend, or whatever you want to call her, turned and shoved me to the ground. A rock cut my hand. There was some blood. I walked back to the swings alone.

I don't know what they talked about, Leslie and that woman—I was too far away to hear—but for some time they talked with great animation, and when the van's back doors swung open, Leslie climbed inside willingly, even eagerly. There was a mattress on the floor of the van, as well as a camp chair, and a bag of books, and a puppy. No one believed that I saw the bag of books and the puppy. They believed me about the mattress though. Leslie waved to me one last time, she was chewing on what looked to be a stick of sparkling pink taffy, before somebody reached around her and gently pulled both van doors closed. "Why didn't you get anyone? Why didn't you scream?" I was asked afterward. I offered many different answers to those questions. None of my answers were the right ones.

The next day, our mothers marched downtown to the mayor's office, where they took over the sidewalks and shook their hand-lettered signs. "WE ARE OUR CHILDREN'S HOME!" they shouted. "HOME! HOME! HOME!" After a week of protest and chanting, the mayor appeared on the front steps to City Hall and promised a crackdown. Police cars stalked the roads around the park. Every white van that surfaced was pulled over, searched, towed. The drivers, now in handcuffs, hollered shrilly about performing a service: all they had done was take some kids to a place [illegible] crime? The police said [illegible]

It was arranged for an [illegible] the playground for the remainder of the summer. Our mothers believed this would cheer us up. Every day we were allowed one or possibly two ice cream treats, depending on the treat you chose: two Bomb Pops or one King Cone. Two Dreamsicles or a Chipwich. I always ordered ice cream sandwiches. "The second for my friend," I promised, though I would climb into one of the maple trees and eat both myself.

From my perch, I could watch the boulevard where the police forced the vans to pull over and park. The drivers who climbed out of the vans were old, as old as our mothers, or older, though they raged as our mothers never did. There was something animal about those ladies, how, under the gaze of the officers, they shook, paced, howled, bristled. One of the women reminded me of a crocodile. It was the way she stared. Or there was the woman who brought to mind a snow leopard—who, in the space beside her van, prowled back and forth, as if readying for a hunt. She wore a smoky-gray jacket buttoned to her chin and a pair of matching gloves, though there was no reason to wear gloves on such a mild day. When an officer began the process of herding her into the back seat of his squad car, she first twisted around to stare in the direction of the park. Nobody had looked at me in those trees before. She looked in my direction and shook her head roughly, sadly, like someone, like me, had already made, or was about to make, a mistake. I've been looking for a portal ever since.

The women and their vans did not come back. As for the girls—as it was mostly girls who had been taken—they also stayed away, often for years. We forgot about many of them. Their desks were filled at school by other children with similar sounding names, and when the portal girls finally did return, they weren't children anymore. I wonder what that feels like, to be watched as a child, to be chosen, devoured, then spit back out. I bet some part of that process is nice. I wouldn't know. Usually the girls were discovered in ditches. They were clothed in thin luminescent fabrics. Often they were crying. It was assumed by our mothers that the girls were crying for their snatched childhoods, that they had wanted to come home all these years but couldn't, despite whatever stories the girls tried to tell at first.

My classmates shied away from the portal girls. "They freak me out," complained a boy seated behind me at their welcome back assembly. This was a common complaint. I think he meant the jerkiness of their motions and their bright eyes. But I had so many questions for them. I went to their houses, and if there was no answer when I knocked, I rang the doorbell repeatedly. Whoever answered the door always looked worried. Sometimes the worried adult right away would order me home. Other times, they said, "Not too long, okay?" and ushered me up the stairs. The girls would be in their bedrooms, lying on their frilly beds. They didn't look normal anymore but it's hard to say why exactly. They looked uncomfortable, though their beds were soft and covered in pillows and quilts. I wanted to know where they went, and what they saw, and why did they come back. Did they have to come back? And whether they were someone different there, and how do they find their portal again, and could they bring me with them next time. They hated my questions. One threw an ugly porcelain doll at me, at my neck. Another faced the wall and wouldn't stop screaming.

Still, our mothers made us invite the portal girls to our sleepovers and special events. At my cousin's twelfth birthday party, the lost girls huddled in the living room, their faces strange. It was hard [illegible]

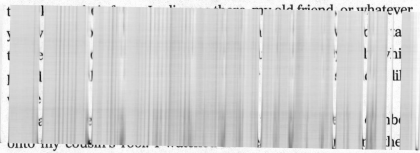

onto my cousin's roof. I watched [illegible] the through the back window, I watched her scale the railing of the deck and hoist herself onto the lower eaves. I didn't stop her or tell anyone. Someone else must have told. My uncle rushed to get the ladder from the garage. He dragged the ladder to the side of the house but before he could reach her, Leslie jumped. We were told she disappeared in the distance between the roof and the ground. An ambulance was called anyway, and we were ushered away from the windows. My mother relit the candles. We had to sing "Happy Birthday" again while the ice cream puddled on the cake.

Several girls who went to that party, not portal girls, but girls like me, jumped from their own roofs in the weeks that followed. I would have tried this too if it had worked. That November, I first found blood on my underwear, and right away I sensed a change in the air, a closing off, and a new feeling of disgust. For a time, it was like all the portals went away.

I grew up. I met someone. I got a job. We bought a house. I tried loving my partner more than a portal. This is what adults grow up to do, correct? What I mean is *wanting*. I tried wanting her more than another world. The day we closed on our home, a 1920s bungalow nestled at the bottom of a hill, I walked around each of the empty rooms. The foyer of our house had a stained glass window that let in a golden light. The doorways between the rooms were charmingly arched. If I felt the possibility of a portal nearby, the first portal I sensed in a long while, I did not turn to look. Instead, I took my partner's hand and led her outside. We looked out on the rectangular swath of land that was now ours. From our deck we watched the setting sun color the sky. "The home of my dreams," declared my partner, and I wondered was this really all she dreamed of. She rubbed her fingers across my knuckles. I looked at her and touched her hair instead of turning around.

I thought becoming a mother would help. A lot of women talk about how motherhood has made them necessary. I convinced my partner that we should adopt a pair of children I heard about online, two siblings from Indiana who needed to be placed in an all-female home. It took half a year to finalize. My new daughter liked me to carry her around the house, up and down and up the stairs, though she was six and it hurt my back to carry her. My son insisted we read to him all the time. He didn't care what the books were about. I read him the unabridged version of *A Secret Garden*, which contained many lengthy descriptions of plants. I read him Studs Terkel's *Hard Times*. He didn't care. Certain evenings we sat in the family room beside the fireplace, eating stovetop popcorn and playing collaborative board games where no one wins. Those were the good evenings. There were other evenings. I think I was expecting to feel happy.

Once I punched the stained glass that hung in our foyer. "Look at this, the window's broken," I pointed out to my partner the following day. We smoothed Scotch tape over the cracks. Neither of us had any idea who to call to fix such a thing. Once I grabbed my son and squeezed him as hard as I could. I don't remember the reason. I remember my son had developed a habit of pretending I wasn't there. Perhaps that was it. Honestly, I think the problem was that people—my children, yes, but also my partner, and my coworkers—kept expecting someone different in my place. If I spoke using my own voice, or acted naturally, acting like who I was, a tangible sense of disappointment overtook the room, like an acidic smell in the air. As if, as long as I stayed, I would be re- [illegible] body believed in them or not.

I began looking for my portal again. "What are you doing?" my partner asked when she found me standing on a stool in my son's closet. I looked in all our closets. I looked in our sugar canister, and in the trunks to both of our cars, and in the gutters to the garage. I crept into our crawl space where no one ever went. Had I found a portal in any of these places, I would have left my family. Surely there were other women out there, less selfish women, who could have easily stepped in and taken my place. There was only sugar in our sugar canister. There were clothes in our closets, and flattened paper bags in our trunks, and dead leaves plus one dead squirrel in the gutters. In the crawl space, I discovered a ground beetle infestation that had to be dealt with by an exterminator who couldn't come until the following Thursday. At night, in bed, my partner coiled and asleep beside me, I sensed doorways creaking open ever so slightly, enough to let through the hint of a foreign breeze, a breath. It had been years since I felt such possibility.

At work, I researched other people's portal stories on the internet. I had to do some pretty fantastic digging, as the news outlets still preferred to report only on the kids who went through, the girls in pigtails, the occasional wide-eyed boy. I wasn't interested in those kids or in the dirty old vans that had returned to the parks. *The portal creepers*, the newspapers still called them. I wanted to learn about the adults who left. After weeks of serious study, my efforts finally paid off as I started to perceive a pattern, or the possibility of a pattern, concerning which adults found portals, and when, and what they were doing when they found theirs. I took copious notes on a yellow legal pad while pretending to converse with potential customers on the phone. My notes went on for many pages and would have gone on for much longer if my manager hadn't rifled through my desk while I was on break and photocopied my research. She brought the photocopies to an HR meeting, along with my computer's browsing history. "But I need my job," I said. My manager agreed as she escorted me to the back entrance, where my bike was chained to a lamppost. She waited on the sidewalk until I rode away.

My partner left not long after. She had become tired of living with a person who wanted always to be somewhere else, somewhere she was not. At least this was how she phrased it. I asked her to take the kids. But the kids had never been her idea. Besides, wherever she was going, it was not a suitable place for a little girl and boy. "Where are you going?" I asked. She kissed me once, hard, on my forehead and promised to send a monthly check to cover the mortgage until the house sold.

The house sold. A week later I was driving west with my children to Illinois, to the place where I grew up. It was the middle of tornado season. There were many more tornados than I remembered. Numerous afternoons that first summer were spent huddled in my parents' basement beside the holiday boxes—ORNAMENTS, WREATHS, LIGHTS—my mom clutching her flashlight that she occasionally shined into each of our faces, making sure we were still there.

Here is how I now spend my day: I wake up. I wake the children up. I tell them to get dressed. I put out a box of cereal, milk, and two bowls, plus two spoons. I remind my children to get dressed again. [illegible] wearing the same clothes they wore the day before, [illegible] I drive them to [illegible] elementary school [illegible] the backseat [illegible] seat with their [illegible] parents' [illegible] cause of my predicament. In the afternoon, my children come home from school, and they are as ravenous as monsters. I am supposed to be finding an office job. I may still be wearing my sweatpants. I put out a box of crackers that are infused with a kind of cheese product. The history of my life hangs in the hallway like an exhibition. The wallpaper of my childhood, the thickets of yellow and red flowers, lies flush against the walls, haunted and waiting.

"I don't have time for this," my mom warned when I first arrived at her house dragging two voluminous black suitcases behind me. My kids were starving from the drive. My mom offered each of us an energy bar that tasted like vanilla sand. This was all my parents had in the fridge, plus a pint of Rice Dream frozen dessert in the freezer. You reach a certain age, my mother explained, and you've eaten everything you've wanted to eat, and you're ready to stop eating. "That's depressing," I said. "Well, obviously, it's not," said my mom. The house was considerably less tidy than it had been on previous trips. There were piles of old *National Geographics* on the countertops. VHS cassettes with illegible handwritten labels were stacked next to the TV. Pill bottles had overtaken the kitchen, and in the family room, the pullout couch was always left in the open position, the sheets twisted into a sweaty prominence.

"That's where your father sleeps now," my mom explained. "There's no point in putting everything away, is there, if you're only going to get it out again."

I noticed other changes between my parents. My mother had begun to yell a lot. Not that I was judging her. I mean, I yelled too. Or, rather, I had yelled, before I started looking for my portal again. But my mother yelled more than I ever had. She yelled at my father that there were grain moths in the pantry. She yelled about that lingering moldy smell in her closet. The shower drain was clogged with hair—his!—again. And so forth. I understood how she felt: the frustration that this world is not as it should be and no one is doing anything about it. My father was losing his vision due to macular degeneration. He spent his day in front of the television watching what was left for him to see of our home movies. My mom yelled at him to turn the volume down. I think she was frightened. I spent entire afternoons on a folding chair beside my dad rewatching my childhood. The past had many more parties than I remembered. "What was I looking for," my dad whispered, "when I pointed the camera like that toward the sky?" My mother yelled at him to pay attention.

One afternoon, when the kids were still at school, I pulled my mother aside. "What's going on with you?" I asked. I guess it was a stressful period in her life. She said it felt like this clock was ticking. "What clock?" I asked. "Stop interrupting," she said. She had developed a growth in her neck behind her left ear. She didn't have a good feeling about the growth. I didn't tell my mother I was looking for my portal again. She probably knew.

The surgery to remove the growth from my mother's neck was scheduled one month out. There was the chance it would affect several important nerves in her face or that the biopsy would come back as malignant. "All a part of life," my mom explained to me, as if everybody at one point must undergo this surgery. We were sitting in the kitchen again, drinking mugs of decaf tea and waiting for the after-school bus to bring my children back. On the television I was five years old (braids, tulle) and dancing in the yard. I asked my mother what she was looking forward to after the operation.

[illegible]

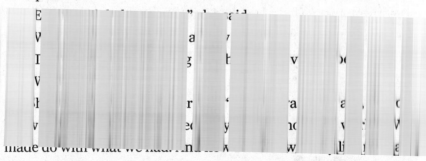

made do with what we had. And [illegible] ter how small it may seem to you. It sounds like an exhausting way to live, how you're living."

"And how exactly am I living, Mom?"

"You're always looking for an alternative." She touched my hand. "I bet this place could feel like home if you tried harder." What I mean is, her hand, for a moment, rested on mine. Her fingers felt bony, skeptical. I think you can love people—children, mothers—and still want to leave them.

On the far side of a portal, there is a place where, instead of having bodies, there is only a bunch of thoughts floating around, and the thoughts interact with each other and entwine. Or there is another world where one's body keeps changing, or else it never changes, or else you get to choose what body you have. And bodies have whatever purpose you want them to have. There isn't just one purpose, and after that purpose is gone, you've failed, and you might as well be dead.

My mother and I took walks together in the late morning. At first we only saw the usual suburban landscape, the lava rocks and the lawn ornaments, the barberry bushes and the retention pond, but a week in, we noticed a white van identical to the sort that once roamed our neighborhood. The next day we saw another white van, and the next day another. I had no idea where the vans had gone these past years or why they were now resurfacing. My mother tensed each time she saw one, though the vans never slowed down for us. "I guess we'll have to tell the children," my mother said. That night, she devoted the dinner table conversation to the dangers of portal creepers. Her talk bored my kids. I wonder if it feels like these sorts of things happen all the time nowadays, children leaving for other worlds. "We know, Grandma," my son said.

The next morning before our walk, I filled an old backpack with essentials for a journey. I wanted to be prepared. It was like I knew. A bank of shredded clouds moved eastward above us and the wind was quickening. There looked to be a storm on the horizon or at least there was a definite drop in pressure. My mother asked to rest at a nearby park under a picnic shelter until the skies cleared, and it was here, while sorting through my bag, attempting to reach a flask of water that had shifted to the very bottom, that I saw my first portal.

Or rather, this was when my mom pointed the portal out to me, as I had walked past it. As it had blended into the shadows of the trees.

But I was the first to walk past it.

It was not how I imagined a portal to look. It looked like a patch of darkness in the shade. "Oh, wow," I said. On the other side, there appeared to be more darkness.

"Hmmm," said my mom.

"Maybe it's night over there," I told her.

A chilly and complicated breeze blew through the portal's doorway, carrying the scent of damp citrus. I heard water dripping onto a hard surface.

"Ready?" I asked.

"No," she said.

I gave her a moment.

"Are you ready now?"

"I don't think this one is yours, dear," she said. At first I won-[illegible] but then it became obvious to me, the citrus. [illegible]

My mom [illegible]

She said she needed my father there.

"But he's not here," I pointed out. This made no sense. Whatever two old people looked like when they loved each other near the end of their lives, my parents didn't look like that. They did not finish each other's sentences. They did not touch each other with affection. In fact, they didn't touch each other at all. "I don't know how long this portal is going to stay open," I told my mom. "Look, it could be one of those healing portals. It has that kind of orange smell about it, doesn't it? If you go through, I think you're going to get better." I motioned to her neck. "It's your portal, Mom. I can't go through it alone."

She told me she was going nowhere unless my father was present.

"Go home and get your dad," she said.

I ran home and found my father napping in the family room while a video played on the TV of my younger self battering a piñata that I couldn't break. "Wake up!" I yelled. It took my dad a while to open his eyes. I shook him awake. My kids were sprawled out on the kitchen floor, drawing pictures of the monsters who lived beneath their beds.

"Kids!" I said. "Do you want to see the portal I've been searching for my entire life?" They wouldn't look up from their drawings, so I put on a documentary for them to watch about other worlds and told them if we weren't back soon, they should go knock on the door of our neighbor Mrs. Geshem.

My father couldn't run briskly anymore. He couldn't run at all, nor could he find his shoes. "Don't worry about your shoes," I said. "Shoes aren't that important right now." I had told my mother if the portal began to fade, she needed to hold it open with her hands. "I don't think it works that way," she said. If she couldn't hold it open with her hands, then she should jump through it, I told her, and keep it open from the other side. My dad agreed to wear his indoor slippers after I promised to clean the soles if we returned home.

The portal was gone by the time we reached the park.

My mother, sitting at a picnic table, was looking into the tumultuous sky.

"I saw a portal," she whispered.

"I'd like to see a portal myself someday," my dad said.

"I'd also like to see another portal," I added, "though it took me twenty-five years to find this one."

"Actually, I was the one who found it," said my mom.

A gray squirrel scurried down one of the trees as my parents discussed where the portal went and whether it would appear here again anytime soon. The squirrel approached the spot beyond the picnic table, the spot where the portal had been, and it stood on its hind legs and looked at us with what could have been pity. Its sad, dark, ringed eyes. "Go away," I told the squirrel, and it vanished into the shade.

Back home, I couldn't find my kids at first. It turned out the DVD had begun skipping, so they ran, sobbing, to Mrs. Geshem's house. It was unclear whether they were sobbing because they finally realized they were left alone or because their space documentary was damaged. "It wasn't even twenty minutes," I told them in Mrs. Geshem's yellow kitchen, my son and daughter clutching onto their mugs of warm milk sweetened with a local honey. We were in that kitchen when the storm hit, hammering the windows with rain. My parents' basement flooded. A lot of boxes labeled CHILDHOOD had to be thrown out. This bothered my mother more than me. She said she felt like she was throwing [illegible]

[illegible] her second dream, she found out her mom, dead for decades, had all this time been saving an apartment for her. The apartment was a one-bedroom and overlooked an alley. It wasn't big enough for a family. My mom didn't know what she was supposed to do with such a place, or what her dead mother was trying to tell her. In the dream, my mom spends hours, days, searching through the closets, and under the mattresses, and in the cupboards, for a hidden message. Neither of my mother's dreams seemed that important. I suppose other people's dreams rarely do.

There were complications with the surgery. NOTHING I DIDN'T EXPECT, my mom scrawled on her dry-erase board since talking wasn't possible for her then. CAN'T COMPLAIN. AFTER ALL I CAUGHT A GLIMPSE OF ANOTHER WORLD THAT DAY AT THE PARK! IF ONLY YOUR DAD COULD CATCH A GLIMPSE TOO, she wrote, then drew an unhappy face. The marker she used was red, which, when paired with the capital letters, added an urgency to her words. She ate bowls of applesauce for lunch and pureed vegetables for dinner.

After a three-day stay in the hospital, my mom returned home. There was a bag attached to her neck via a plastic tube that my dad drained every day in the powder room sink. No longer having the energy for our morning walks, she took brief afternoon strolls with my dad instead, not long, to the end of the block and back. They went even when the storm sirens were wailing and the sky looked sick. My dad wore a pair of binoculars around his neck while my mom held a notebook. On their initial walk, they spotted two portals glinting in the distance. On their second walk, they saw five. One of the worlds through the portal looked very soft, my dad said. Like if you took a step onto that world, you would sink right through to its very center. One of the worlds contained only the colors of a sunrise.

I didn't understand why portals kept appearing to my mom. Because she was closer to dying now? Because the portals were getting tired of their usual fare, all those energetic children, so they wanted someone old and dying? I trailed my parents on their walks. "Where are you going?" my daughter asked. I learned how my mother's portals seal up if anyone but her gets too close. How they dissolve in a gentle rush of air. Once there was a row of them, each a varying degree of brilliance, the last one blinding. When my mother saw such portals, she pointed and laughed, jotting an observation in her notebook, as if she had just spotted a mildly interesting bird.

My mother never recovered from that surgery. Last week, she barely had the energy to get out of bed. Her daily walk consisted of strolling from her bedroom into the kitchen with my father at her side. Her portals have begun to line the hallway of this house. They appear in the kitchen windows. I would have gone through any one of them with her.

STAY AWAY FROM MY PORTALS, my mother wrote. YOU ARE NEEDED HERE.

But no one is that precious. Each of my mother's portals is, in my opinion, becoming more beautiful, like an attempted seduction is going on. At times there is a portal in every window of our house. This makes it difficult to distinguish the actual world outside. Certain portals appear to be constructed out of translucent silk. Other portals undulate as if made from waves. They smell of mountain passes or rain. Sometimes I can't help reaching out to touch them. If rea t ou t e n, ey c u e di ss e. oc *h*

My nc er va s h beau if l e a y. e n s a lc l tc mu h e n s. Y U K O V N E I D F N Y. A VAY F T C N U H L A D M T, L K V C U she wr in e t ic red l tt ri . f th r r , e s s ppe w rin h n eup. I o l 't co e e r e S stopped dyeing her hair as well. At this point, there are too many portals gathering around her, and she no longer keeps a record.

My daughter tells me the windows of the white vans cruising past her and her friends have begun lowering. She has gotten the feeling that someone, or something, is looking for her. "That doesn't have to mean anything," I tell her. I don't know what to tell her. Right now I am trying to construct a map of all the places my portal isn't at a specific moment of time. The leftover spots will indicate where my portal might still be. It is, I hope, only a matter of probability.

"Going through a portal isn't giving up," I told my mother. "It isn't abandonment at all. It's about radical love and second chances. It's about believing in the possibility of other worlds and finding the world where you belong."

ABANDONMENT, my mother wrote.

She wrote, GIVING UP.

At the bottom of her marker board, she drew a complicated shape in outline with numerous sharp angles. It could have been a maze. It could have been creeping vines, the kind that strangle you in your sleep, or else the kind that grow a single starry flower. There seemed to be no beginning and no end to the object she drew. I think it had a heart in its center, though my mother has never been much of an artist so it might not have been a heart. Then the timer on the microwave went off, reminding me to pick up my children at the end of the block. It was another windy day and the squirrels stayed away from me.

Do you know what it feels like to be on the verge of leaving the world? It feels like a part of you is finally about to be torn open, a part of your face, the fake part, the part that's smiling. I am not going to be surprised when that happens. On the way to the bus stop, I watch a white van, mud splattered all over its side, drive down our street slowly. At the corner, where my children wait in the morning, or where I wait for them in the afternoon, the van pauses. The wind blows harder. A piece of trash, a generic yogurt container, is picked up by the wind and taken.

HOW TO KISS A HOJACKI

The first thing you should do, assuming you're the normal one: You should open your mouth. You probably [illegible] this should [illegible] already. But don't [illegible] the way [illegible] you [illegible] kiss [illegible] your partner [illegible] different [illegible] or whoever [illegible]. Y[illegible] to [illegible] anybody away. [illegible] mouth [illegible] a [illegible] le, [illegible] trying to make your lips pliable and warm[illegible]s. A[illegible] help show how friendly you are and [illegible] how will[illegible] increasing list of [illegible] zones. Next, the Hojacki, or the Smith Smith, or the Tanger—the person who is becoming one of these Wonderfuls—needs to open their mouth too, at least a little. Or else it will feel like you are kissing a fleshy wall. At the very least, they'll need to stop acting as if their lips have been sewn together by an invisible thread.

Michael had printed these instructions off some website. He was trying to make things work, but he didn't know how to get his wife to do this last part.

• • • •

If you try to touch me with your tongue, I will scream, Michael's wife wrote on one of her ugly yellow Post-its. The two of them were in the kitchen. Nailed to the kitchen wall was a calendar featuring photographs of funny long-haired cats. There was a red bowl in the center of the island meant specifically to hold apples. The bowl was empty, as the apples at the supermarket these past few days had been of low quality. "How are you going to scream if you can't talk?" Michael asked. *I don't want to feel your tongue, okay?* she wrote. Michael added that to the ongoing list in his head. *I will not touch my wife's stomach. I will not touch her breasts. I will not touch her genitals. I will not touch the insides of her thighs or any part of her thighs. And I will not touch her with my tongue.* His wife wore her hair braided, as the Hojackis tended to do in the photographs online. A loose green dress hung from her shoulders. The dress looked like a green sack. All of her clothes were sack-like on her now, as she no longer ate solid food. He was still in love with his wife. He was in love with a previous version of her.

"You used to like doing this," Michael reminded her.

His wife wrote something down on her pad of Post-its. He stuffed the note, unread, into his pocket. She smelled of cloves and disinfectant.

"It means a lot to me that you're trying," he said. This was what he had read he should say whenever he attempted intimacy, even if his wife wasn't trying. Again, his wife wrote something down on her Post-its. He walked into the yard and raked the dead leaves into several wet piles. The woman he married existed somewhere, he believed, in some hidden well of his wife's current body. His wife had told him otherwise, but he knew his wife better now than she knew herself. He had known her and loved her for twenty-two years. He needed to find that well and reach inside, no matter how dark the place was, or strange, and bring her back to him. Using the rake, he kept scraping the same spot of lawn until he was tearing away at the grass and the soil below the grass, and he made himself stop.

When he came back inside the house, the kitchen was empty. "Hello?" Michael called. The family room was also empty, but the evening news was on. A reporter on the feed was asking Cheryl Mooney about her opponent's proposal of a mandatory quarantine for confirmed Wonderfuls. A temporary quarantine, of course, only until somebody, some agency, understood what was going on. Mooney asked the reporter what he was afraid of. The reporter replied, "I think it's more about protection, about 'protecting what we identify as human.' I'm quoting Georgie Kloburcher here." Mooney asked, "Is our definition of humanity so narrow that it cannot include me and people like me?"

Mooney and Kloburcher were running for governor that fall. Mooney was in the early stages of changing, while Kloburcher was not changing like that, nor would he ever allow himself to do so. Some people guessed Mooney was changing into a Tanger, but Michael thought a Hojacki was more likely. Already her eyes looked different. Her eyes looked like the eyes of Michael's wife, like she saw something, something better in addition to what everybody else could see.

The reporter said to Mooney, "Yes, that's right. We have a narrow and science-based definition of what is human," and Michael turned off the screen.

Kloburcher had entered the race as an independent, promising "to call shit, shit." He labeled the Wonderfuls as a threat to future normalcy and stressed this was a state issue, a New York issue, as New York had the highest transformation rate by far, followed by Wyoming, which wasn't even that close. His stump speech stressed his commitment to scientific rigor, plus mandatory participation in government studies, and also quarantine and sterilization if it came to that. Michael did not want his wife sterilized or interned, but he understood what Kloburcher was getting at: Here was a problem that needed to be solved.

It was mentioned that a governor might not possess the power to enact any of Kloburcher's suggestions. "Limits have been known to fall away in times of great adversity," Kloburcher replied.

It started out as a small, weird story in the UK, with several women in Framlingham displaying identical symptoms of stabbing back pain, discolored tongues, and a nonexistent libido. Rogue bacteria in the water supply were blamed, or else it was the changing hormone levels of the middle-aged females. The women's symptoms escalated to include visual hallucinations, selective mutism, a repulsion to sex with any gender, and weird physical alterations of the body, such as a bluish tint to one's skin. They believed they were changing into something. At the government's expense, they were transported to London via a secure van and examined by experts. Poisoning by heavy metals, a psychosomatic illness, an infection from a tick-borne parasite, insanity, a supernatural occurrence, forbidden travel between two worlds–before any accurate conclusions could be made, the women unstuck the wires from their skin, rose out of their hospital beds, and left.

In the photos on their Patreon page, they wore matching green dresses that brought out the sudden deep green of their eyes, the hems falling far below their knees. *No longer are we seeking explanations for what is happening to us*, they explained in their overview. None of them looked so unusual in these early photographs until they opened their mouths.

The initial story on the Framlingham Hojacki aired on an unpopular BBC radio show. Michael's wife listened to the show every evening while drying the dinner dishes. By this point, the group of women were refusing to speak or else they couldn't, so in the studio, on air, live, they rapped against a set of wooden breadboards, an urgent, angry rapping. Michael's wife complained about her own symptoms not long after, as if the show itself were a contaminant. The backaches, the itching tongue, the vivid daydreams. Later, she insisted she always ached in such ways.

Michael remembered his wife otherwise. He remembered her naked and swimming last May across a rural pond thick with pollen. She swam toward him, her body fluid and careless, the only beautiful thing in that water. When she pulled herself onto the dock, she had been fully visible to him.

Michael's wife did not remember the pond like that.

She went online and stayed up most of the night, searching for other possible causes for her symptoms. There were no other possible causes. She woke him at three in the morning. "Look at my hand," she said, holding out her hand. She was still talking to him then, though her voice was hazy and already half blocked. She tapped her nails. "The color," she said. A pale blue tint. It did not look severely blue. It did not look like a big deal. "Come back to bed," Michael said, reaching for her. She did not come back to bed.

The next morning, in the kitchen, after the kids headed off to school, [illegible]

QUESTION: [illegible]

ANSWER: [illegible]

QUESTION: *Is the fact that my partner is now a Hojacki partially my fault?*
ANSWER: *Maybe. We are researching the causes.*

QUESTION: *Is this a phase my partner is going through?*
ANSWER: *No.*

QUESTION: *Is it true that at some point my partner will stop speaking to me and, after that, her voice will never come back?*
ANSWER: *Yes.*

Her breath smelled of peppermint and something sour. She didn't look at Michael. She looked in front of him. She looked over his right shoulder. "What are you looking at?" Michael asked. She said she saw things now. A hive of silvery cells hanging off their fence post, or a flaming bird that could block out the sun if it wanted. None of that stuff was there. Despite the Q&A, he assumed his wife would grow out of it. "I want to find a way to keep loving you," he said, and, throwing the handout aside, he pulled her to him, and he kissed her. In order to kiss her, he needed to pry her mouth open with his tongue. He lost track of their boundaries, which parts belonged specifically to her, and which were his. He loved this confusion. His wife complained of a coating in her throat afterward. He made her cups of tea laced with manuka honey.

By the end of the summer, his wife had struck their monthly night of intercourse from the calendar. She had also stopped talking. *I am changing into something else! Something that cannot have sex*, she wrote. "I'm your husband!" he insisted, rewriting their sex night onto the calendar. She crossed it off with a thick black marker. He wrote it on again. Each calendar month featured a photograph of a long-haired cat wearing a fancy hat. It was a ridiculous calendar. September's cat wore a top hat. His wife tore the calendar from its nail and threw it into the garbage. On top of the calendar, she piled watermelon rinds and tomato seeds. His daughter cried, having imagined the calendar's cats were her cats.

Michael told his wife that she should see a psychiatrist.

"I'm not the one who appears to be afraid," she replied.

• • • •

When Michael and his wife first met, and all through their engagement, they had sex every night. He had a drinking problem then. For years they dated and fucked, he often drunk, his future wife not. He was her first boyfriend. If they were apart for longer than several days, he wrote her letters, and in these letters, he professed his love and sketched crude drawings of the two of them in bed. This was before cell phones or email. She had written him back. She had written, *If we weren't together, I think some bad thing would happen.* He kept her letters in a shoebox at the bottom of his closet, planning to pass them on to their future children. Michael did not know what happened to the letters he wrote his wife. There were no shoeboxes on the floor of his wife's closet.

A month before the wedding, he stopped drinking. This made him a better person, he assumed, at which point his future wife stopped agreeing to have sex with him every night. This was, to Michael, confusing. He told a friend about it. "You mean, *you* stopped wanting to have sex once *you* stopped drinking?" "No. [illegible]

When sex dwindled to a biweekly event, Michael bought books for them to read, a stack for her and a stack for him. This was before anybody had heard of the Hojacki. His books dealt with how to pleasure one's partner in bed. His wife asked him to stop touching her there if he tried a new idea. She was probably becoming a Hojacki during this time, she later told Michael, but she hadn't known. "That's ridiculous. The Hojacki didn't exist back then," he told her. She didn't want him to use his tongue on any part of her body.

The books he got for her dealt with rekindling desire and included fun things to do with him in bed. He didn't force her to read them, so she didn't. Instead, at night, she read graphic novels meant for children, the books their son would go on to read, about boys who put on magic scarves and suddenly they could leap through transcendent walls of light and fly through clouds.

They married on Columbus Day. Michael's mother, a schoolteacher, had thought this in poor taste, while Michael's father said, winking, "Be prepared for wild seas and savages!" After the reception, Michael drove his wife to an upscale chain hotel in a suburb of Syracuse where his mother-in-law had reserved the nicest room. Everything around him that night looked permanent and long-lasting: the heavy fabric seats of his car; the firm, indestructible hotel mattress; the flame-retardant bedspread. He removed his wife's wedding dress and folded it into a neat pile of organza or whatever it was, and he dressed her in a pale silk negligée. He was seeing things he had never seen before. He saw the connections between things. He saw that his wife's body and his body were connected by permanent threads of light. He was able to touch that light, those threads!

In the years following their wedding, they traveled a lot. They took a cruise ship across the Atlantic. They drove through the vast midwestern states until they reached the Rockies. They huddled in some mountain pass in Italy at the beginning of an early snowstorm, the scenic vista gone, replaced by a cold, impersonal white. They tired of traveling, so they had children. Then came the heavy satisfaction of watching one's child fall asleep, the hushed conversations on the couch once the children were sleeping, and the closeness that comes from creating a human being together. Michael and his wife began to know each other deeply, and he was patient and understanding, and it was only once the kids started school that he expected sex to return to a greater frequency, and he expected it to also become more profound. This did not happen.

"I was becoming a Hojacki then too," his wife later claimed. "No, you weren't," he insisted. He put the kids to sleep on certain evenings so his wife would stop acting harried and resentful. This was an idea from one of his books. Michael took charge of everything those nights, the food, cleanup, bathing, hugs, kisses, the kissing of each stuffed animal belonging to his daughter, kissing the stuffed monkey, kissing the stuffed turtle, plus the finding of his son's escaped chameleon, while his wife took an evening swim aerobics class at the Y. He expected sex on those evenings in return. His wife claimed she was worn out from the swimming. "Right," he said, leading her upstairs. In bed, he rubbed the bony protrusions of her hips and the area around her tailbone, which had become mottled. Having sex with someone who doesn't want to have sex with you is not ideal sex, but it is at least something. When positioned behind her, holding on to her stomach with his left hand and gripping her right breast with his other hand, he felt so much love for her. He wrote her a new love letter. Once he wrote on his chest using a permanent blue marker: *Love me!*

Her lack of enthusiasm was noted.

"Do you not want me anymore? Is it because I gained some weight?" he asked. "I can lose the weight."

"I want you now but in a different way," he said.

"That way doesn't count," he said.

His wife printed out forum posts for him to read. Her favorite posts read like fairy tales, such as a Hojacki woman who claimed her partner had given up all expectations and all intercourse, and in return discovered a new and satisfying closeness, a love that expanded beyond our current rigid definitions of love. How Michael hated those forums! "These people can write anything. They can make shit up. They *are* making shit up. You know that, right?" he told his wife. He refused to read any more forum posts. "I'm changing whether you read those posts or not," she insisted. Around her was an aura of achiness and complaint and anticipation. He said,

"You need to make it stop. This is not a real marriage right now. I don't know what the fuck to call it." He was scared that she didn't want it to stop. Certain Hojacki symptoms—the shadowy eyes, the darkened eyelids, the hollowness of her throat—suited his wife, adding a delicateness to her features.

The night before his wife stopped talking, she had brought him out to the deck and stood beside him, looking into their darkened yard. Even in the dark, Michael could see the lawn was a mess and in need of mowing. They had a push-mower that smashed the grass and clover instead of cutting anything down, no matter how often he had the blades sharpened. The mower had been his wife's idea. She said they would be helping to save the world.

She had not made dinner that night, though dinner was her responsibility. The kids ate bowls of chocolate cereal shaped like rabbits; Michael did not like cereal, so he didn't eat. He turned toward his wife on the deck. "There is an expectation that you cook the meals," he said. His wife replied, "I don't think you understand what's happening to me. One thing you don't understand is I want to change." A certain stillness surrounded her, a thickening of the air. He moved to stand in front of her. Otherwise she wouldn't have looked at him. "What if I don't want you to change?" he asked. Even though he stood right in front of her, she acted like it was difficult to lift her eyes in his direction. Her hair was in her eyes. She no longer bothered to push her hair away. "I'm going to become better than I was. Or truer," she said. She used to pull back her hair. "Do you understand what you'll be giving up?" Michael asked. "I won't give anything up," she said. "Hojackis aren't mothers," he said. "Says who?" she asked. "The newspapers. The video feeds. Come on, they aren't wives either," he said. "Well, then, let's rewrite the definition of a wife," she said. "You can't do that," he said. "Yes, I can," she said. He used to be able to study and adore her ears. He would touch the soft flesh of her earlobe and touch its three closed holes left behind from previous piercings. "You're going to become a fucking monster," he said. "Don't use that word. It makes you sound ignorant," she said.

She began writing notes to him the next day. Michael said, "No way. You talk or we don't communicate at all." She left notes for him on the bathroom mirror, twenty-five hastily written *I love yous*. He crushed the notes, then he took away her pen as well as her Post-its. "Talk to me," he said, quietly and calmly. She drove to Target and bought more sticky notes. She claimed her mouth had been sewn shut. "It's not sewn shut," he said. He held her head with one hand and, using his other hand, he pried her lips apart. This was difficult to do because she had tensed her jaw muscles so tightly. He ended up hurting her. "I'm sorry," he said, offering her a baggie of ice wrapped in a washcloth. After that, she only opened her mouth enough to accommodate a straw through which she sipped a high-calorie chocolate-flavored liquid. The straw was narrow. It took her a long time to finish a can. Other days she used a nutrition patch. She used to sleep curled up in her underwear. [illegible] used to s[illegible]ep [illegible]led up and faci[illegible]g M[illegible]ael. The[illegible]e [illegible] e b[illegible]ween [illegible] [illegible]d *wo[illegible]'t*," he told h[illegible] on [illegible]um[illegible]- [illegible] when he b[illegible]ga[illegible] [illegible] remo[illegible]e his pan[illegible]s an[illegible] she [illegible]ack[illegible]d [illegible]. [illegible] could no[illegible] [illegible]agine his father in [illegible]s si[illegible]ati[illegible]n, [illegible] or an[illegible] of [illegible] married uncles. His [illegible]the[illegible] wou[illegible]d [illegible] to [illegible]ho[illegible] off and taken her [illegible]fore. *T[illegible]s [illegible]*, she wrote, pointing to where she was standing, fully clothed on the other side of the room. He remembered how carefully she used to dress in the morning. He used to lie in bed and watch her dress. She used to shake the creases from each piece of clothing before pulling it on. She had worked as an office manager at a design firm until they fired her.

Her name on the forums was Mentomyll. Her avatar was a cartoon beast with green eyes and matching hair. If he could touch his wife in a certain and familiar way, he believed he could bring her back. *Coercion*, his wife wrote on a Post-it after a different night when he had almost gotten what he wanted but not quite. "You're making me sound like a creep. Actually, it's marriage. It's love," Michael insisted. Though that word she used was such an offensive one, heavy and criminal. It was a hard word to get rid of. Once, when they were dating, he drove her to a lake, and in the soft grass beside the lake, his arm wrapped protectively around her, she fell asleep.

That fall was ugly and unnecessary and windy. The kitchen calendar, were it still hanging on the wall, would have featured that month a cat in a bonnet looking out on them with ridicule and disappointment. The wind blew in every direction all at once, and Michael started walking funny, like he had a slight limp. Glossy campaign signs sprouted in the kept lawns of the neighborhood and also in the front windows, as if the houses were shouting out opposing names. And all the pumpkins left on their front steps rotted, squirrel bites in the orange flesh, and the cheesecloth ghosts hanging from the maple trees started to smell like mold. Michael had difficulty looking into a woman's face. The porn he had downloaded weeks before to his phone made him angry. It made him want to throw his phone.

"Why doesn't Mommy talk anymore?" his daughter asked in the checkout line of Trader Joe's. Michael had discovered recently, underneath his daughter's pillow, a hoard of his wife's sticky notes, each one carefully smoothed and made precious, the stack preserved in a Ziploc baggie. She must have pulled the notes out of the recycling bin. He tried to meet the eye of the store cashier, a college girl who wore her hair pulled into an unbalanced braid. The cashier wouldn't look at him. She must have known he wasn't getting any at home. The entire world was fucking, he knew. In every movie, there were couples in pillowy soft beds, fucking. He made his wife rewatch those scenes with him, and when he turned the movie off, he listened to the neighbors in the next house over moaning through the windows while their bed creaked. The squirrels outside humped each other on the tops of the trees.

He would be a different kind of husband in another life. One who woke early to cook a nourishing breakfast for the kids and his wife, who was not the wife he had currently but a woman who desired him, the woman he married. In this other life, he would be patient, and never raise his voice. He would, in hushed tones, praise everybody and everything.

Praise to the supermoon!

Praise to the bruise on the side of his wife's leg!

Praise to the milk splashed against the dining room wall, and the foyer's mildew, and the oily handprint on the window!

He made his wife get her hormones checked. "I know, we'll get our hormones checked together," he said. He wanted to make sure she [illegible] H[illegible] D[illegible] A l[illegible] el[illegible] w[illegible] [illegible] but [illegible] ill [illegible] th[illegible] rea[illegible] of [illegible] mal

[illegible] obu[illegible] he [illegible] va[illegible] t [illegible] is ne[illegible] t ra[illegible] ly [illegible] f[illegible] ow[illegible] week [illegible] th[illegible] we[illegible] er[illegible] d[illegible] [illegible] te. M[illegible] ich[illegible] a[illegible] l [illegible] d a[illegible] ed [illegible] wi[illegible] e i[illegible] [illegible] an[illegible] d t[illegible] go. *d[illegible] o[illegible] [illegible] fo[illegible] um [illegible] os[illegible] l p[illegible] te[illegible] t?* sh[illegible] wrote on a Post-it. He ended up streaming the event on their living room screen. His wife stayed in their study on the computer, printing out more forum posts.

The rally was held in a private and windowless airport hangar. The men and women who stood on the concrete floor had hopeful, needy faces. Some men hoisted children onto their shoulders, and the children cheered at inappropriate moments. "The governor is going to be a part of you, and you will be part of the governor," shouted Kloburcher. The children cheered. "Do you really want Cheryl Mooney to be a part of you, and vice versa?" Again, the children cheered. The crowd shouted obscenities. Michael heard what sounded like his own voice in the crowd. His daughter wandered into the room and sat beside him on the couch.

"That man would like to be our governor," Michael explained to his daughter. "You have to be eighteen to vote. I'm voting but I don't know if your mom will. Voting is a right, and everybody should exercise that right when they have it. For a long time, women couldn't vote, but then they could vote starting a hundred years ago." He didn't usually talk so much. He was worried about his kids, who were growing up in an environment where radical change to a person was seen as acceptable or even desirable. He felt like there were a lot of things he must now teach them single-handedly, such as the value in stability of character, and how to say *no thank you*, and the importance of keeping your promises.

"I don't want to vote," his daughter said. "Well, you can't, anyway," said Michael. The girl clutched a dirty bear made out of alpaca fur. Every week, Michael had to blow-dry the bear's fur to make it fluffy again. This was supposed to be his wife's job. His daughter pushed her face into the dirty fur. "What's happening?" she asked, her voice muffled because she was speaking into the belly of the stuffed animal. Michael put one of his hands on his daughter's neck, and the other hand he put on top of the bear.

Kloburcher said, "Who doesn't want to be different, okay? Who doesn't want to change a little? But we have to let it be known that certain ways of changing are not okay. They might be okay in Canada, or in Syria, or in Vermont, but not here. We are going to fight this shit! Whatever it is that thinks it's okay to take the people we love and turn them into something we don't understand—we are going to stop it."

• • • •

They found a therapist. Michael's wife found her on a forum. Because Dr. Sabrina lived in Ohio, she conducted the sessions over Skype, meaning Michael and his wife could sit on the couch in their family room, Michael holding the portable screen, while Sabrina sat in her home office. The forty-minute therapy sessions were funded by the government and therefore free. This was the only reason Michael agreed to it. They had to sign a waiver allowing the NIH to publish articles about them at a later date. Dr. Sabrina promised pseudonyms would be used. Neither Michael nor his wife would get to choose the pseudonyms.

For our anniversary, I bought my own flowers, Michael's wife wrote on her marker board. *I bought them from Trader Joe's.*

"You bought yourself flowers," repeated Sabrina. She sat very still in a swivel office chair. Behind her, pinned to corkboards on the wall, hung childish drawings of stick figures and monsters. It was difficult to tell the two apart in those drawings. The monsters had enormous hearts; the stick figures had fangs. "Michael, did you know your wife wanted flowers?"

"This does not seem like our biggest problem here," said Michael. "I have been celibate for months, okay?"

"You won't buy [illegible] f[illegible] o[illegible] v[illegible]?" Sabrina asked.

Michael's wife w[illegible] *re-lationship. To me,* [illegible]

"Look, having se[illegible] al, and it's powerful, an[illegible] wanting it, especially wanting it with one's wife. I just want to love you, okay?"

We need to redefine love too.

"Do you know what I actually need? I need my wife to take off her clothes in front of me with the lights on. I need my wife to want me or at least pretend to want me. I need sex with my wife because I love her and I am going insane. I need—"

Sabrina interrupted Michael. "We *need* oxygen. We *want* sex. Nobody has ever died, as far as I know, from a lack of intercourse."

So what you're saying is that you can only love me in one particular form. In one particular way? his wife wrote.

"What if I were the one who turned into something?"

I would still love you.

"What if I turned into a Smith-Smith right fucking now with those rancid fingernails." Michael's wife shrugged. "Do you even know how the Smith-Smith smell and what they eat?"

She pointed to herself. With her fingers, she jabbed at invisible points on her chest. Michael turned toward Sabrina. The therapist's legs were crossed, her notebook open on her lap. "Shouldn't you be writing some of this down?" he asked. Sabrina wrote something down. She called the two of them courageous. She told them that any problem worth solving could not be solved within one session, but already they had made progress. "Do you know what I've learned about you so far? That you each are holding on to a different and equally acceptable definition of love. And you know what? Love is large enough for both of your definitions." Before signing off, she gave them their first homework assignment: to hold a photograph from their wedding and recall several details from the day.

They could locate only a single wedding photo, the one that hung in the gold frame nailed to their family room wall. "What happened to all the albums?" Michael asked. They had spent a small fortune purchasing hundreds of semigloss photographs as part of a package deal. Michael's wife pointed to the window then she left the room.

The remaining wedding photo had been taken on the deck of a county park lodge. Michael's wife had thought the park's changing trees would create a memorable backdrop, but the trees changed early that year because of the drought. By the day of their ceremony, all the leaves had already fallen, leaving the branches of the trees empty, though the ground appeared to be carpeted in golds and reds. His wife was disappointed. Michael was not. Under a trellis, in a white wind, he promised to love her forever. Nothing about that day had been monstrous. His desire for his wife was considered normal, and loving, and good. He had felt chosen. There his wife was, choosing him out of everybody. He felt a spotlight, a kind of radiance, shining down upon his head. She had worn a strapless dress made out of multiple layers of material. Her sister dusted her shoulders with a powder that made her skin glisten. They looked too young in that picture to be making any permanent decisions. He looked like he was grabbing her waist. She clutched her yellow flowers. The bridesmaids, lined up in a row behind them, wore matching black dresses and black shoes.

The morning after the wedding, they left for a honeymoon in the Rockies, renting a cabin in a new development north of one of the national parks. The cabin had a croquet set in the garage, which they never used, and a badminton set, which they assem- [illegible] in a woods near their home. Michael had assumed, wrongly, that every cabin in that area would have scenic views. Each day of their honeymoon they drove—to a trailhead, to a lake, to a vista—and every night they had sex, he remembered in shimmering detail now, in their cabin's loft whose windows overlooked somebody's unadorned yard. For those two weeks, she had done so willingly, he thought. They lay tangled and hot on top of the moose-themed comforter, his legs twisted around her legs, as they stared into their neighbor's yard, which had been losing form in the dark. But this was supposed to happen, as it had been growing late.

"Does it have something to do with the way I wanted to have sex with you?" Michael asked once. "I know it wasn't . . . the positions, or—we don't have to have sex that way anymore. I know I used to say that we did, but we don't."

Their second homework assignment was to sit beside each other in a comfortable neutral territory, without judgment or expectation, and observe what happened. They sat on the deck in the backyard and looked out onto their strange and wild yard whose landscaping had cost them a lot of money. Their landscaper had been some big shot from outside of Rochester whom Michael's boss recommended. The guy worked alone, digging up the existing weeds and clover with a shovel, then he raked and planted the prickly flowerless bushes and native perennials around the border, inspired by a dream he had. He left them with an identification map, sketched by hand, that made the yard feel like some allegorical other land. Michael lost the map. They no longer knew the names of the plants that were supposed to be out there. The plants were all dead or dying this time of year anyway. It was late October but warm. Michael missed the sound of his wife talking. She used to talk to other people like she was reading them a story. To him, she used a private voice, low-pitched and gentle, when they weren't arguing. He had no proof of this. In her lap, she held on to a stack of Post-its, a gentian blue this time.

She wrote, *I wish we could be the same thing.*

Deer were scrounging that evening in their neighbor's yard, feasting on the hearty late-season kale. The animals triggered a motion-detector light as bright as a searchlight that the neighbor recently installed over his garage. The light illuminated both properties, the neighbor's decimated patch of winter greens and their own weird growings. Michael wished the deer would come into their yard too and eat their unidentifiable plants, but the deer couldn't do this, as the previous owners of their house had built an impenetrable cedar fence along the property line. The kids were inside in their beds, nestled around their devices.

His wife wrote, *I think my skin has these enormous pores that let certain things through, like the wind, and some seeds.* She had grown taller these past months, her spine lengthening, and a powdery metallic substance had begun to collect on her tongue, occasionally staining the corners of her mouth silver. Though other of his wife's symptoms could still be hidden with a scarf or some makeup.

The neighbor, the one with the herd of deer in his yard, stood at his patio door and stared onto Michael's deck. The neighbor lived alone. Michael's wife used to set leftovers on the neighbor's stoop when she had made too much stew or when no one liked that [illegible] back and applaud, pretending [illegible] turning into something that is not human," he had told Dr. Sabrina at their previous session. Women did not use to believe they were turning into something else. If they turned into something else, it used to be not okay. The boundaries of what was human and acceptable used to be very clear. Michael liked how things used to be. There used to be a time when, if you were born human, it was difficult–impossible?–to leave your humanness behind. "Define *human,*" Dr. Sabrina had challenged him, raising her eyebrows like this was a complex argument, one that would really stump Michael. "Define *wife,*" he had shot back. "Define *husband.* Define *spouse.* Define *conjugal obligations.* Define *making love.* Define *the legal definition of a marriage.*"

He wished he knew that neighbor's name. He could have shouted the name out loud and started a conversation with the man. Then maybe his wife would stop writing about herself. He could feel his blood bulging against the inside surface of his skin. The neighbor slid open his screen door and stepped outside onto the patio holding a spray bottle. He pointed the bottle at the deer and bellowed like an animal.

The next day, Michael broke a mug at work while trying to wash it in the sink. The handle fell off and broke into two pieces that could have been glued back together again. But who wants to use a mug with cracks in the handle? The day after that, his workplace ran out of coffee. Nobody had any ideas about how to fix this problem. Though it was not that difficult of a problem. But nobody knew whose problem it was. *You have nothing to be afraid of,* he wanted to tell his female colleagues when he met with them alone in the cramped windowless conference room. *I am emasculated.*

In addition to the Hojacki, there turned out to be the Melones, and the Drosis, and the Smith-Smiths, and the Tangers, and the Pourishes. New variations popped up almost every month. Someone else's happiness used to look recognizable. Now the happy Asbells had light shining out of their knuckles. The tips of a Chacier's ears were supposed to change color. Michael's wife sat by herself in the garage with the door closed. Was she happy? What would her happiness look like now? She held some kind of tool in her hand and used the tool to repeatedly strike a piece of wood.

Everybody else on their side of the street had already raked the yellow and red leaves to the curb. Their lawns appeared pale green and sickly while Michael's lawn looked carpeted with gold from the trees. “What happens if I don't want to rake this year?” he demanded to know. He was saying this to his wife. “What if I stop taking out the garbage? What will happen if I start eating out every lunch? What if I don't unclog the bathtub drain upstairs?”

Graphs were released showing estimated infection increases of 17 percent. The evening news ran stories of the Wonderfuls, the Hojacki in particular, who were being kicked out of their homes in substantial numbers, and it wasn't as if they had somewhere else to go. It wasn't as if they were kicked out of their homes gently, with adequate support and preparation. Occasionally there was mention of one of them seeming to disperse in an expansion of light, but more common was the appearance of their bodies sprawled across a stoop or thrown down a stairwell. During one interview, Mooney held up a photograph of a Hojacki on the sidewalk with her skull bashed in, her strange blood pooling iridescently around her head. Speaking very slowly and very clearly, Mooney stated, “So what if we don't understand their purpose? We must accept the W[illegible] have an inherent value.”

[illegible]

trigger was a lack of effort, a certain giving [illegible] ously would have been considered inappropriate.

“You are becoming a monster,” he had told her, standing on the deck on the last night she had used her voice.

“I am not a monster,” she said.

“But you're becoming one,” he said.

“I am not becoming a monster.”

“What do you think you're becoming?”

"I don't know. Myself, maybe."

"You don't know what you are."

"And, what, you can't love somebody unless you know what they are?"

The first debate aired live Tuesday night. Michael's wife refused to let him turn on the screen in the living room. She blocked his view, the remote shoved into the front pocket of her green dress. "I could push you out of the way," he said. He didn't do this. He went, instead, into the study and watched the debate by himself on their old desktop computer.

The opening question concerned the decline of economic development in the Rust Belt. Michael flipped through a stack of catalogs while the politicians droned. Twenty minutes in, the moderator read a question emailed from Jane M. in Solvay concerning whether Wonderfuls should share the same rights as regular people. *For example, should someone, or something, that doesn't appear human be allowed to vote in the upcoming election?* Jane M. wondered.

Mooney wore oversized sunglasses and a navy sweater that covered her neck all the way up to her chin. She kept her hands out of sight behind the podium. She spoke about fairness and goodness. Everything she said was vague. What she was saying made Michael want to get up and leave the room. "The Wonderfuls still belong here," she said. "'Here' meaning this planet, this country, this state, and this community. It's our job to make sure there remains a place for them. How we treat them is a clue to how all of us will be treated when the time comes."

"When the time comes?" asked the moderator.

Kloburcher cut in. "It used to be that people were born human and stayed that way. Now the Wonderfuls—who chose that name, by the way?—the Wonderfuls, they come along, and what the hell is happening to our families? What are we letting happen?" Kloburcher turned toward the left side of the stage and motioned briskly with his hand. "I have some people I'd like to bring out. Some people I've gotten to know, people like you."

"I don't think that's allowed." Mooney glanced at the moderator for confirmation. "Is this allowed?" A man and a woman walked out from behind the gold curtains. The man's hand rested on the woman's arm. He led her to Kloburcher's podium and tilted the microphone until it touched his lips. The spotlight was not shining onto the woman directly. It was shining on the man. In the half-light, the woman looked creepy and distracted, the look of a Hojacki on heavy medication. The woman either wanted to be medicated or else her husband had forced her. "My name is Anthony Papp," said the man. "When my wife became a Hojacki, she stopped caring about me. She stopped caring for her kids. I lost her, and my kids lost her. We don't need this new whatever-she-is. I need my old wife back. I don't know how to bring her back. Can she come back?"

Dr. Sabrina's third homework assignment was a page of exercises for them to do in bed. The list of exercises was labeled *Phase 1*. They tried following the handout's instructions. At least, Michael tried. They were to touch each other in a way that felt good to the person being touched. What was bearable to Michael's wife that night was his hand, unmoving, on her wrist. If he moved his fingers up her arm, light touches, gentle touches, she started to cry. *I don't want to be touched anymore*, she had written. "Come on," he said. *I don't want to*, she wrote. "This is me, loving you," he had said. He didn't know which version of his wife was crying in bed, his real wife or whoever she believed she had become.

After the exercises, they were to lie next to each other. His wife reached for her laptop, typed, then tapped at the screen: another happy forum post. "I don't want to read about those people anymore," Michael said. He noticed his wife's eyes had changed. When had they changed? They used to be a familiar blue ringed by gray. He hated his wife's new eyes, and as he lay in bed staring at her, his hatred turned into anger, and his anger spilled out from his chest like an actual force. It expanded throughout the room. It expanded throughout the house until it became larger than the house. It loomed and menaced above the roof, but harmlessly, without consequence, as there was nothing appropriate these days for a man to do with such unsuitable emotion. A man like Michael should have buried any anger he possessed in his reusable lunch sack. Never mind its insane howling. *Look*, Michael was supposed to say, *everything is always okay!* Don't worry, no one wanted to punch his fist through the drywall of his bedroom. Michael did not even think about that! He did not want to take the grocery clerk with the tattoos running up her arms out behind the dumpsters, and tear off her skirt, and fuck her from behind. The same clerk he saw every time he ran into TJ's to get whatever his wife told him to get. It wasn't the fall. There weren't a lot of dead things in the gutters. Someone hadn't started shooting the deer in their neighborhood and leaving the carcasses in the street.

He watched the second gubernatorial debate alone. He didn't know where his wife was. The children were upstairs in their separate bedrooms. He didn't know what they did in their bedrooms. The focus of this debate was security.

"Years ago, I used to think safety would look like a wall," spoke Kloburcher. "Isn't that hilarious? Do you remember the time, back when a wall and the securing of state borders could have been the solution? But a wall isn't going to cut it anymore, people. Because guess what, they're already here. They're on the inside. They're in our homes. They're in our workplaces. They're in our beds.

"I want to protect you and the sort of life you thought you were going to get, a life where you can walk down the street of your hometown and recognize where you are. I don't think that's too much to ask, to recognize what's around you. Once elected, I promise you, I am going to gather them up, and I am going to put them someplace else. Someplace enclosed and protected, and I will protect them, and I will protect you. Then we can all stop talking about them. And I mean *we stop talking about them*! So we can start focusing on other things, like our jobs, our schools, our defenses, and what we were afraid of, and why we don't have to be afraid of that anymore."

"What are you talking about?" Mooney asked. She wore the same pair of sunglasses, though this time her turtleneck sweater was a soft gray. Her hands were covered by gloves. "I mean, what is he talking about?"

"I believe he's talking about building an enclosure for the Wonderfuls," said the moderator.

"You want to intern them–is that legal? How would a governor even do that?"

"I'm not afraid to say out loud how you feel," said Kloburcher, and he looked into the camera, and he looked into Michael's eyes.

Michael's wife was asleep, and he wasn't because he couldn't sleep. So he lifted up the sheets and looked. She slept wrapped in her worn brown bathrobe. "I miss you," he whispered. The last time he had been physical with his wife, it hadn't been actual intercourse. He didn't know what to call it. She had refused to take off her underwear in bed. He hadn't the energy to rip her underwear off of her, so he had humped against her beige cotton panties. His wife once wrote to him in a letter, *The fact of us being together is keeping the world going.* This was a long time ago but that image had stayed with him all these years: love, their love, literally causing the earth to spin.

He undid the knot on his wife's robe and slid off her underwear. Using the light from his phone, he looked at her again. She was his wife. There was nothing wrong with him looking at her. He separated her legs. She had always been a deep sleeper. Her hair down there had thinned to several loose curls, and the lips of her labia had flattened. Where the opening to his wife's vagina used to be, there was only a tiny crevice no longer than a pencil eraser. He slipped the tip of his finger in her to see if he could widen the hole. He moved slowly, acting as gentle as he could. When his finger had worked partially inside of her, she began to stir. Half awake, she swatted at his arm, her face fearful and panicked.

Her fear confused Michael, as he loved her so much in that moment.

"It's only me," he said softly, though he removed his hand.

He watched her until she fell back asleep. His finger that had touched her there smelled like ocean water for the remainder of the night.

The election campaigning turned ugly. This was actually a relief. Violence erupted at Kloburcher's rallies, and it was a relief to see people from both sides finally acting like they felt. Pepper spray in the eyes, sucker punches, a lunging dog, threats chanted through megaphones, thrown rocks, choke holds, a tackling to the pavement, riot gear, swear words, screamed epithets, all of it filmed shakily on somebody's cell phone. "What country is this? Is this the United States of America? Because I can't recognize it," said a commentator, sharing another smoke-filled protest video that resembled the kind of riots usually seen only in poorer nations.

All the videos looked the same. Everybody in them shouted,

everybody's face contorted in rage. People's hands formed fists, and somebody was always panting and shaking the phone while running toward, or into, or away from the action, while one of the candidates went sneaking in through the back doors. There went Kloburcher, sneaking along an overpass and through the back door. He wanted the protestors arrested. He demanded they be roughed up and thrown out and their tongues cut off, but then, he raved, they'd probably go around moaning, tongueless, into their bullhorns and their livestreams. They would find some way for sure to continue making an irritating noise. "Do what you need to do!" he ordered the crowds who came to venerate him. "I'll cover legal fees, okay?"

Mooney, meanwhile, walked through the main entrances of her venues. She walked along the line of protestors who shouted at her and threw things, objects, some of the objects sharp and homemade. A look of disgust on the protestors' faces, or maybe it was fear. Not that people were afraid of *her*. She resembled somebody's grandmother, or she used to. It was what she stood for, what she and her body were suggesting. She was a ghost from a distinct future in which people's wives, and their mothers, changed form, and that was supposed to be okay, while husbands sat on their hands and nodded, or maybe they were supposed to clap their hands with enthusiasm while at the same time, embracing an increasingly unfamiliar world. Mooney described that future as a desired one. She would not talk about the ugliness of it, which meant, to Michael, she was not being honest. She accused Kloburcher. She accused his supporters, pointing at them in the crowds, pointing and jabbing her elongated and gloved fingers. "You think you are living in one world and I am living in a totally different world. But guess what, there is only one world, and we're living in it together."

"I hope somebody shoots that woman in the mouth," Michael said. He didn't want Mooney's version of the future either. His wife looked up. At least, he thought it was his wife. Was it his wife? That depended on what defined a person anyway. "Stop staring at me," he said. He wanted his real wife to come back and thank him for bringing her back. He wanted Mooney to stop talking. The politician noted her security guards were unarmed. "Do you wish to become a martyr?" asked one reporter. Mooney replied, "I will not tolerate any politician who plans to tell me, or people like me, that I'm no longer human. What part of that do you not understand?"

When Michael arrived home from work, the first floor of the house was dark, though he could see a light on upstairs in his daughter's bedroom. He set the carton of extra-large brown eggs and the gallon of milk and the boxes of macaroni on the kitchen island, and he climbed the stairs.

His wife was in the glider. His daughter was in his wife's lap, a fleece blanket patterned with stars draped over the two of them. The girl was too big to sit like that now. Parts of her, the ends of her limbs, could no longer be contained by the glider's frame or his wife's body. A lamp filled a portion of the room with a warm, artificial glow. The other parts of the room were dim. "Why don't you talk to me anymore?" his daughter asked. His wife's eyes remained closed. Her hand moved so it rested on the back of his daughter's head. The gesture made her look, for a moment, like a mother again. He imagined himself cracking open her stranger's body, removing the excess tissue, or fluids, or whatever it was, until the mother and wife he had known and loved was revealed.

"Can I stop talking too?" asked the girl. His wife used to read to his daughter in that chair all the fantastical classics, the books where children slip through cupboards, or rabbit holes, or a violent weather system into other worlds and their parents never notice they're gone. In such books, it was never the mother who left. His wife, or whoever that was, opened her eyes and chose a book from the top shelf. She did not put much thought into which book she chose. She placed the book into his daughter's lap and tapped its cover. A book about a bear who lost his way in the snow. His daughter began to read to herself. She was a good enough reader now that she didn't have to read out loud, though her lips still formed the shapes of the words.

Michael's son did not approach his mom to ask what was happening to her. The boy was older than his sister by several years, busy with soccer and rarely home, preferring most nights to have dinner at a friend's house elsewhere in the neighborhood.

Mooney was attacked at a rally. Her security guards did their best using their hands and their brute strength, but the attack had already happened by that point. A man wearing a baseball cap embroidered with a golden "K" punched Mooney in the side of her face with brass knuckles, then used a knife to slit open her arm. "Alien! Alien! Alien!" the man shouted as he did this. He meant the extraterrestrial kind, which wasn't accurate, as far as anybody knew. People had their phones out. The videos they took showed that Mooney did not raise her arms to shield her face, though she allowed a guard to cover her with his body. Another guard tackled the man to the sidewalk, slamming his head against the concrete, while Mooney supporters stomped on the fallen man's fingers, breaking numerous bones, then another man wearing steel construction boots kicked him in the left side repeatedly. The attack looked similar to the other videos of violence occurring outside of the rallies. The difference here was Mooney on the ground, her skirt hiked up, bleeding, and her blood didn't look normal, and she wouldn't cover up her weird-looking blood. It was argued that she had, in fact, smeared her blood over the sidewalk with fluttering movements of her hands to make a greater impression.

Mooney's campaign issued a statement: "What was done to me is of little relevance to my bid for governor. I believe, still, in equality, respect, protection, acceptance, an embrace of change, and an acknowledgment that who we are now as a society does not look the same as who we were a decade or even a year ago. I will still fight for these things. The difference being I will fight for them harder than before."

Kloburcher issued a statement explaining his previous suggestions of violence were not, in fact, invitations to violence. They had been more metaphorical: a metaphorical expression of the anger of his supporters, whose anger was understandable, as look at everything that had been taken from them. Kloburcher listed everything that had been taken from them. Crimes against the Wonderfuls, he noted, had increased 300 percent during the past six months. Solutions other than breaking the bones of the attackers must be considered, he said. Get at the root of the problem rather than hacking off the branches. At the same time, he reminded everybody that violence, or let's call it force, can be a means of communication when nobody in power is listening to you.

At ten o'clock on a Tuesday morning, which happened to be Election Day, Michael and his wife met with Dr. Sabrina for what would be the last time. Sunlight entered the room through the kitchen window and made the countertops glare white. *Am I not a man?* Michael had begun to think. *Am I not a person anymore?* He said, "I will make you leave this house, and this family, unless we start having sex again."

"Whoa! Okay!" said Dr. Sabrina, holding up her hands. "So we have something to talk about now. We have a place to start. Let's talk about your definition of sex. Define *sex*."

"I think you know what my definition of sex is," Michael said to his wife, who slumped beside him in yet another green dress. He was sick of seeing that color on her.

"Yet sex can mean a lot of things to a lot of people. Correct?"

Michael said, "You can't change the definitions of words like that." His wife clutched a pad of Post-its in her lap. She had not written a word all day. "I don't think I expect too much from you. You want to stop talking to me? You want to start drinking your meals through a straw? You want to sit around instead of taking care of the kids and the house? Fine. But part of being in love is that we are intimate in bed. I do expect that from my wife. I'm not forcing you," he said to her very clearly, not wishing to be accused of anything vulgar or illegal. "Whatever you decide to do, you are making the choice. If you refuse to have sex with me, you are choosing to get divorced. If you choose to get divorced, you are no longer welcome in this house. Think seriously about how you will get by as a Hojacki, or whatever you want to call yourself, without my financial support." Michael did not want to do any of these things. He did not want to take the children, or kick his wife out of his house, or withhold money from her. He hoped his threats would force this woman to start acting, again, like his wife. He loved his wife, only not this version of her.

"Michael, you do realize the changes Hojackis go through in certain areas of their bodies? You realize how they feel about intercourse, right?" asked Dr. Sabrina. "I am assuming you are equating sex with intercourse."

"Likewise," Michael said to his wife. "If you choose to have sex with me, then you are choosing not to get divorced. I am not ruining anybody's life."

Dr. Sabrina said, "You're angry."

"I am not some monster. This is what married couples do. They desire. They are desired. It's normal. It's called *love*."

The therapy session ended. Sabrina suggested they talk again tomorrow. In the meantime, she promised to send over a new handout with some fresh ideas. Michael closed the screen and told his wife that he still loved her, and he hoped she would make the right decision. Then he left for work, stopping on the way at the local community center, where a line of voters moved sinuously across the polished wooden floor marked for basketball games. Everybody there had an opinion about the election. Mooney was good, and Mooney was not good, and Kloburcher was good, and Kloburcher was not good. Not all these statements could be correct. The clump of women who waited in line behind Michael wore loose green dresses cinched around their waists with canvas belts. They wore buttons pinned to the collars of their dresses: *Time to change!* The argument being that someone, because they changed, or were changing, would make a better governor, or wife, or mother, or person. This was faulty logic, Michael knew. The extraordinary people were those who did not change. The people who said no! He waited behind two men who called Mooney childish names. Michael reveled in their shared humanness. The exit polls suggested it would be a close race. It didn't feel that close.

They were lying in bed on election night with their heads set upon separate pillows. Michael had given up looking at his phone. None of the news outlets would call who won. His wife rolled over to face him and nodded, her new eyes wild and curious. Or else her eyes were faraway and frantic. He had trouble reading her expressions. But it was a real nod. He did not make this up.

"I appreciate this," he said, reaching to rub her shoulders and her stomach. She tensed when his fingertips moved to touch the delicate skin around her abdomen. He said, "I appreciate you. I love you. I've always loved you. I never stopped. Give me a few minutes."

Downstairs he took hold of the bag of tea lights leftover from the Halloween pumpkins. He placed two candles in each bedroom window and lit them with a lighter neither of them used for cigarettes anymore. The room flickered. She blew every candle out. Michael removed his sweater, his T-shirt, his belt, his pants, his underwear, and his socks. He took off her green dress, her bra, and her underwear. She did not allow him to remove her socks. "It's totally okay to keep your socks on," he said. He believed his real wife was about to come back to him, at least a part of his real wife. He believed she wanted to come back and that she was able to.

His wife appeared to be fine at first. She seemed to be rocking silently along with him as he rubbed against her. He asked if she was okay as they rocked. "Are you okay? Is this okay?" he asked. She didn't shake her head to say *no* or *stop*. It wasn't as if a different version of her life existed that would take her in as she was. He leaned back and spread her legs apart then hesitated, unsure if it was technically possible to enter his wife. That hole he saw had looked so small! But also expandable. It was worth trying. In his mind, he had already tried.

He had been looking at other parts of her body as well as he could in the dark. Now he looked down at her face. She must have been biting hard on her tongue all this time. A bit of silver blood was gathering in the corner of her mouth. He brought his fingers to her mouth, intending to wipe away the blood. "Are you—?" he asked. She flexed her knee, her left knee, and she kicked him. He fe[illegible] backw[illegible]rd o[illegible] the m[illegible]ttress. Even [illegible] it [illegible] th[illegible] ca[illegible]es [illegible]e w[illegible]rld was [illegible]ick[illegible]e[illegible] as if [illegible] was in dan[illegible]e[illegible] g[illegible]t. [illegible]or[illegible]" he said. H[illegible] got [illegible]k on [illegible] of he[illegible]. Sh[illegible]e [illegible] k[illegible] a[illegible]-[illegible]r[illegible] time. Had sh[illegible] wanted [illegible]m to s[illegible]op, [illegible] h[illegible] [illegible]ed [illegible]n ag[illegible]in, Mich[illegible]el kn[illegible].

Th[illegible]at ho[illegible]e in [illegible] appea[illegible] to be stret[illegible] [illegible]u[illegible]. [illegible]w[illegible]t bone-dry down there either, he noted with relief. Still, it was difficult at first. Then it wasn't. "I love you," he said. How he meant this. He said it again, confident this was the best love he had ever offered anyone, a love he could only feel here, in a private place inside of the woman who was his wife. He held his wife, his real wife, in position on the bed on her back so she would stay in this special place with him. Her eyes were closed. "Lisa," he said, wanting her to open her eyes.

She did not open her eyes. Instead, an abrasive noise, a squeal—like a stuck animal!—eased out from behind her closed lips. He rubbed her arms, her hair, trying to quiet her. "Shhh," he whispered. Her noises increased in intensity. She was going to wake the kids if she kept that up. He rested his hand over her mouth. Every place they touched, those places were shining. She must have seen that too. After a certain point, her squealing stopped, or he couldn't hear her anymore. Who wouldn't want to shine like this? His hips shined against her hips, her mouth shined against his hand. Then the light between them became a sound, and he pushed that sound far inside of her.

Afterward, she rolled onto her side to face the window, which earlier in the evening Michael had closed and locked. The blinds were pulled. No one could see inside their room. Michael nuzzled against his wife, holding on to her from behind. She deepened her breathing and he assumed she fell asleep. He let go of her, put on his clothes, and left the house, wanting to take a walk. There were streetlamps in their neighborhood up to a mile out, after which there was nothing to see. At an empty intersection, he checked his phone. The news reports were useless. *Kloburcher!* said Fox News. *Mooney!* said the *Times*. The night was clear and cold, and Michael was underdressed. His fingers grew numb. At the same time he felt an expansive heat, a certainty in the pit of his body, which kept him comfortable. All the stars appeared to be out, covering the sky with a natural light. The only constellation Michael recognized was Orion because of the hunter's tidy three-star belt. The other constellations had never made sense to him. It was like somebody a long time ago thought they could gaze up into the stars and see whatever they wanted to see—the gods, the winged horses, the queens—and they thought what they saw was so important that they believed everybody was going to see the same things forever as well.

Back home, he removed his shoes at the front door and crept into the bedroom he and his wife shared, listening for her damp familiar breathing. Instead of his sleeping wife, he found a woman, or something, an individual sitting upright and naked on the edge of their bed. The blinds had been pulled up. Anyone could have looked in. Her–its?–body was illuminated by the porch light outside. Michael didn't recognize its features. The strands of colorless hair, the blank back that did not show the curve of any bones. It seemed an inappropriate dream, considering what had recently taken place in that bed.

He looked again.

He saw his wife, naked, her legs crossed at the ankles.

A trick of the light.

She had laid out several photographs on top of his pillow. "I thought you were sleeping," he said. "You should be sleeping." At first, he thought the photographs were close-ups of a butterfly's chrysalis stage taken at an unusual angle. He leaned in. The cocoons were enormous, and each one had been set upon a bed. Inside each cocoon was the outline of a woman's [illegible]d to her knees. The last picture showed an appendage [illegible]o, it was too odd to tell [illegible] worming its way out.

His wife wrote something down on a yellow [illegible]el did not read what she wrote. He gathered the ph[illegible]d them as best he could and threw them away. "I don't [illegible]ok at shit like that anymore."

She wrote something else down.

"I want to look at you."

She wrote something else.

She wrote something else again.

His pillow was filling up with Post-its.

"I love you so much right now," he said. "Are you listening to me?"

She wrote again. He took away her pen, and she moved to the window on her side of the room. The kids had abandoned their bikes in the driveway though snow was predicted overnight, an early blizzard. But for the moment, the ground was bare and sterile. Michael stood on the other side of the bed looking out the same window, though from a different angle so he couldn't see the bikes. *People's lives don't need to be magical to be worthwhile*, he wanted to say. *We are enough as we are. You were enough for me.* He would tell her this tomorrow. "Come on, let's go to bed," Michael said, brushing the notes from his pillow. The small square papers fluttered like lost yellow wings to the floor. His wife lay on her side of the mattress. She faced the window. He lay beside her on his back. When they woke the next morning, the world was buried.

LONG MAY MY LAND BE BRIGHT

1. My Background

For much of my life I have cared about several things, including the genealogy of my Eastern European ancestors, who immigrated here to the United States of America between 1911 to 1914 from various Polish villages, and also what preventative measures I can take now to ward off future and personal diseases, but I have not cared about politics in this country. I did not come from a family of influencers. I came from a family of people who watched other people's children for a living, who haggled at the Sunday flea markets, whose sphere of influence spread no farther than the other side of the block, if even that far. However, the recent rifts in our shared reality—the distance, both figurative and literal, inserting itself between the houses in my neighborhood, and between the rural and urban geographic regions of my state, and in fact throughout our entire country—have become impossible for me to ignore. There is a rift tangled in the lilac bush outside my home. Another rift is growing between my struggling hostas and Mrs. Slevensky's detached garage. Another rift is tearing into the asphalt in the street. If I look across my street, I no longer see the houses on the other side. I see a gash of nothingness, a fissure of silence. Each day the silence grows a little larger.

2. The Goal of This Essay

I want to leave a record so that, in case the inevitable happens, the people who come after us, the future generations, can know that once we all lived in the same country. That it was possible, once, for us all to live in a shared reality. If they can understand the process of our separation, perhaps they can figure out the process of rebinding, if there is a process of rebinding.

3. Some Notes on the Beginning of the New Compromise

The first presidential inauguration of 2017 was held on January 19, when Carl Elliot was sworn in as the Odd Day President of the United States. Although this was an unorthodox move—never before had a presidential inauguration been held on January 19!—the ceremonies and festivities closely followed tradition. Mr. Elliot attended a morning prayer service, followed by a visit to the White House for coffee with the departing president. Later he listened to invocations and blessings, as well as anthems sung by a white choir from Utah, though the fanfare was dampened by the lingering gray haze of the sky and the inconsistent drizzle. When Mr. Elliot was sworn in a minute before noon, his hand pressed down upon two Bibles. He moved to the podium, coughed into his fist, and declared from now on this was a new America—an America-First America. To those viewers who voted for Mr. Elliot in the November election, this proclamation was a relief. No longer would they have to feel responsible, neither as individuals nor as a country, for the world's expanding list of travesties, which included disease epidemics, radical Islamic terrorism, climate change, refugees, and child soldiers. "A new national pride will stir our souls, lift our sights, and heal our divisions," said the Odd Day President, and the crowd cheered. The crowd that was racist, provincial, and ignorant, according to the Evenists who watched the day's ceremony with increasing alarm.

Standing behind the presidential podium, Mr. Elliot did not speak beautifully. No one expected him to. He did not intend on being a beautiful president. He promised that proper Americans, like the people in the crowd wearing the baseball caps, would all have jobs. He mentioned feeling good about one's self but did not mention universal health care, nor did he bring up the prismatic glimmer that first appeared in the corner of one of the bulletproof panels. Perhaps he didn't notice the hungry light. He made a fist with his hand. The light mounted his hand and had anyone known what to look for, no one did, they would have seen the light had teeth, how strange, and the tiny teeth ripped into the surrounding air, leaving behind a laceration and what I believe to be the beginning of our first modern rift.

There had been talk of a revolution—or was it a counterrevolution?—planned for the afternoon. All that happened was a Starbucks had its windows smashed and somebody's limo was set on fire. Riot police tackled the responsible revolutionaries (or counterrevolutionaries?) to the ground. The media took a few smoky and atmospheric pictures, then left to cover the parade, which had better visuals and more tractors.

The following day, at the second inauguration for the country, Lillie Jetrin was sworn in as the Even Day President of the United States. The ceremony was similar to the day before. Mx. Jetrin went to church, enjoyed coffee, attended a luncheon, received blessings, and delivered their speech. And, like Mr. Elliot, a light appeared, this time near Mx. Jetrin's right ear, a light again with teeth, which nobody noticed, which ripped the air, causing, from what I understand, our second rift. "We will not a build a wall," announced Mx. Jetrin. "But we will tear walls down. We will not ban a religion; we will welcome all religions. The American Dream is big enough for everyone!" Mx. Jetrin's crowd cheered and at the same time was written off by the Oddists as globalist, godless, and entitled. This idea of dual presidencies–more specifically, alternating-day presidencies–had been the compromise the country painfully worked out after the results of the 2016 election had dissolved under accusations of ballot forgery, gerrymandering, foreign influence, and voter suppression. The parade that second day did not have tractors, but it did have additional marching bands and two astronauts. Still, viewers who surreptitiously had streamed the two-day inaugural coverage on their workplace computers found themselves bored and ready for the festivities to end.

4. *What It Is Like to Live in the New Compromise*

"You aren't ever safe," President Carl Elliot told us in his first official address. He seemed very sure of himself and very scared for us. After he read the names of people whose family members had been murdered by those who didn't belong in this country, it was difficult to look around and not be frightened. Even in the Upstate New York village where I live, there were people I didn't know, and twelve miles east was Syracuse, a city filled with strangers, many of them from elsewhere.

Two days later, in his second official address, Mr. Elliot explained that, in addition to our present lack of personal and national safety, we were also being used and misled by other countries. Putting America first meant withdrawing from any suffocating international agreements, including the Paris Agreement, which had been the previous president's environmental triumph. Global warming wasn't that important of a topic, not when America had more pressing issues to worry about, like the state of American manufacturing. Youngstown and Detroit should matter more to us than Paris or the Maldives. This all made sense. "As someone who cares deeply about the environment, which I do, I cannot in good conscience support a deal that punishes the United States," said Mr. Elliot. He said, "We need our coal mines, so we are going to get our coal mines."

In President Lillie Jetrin's first official address, they said, "We are not afraid of the future, so we are not afraid of each other." They reminded us that we began as a nation of immigrants, and the embrace of immigration and refugees is a fundamental American value. They cited data that immigrants, legal or otherwise, are less likely to commit a crime than native-born Americans, and I found my fear from the previous odd days temporarily lessening. I was beginning to learn how to adjust my thinking and my beliefs depending on which day it was and whether certain facts were being highlighted or withheld. Two days later in the White House Rose Garden, Mx. Jetrin explained that, despite what Mr. Elliot previously told us, the entire world is interconnected, and we would remain part of the Paris Agreement after all. "No nation, not even one as powerful as ours, can solve the challenge of global warming alone. We must face this challenge together. This is our most important mission," said Mx. Jetrin. Mr. Elliot released a statement the following day saying, "No, the Paris Agreement remains stupid, and we will not be part of any stupid agreements." Such back-and-forth continued for days until the two presidents were reminded by the Administrative Office of the New Compromise that they were presiding over separate realities of this country. They were encouraged to move on to some other topic. The administrative office noted it was Mx. Jetrin's turn to choose the topic.

Mx. Jetrin issued an executive order requiring federal agencies to avoid using gendered pronouns on even days and also to avoid binaries when possible to promote inclusivity, avoid misgendering, and reduce the importance of gender in our lives and identities. A portion of the executive order urged the public to participate in degendered nonbinary language as well. My spouse asked, "Is this a joke? Because our lives have become one big fucking binary." When it was Mr. Elliot's turn to speak the following day, he said, "I'm not going to respond to that idiotic proposal of hers." When it was my turn to speak, I told my husband about my dream, where I stood among a crowd of people on a beach where everyone touched each other with great care. Or else they didn't touch each other and kept their hands relaxed at their sides. The healthy rapturous oceans crashed in my dream cheerfully upon the reinforced shores. "Sounds like a nice dream if you like water," my husband told me.

The next time my spouse went grocery shopping, they bought me a bouquet of flowers for no reason. It was an even day. It was the beginning of February and the flowers had been flown in from South America. The act of purchasing flowers from South America seemed more an odd-day activity due to the carbon consequences of winter bouquets, and I told my spouse this. We were still figuring out how odd/even differences would affect our individual lives; mistakes were bound to happen. "Do you want me to return them?" they asked. Returning them would have resulted in a further waste of petroleum so, regretfully, I set them in a vase in the corner of the kitchen, where the shiny yellow petals reflected the room's artificial light.

By this time, multiple rifts were probably around us already, waiting and listening, but no one knew yet what they were or how to recognize them. Also no one wanted to deal with them. If we did notice them, we told ourselves they were particles of dust or a remnant of a smashed insect.

• • • •

Not long after the joint elections, my spouse and I joined a book club for adults who wanted to continue processing our new form of governance. The meetings were held at the Slevenskys' house, where we snacked on kettle chips and drank flavored sparkling water. The flavors of water were unusual, such as toasted coconut. The first month we read an investigative narrative about the United States' historical transformation into a plutocracy in conjunction with the rise of the Far Right. The book showed where we might have been headed, toward a unified apocalypse of policy determined by a tiny group of mega-rich men. I felt grateful for the New Compromise, where, on the surface at least, there could be a sense of balance. The next month's pick concerned the history of the white lower classes in America over the previous four hundred years. Mrs. Rettig, who liked the book, said, "I wish all the illegal immigrants would read this book. I think this book would help them understand why some of us think they're cutting ahead of us in line. We want the American Dream too, just like them, only we're not allowed to cut in line." Mrs. Slevensky, who did not like the book, said, "I think undocumented immigrants have better things to do than read a book about understanding white people. I don't think that's a group of people anyone needs to be understanding better right now." It happened to be an odd evening, which meant Mrs. Slevensky's comments came off as alarmist and shrill. Mr. Rettig, who hadn't finished the book, said, "I think lower classes can become middle classes if they try hard enough. When upward mobility fails in America, I think you have to look at limitations of ability and initiative." Mr. Slevensky, who hated the book, mentioned he also personally hated the label "white trash." He said no one, including the author, should be permitted to use labels like that. Ms. Deenen, who liked the book, suggested we find some lower-class readers to join our group. I, who was on the fence about the book, said nothing, trying, even at this early point, to remain a neutralist. A large part of being a neutralist is saying nothing. On the walk home, I thought I saw a glint of displaced light beside the book drop for our neighborhood library. I thought I saw, outside of my bedroom window, a hard shimmer flapping in the evening breeze.

My neighbor Mr. Granell built a wall in his backyard on top of the boundary line between our properties. His wall looked like a chain-link fence to me. He said no, it was definitely a wall. Walls have been in the news lately. Here is a quick list I made of other walls:

- the wall being built along the southern border of the country on odd days, at times built out of concrete, other times made from steel slats. Mr. Elliot ordered the wall to be built. He said, "We've already let a lot of people into the United States over the past two hundred years. It's time to stop letting people in."
- the wall being torn down along the southern border of the country on even days.
- assorted bumper stickers related to walls:

  "Build the damn wall"
  "Build the wall and deport them all"
  "Don't build the wall"
  "Build Bridges Not Walls!"
  "It's not a wall, it's an investment"
  "Heaven has a wall and strict immigration policy. Hell has open borders"
  "No ban, no wall, America for all"

- assorted T-shirts that said the same thing as above.
- The Whole in the Wall, a vegetarian restaurant eighty minutes south of Syracuse famous for its pesto.
- *The Wall*, a novel by the Austrian author Marlen Haushofer. The wall in this case appears suddenly in the middle of the night; it is an invisible wall, and on the other

side of the invisible wall, everyone is dead. This is one of my favorite books. I just reread it.

Mr. Granell liked to talk to me over, or maybe it was through, his wall. He said, “I don’t mind a handful of refugees coming into the country, but I want them to come into the country the same way my great-grandfather came into the country, by filling out paperwork, waiting in a long line, and only then walking through a narrow point of entry.” I nodded and said nothing. According to election results, 257 people in my district had voted for Lillie Jetrin while 254 people voted for Carl Elliot.

The flowers in my kitchen showed no sign of fading. Finally I threw them away while my husband was at work. It was an odd day, and I was tired of how they looked.

“We need to remember how to stand in somebody else’s shoes and see through somebody else’s eyes. Or else here’s what we’ll lose: our ability to understand each other,” said Mx. Jetrin in their weekly address to the nation. They suggested those living in America be required to all read the same book as reading is an empathetic exercise in disguise. They recommended *The Jungle*, or *Americanah*, or anything by Patrick Modiano or Orhan Pamuk for starters. Their idea of a mandatory national book club did not catch on, however. Many people already belonged to a separate book club or else they didn’t want to belong to a book club. Mr. Elliot did not want to belong to a book club. He did not read for pleasure, and anyway he did not think empathy had anything to do with reading. He said, “An act of empathy is going out there and holding somebody’s hand, somebody whose daughter was shot by an illegal immigrant, a murderer who shouldn’t have been in this country, and you promise that mother, with tears in your eyes, that she will get justice. You promise her this country will get better.” The following day, Mx. Jetrin said such talk of murderers and vigilante justice will only make the divides between us vaster. They talked of the divides between us like they were physical and widening crevices. People assumed Mx. Jetrin was speaking metaphorically. They said, "I am not speaking metaphorically." This was the first time a part of government publicly acknowledged the rifts, which were, by this point, multiplying and, admittedly, difficult to ignore.

A joint governmental task force pulled together experts from a wide range of fields. The experts included political scientists, fabulists, scholars of literature, historians, environmental scientists, physical geographers, and volcanologists. Eventually they issued *The First National Rift Assessment: Impacts, Risks, and Adaptation*, a report that Mx. Jetrin, Mr. Elliot, the press, and most people ignored, everyone having other more pressing issues on their minds, such as the budget deficit, drug addiction, structural racism, tax reform, tax evasion, social justice, and whether landowners had the right to shoot critically endangered red wolves when the animals wandered off protected lands. Mr. Elliot added that he didn't believe in things like rifts as a general principle anyway.

The noises rifts emit range from a thin wheezing to a low-pitched shuddering, or perhaps it is more of a creaking. There is the possibility such noises mean the rifts are trying to communicate with us. There is also the possibility that these noises mean nothing and are more an automatic process similar to digestion. Early on, people thought the arrival of a rift near their home meant something good about them as individuals. It meant they were right and whoever was located on the far side of the rift was wrong. It meant the person on the other side of the rift was causing the rift and should be blamed.

Here are some smaller differences I noticed between odd and even days. On odd days, I was allowed to shoot anybody if they walked in a menacing fashion onto my lawn. I also ate more Cavendish bananas. People in general drove more. My husband drove more. On odd days, my husband insisted the ceiling lights stay on when he left the room, and he took long drives through the industrial countryside. Mr. Granell glared at Ms. Deenen on odd days if she walked by his house holding her wife's hand. There was a puppet show at the library on an odd day where a girl puppet dressed up as a boy puppet and danced at the ball with a girl puppet, and this was supposed to be funny. *Hazily* was a popular odd-day TV show in which white special agents attempted to stop minority terrorists (the exact minority differs from season to season) from blowing up important American monuments. Each odd day on my calendar was circled in yellow highlighter.

On even days, my family had comprehensive health insurance. I could take my child to a doctor after they broke their arm instead of watching how to splint an arm with newspapers on YouTube, then splinting my child's arm with newspapers. Heteronormative students, or students belonging to the racially dominant culture, were encouraged on even days not to register for classes at the Writer's Center downtown, as their stories had already been told. Local business owners noticed an uptick in sales, and there were fewer Amazon boxes piled beside people's doors. *The Night Shift* aired, a popular TV show in which all wealthy characters were metaphorically evil. Each even day on my wall calendar was circled with a thin permanent black pen.

Larger changes were also happening, but they tended to happen elsewhere, so it was almost as if they weren't happening. I would hear about such changes on the news. The U.S. placed extreme odd-day tariffs on a lengthy list of Chinese products including semiconductors, microscopes, and floating docks. On even days those tariffs were lifted, and the port waterways clogged with container ships while dockworkers labored with required overtime. Undocumented workers, on even days, picked fruit openly in the surrounding countryside, while the same workers hid in their apartments with the blinds shut during the odd-day ICE sweeps, leaving the fruit to rot in the fields. Migrant children were either separated from their migrant parents while trying to enter the country illegally from Mexico or those same children were reunited with their parents briefly, depending on the day. I heard about large swaths of federal land that were no longer protected or the land was suddenly re-protected. In Syracuse, on even days, refugees settled into the north side with truckloads of volunteer help, and on odd days, people just wanted those refugees gone—but either way I didn't live in Syracuse. I rarely had reason to drive into the city. The only time I interacted with the new refugee community was at the occasional even-day pop-up restaurant event, where they spooned different and flavorful food onto my plate, and I looked them in the eye, and I said "thank you" clearly and loudly. Those pop-up restaurants happened once every three months. My own neighborhood had only one refugee family from Bhutan, the Dorjis, who lived at the far end of my block, which is a long block. I waved to the Dorjis on even days and ignored them on odd days like everybody else.

Mr. Granell continued to fortify his wall, which also became my wall—our wall?—as it sat on the border of our yards. He fortified our wall with sandbags and a windscreen and a tuft of razor wire, which was legal only on odd days. At various neighborhood locations, the rifts glimmered and shifted, but they were still small. While they were small, they did not seem like much of a problem, only a change.

Rifts can be beautiful when seen from indirect angles. They may shimmer indiscriminately in silver and bright coppery tones. Because of such shimmering, a lot of people in my town used to act like the rifts were magical. People acted like we were in a magical story where bright magical silvery things and coppery things happened to us, versus the story we were actually in, which would be properly classified as political nonfiction.

When looked at directly, rifts are violent and frightening and realistic, even the smallest rifts. Even the ones that sounded like baby cats. Nobody looked at the rifts directly at first.

Editorial boards from major newspapers suggested geographic reorganization. The Evenists could congregate down south while the Oddists moved up north. The other way around would work as well, the Oddists down south, the Evenists up north. It was easy to idealize a place that didn't exist, where all the days would be filled with people and opinions and laws and politicians and regulations that agreed with you. In an evening interview, Mr. Elliot told the story of an illegal immigrant who robbed and killed four innocent people in Nevada. The next day, Mx. Jetrin told a reporter about a refugee family from Northern Nigeria whose eight-year-old was becoming a child prodigy at chess in Queens, New York. The next day, I ran into Miss Boersema, my son's even-day science teacher, in the freezer section of Nojaim Brothers. She said her brother needed to hire a janitor for his print shop in the city, so he hired a Syrian refugee to mop the floors. The refugee was supposed to do whatever was needed and be grateful, but Miss Boersema's brother kept finding the refugee in places he wasn't supposed to be, like the second hall stairwell, where he was often talking on his cell phone. The floors of the shop remained filthy. The brother had to fire the refugee after only a week. The refugee threatened to send federal and/or state agencies after the business. "I was surprised to learn such a person could be choosy about employment options," said Miss Boersema softly. She thought a generalization should be made from her story. The suggested generalization was that refugees were too choosy about their employment options. I felt like I needed a wider perspective, so I started up a conversation with my refugee neighbor.

ME: "What do you think about this country's new political system?"

Mx. DORJI: "It is disappointing. I believe something bad will happen."

ME: "Thank you."

I considered asking Mx. Dorji to join the book club but I didn't end up asking them.

Mr. Granell picked the next book for our upcoming meeting. The book he picked, about Louisiana Oddists, was written with much sympathy by a sociologist. The sociologist claimed she was an Evenist, but most people doubted this to be true. Mr. Granell's opening question: How did feelings of marginalization culminate in the partial election of Mr. Elliot?

There was a rift in the Slevenskys' fireplace. I wasn't sure if it had been there the month before. The rift looked like it was chewing on something. It looked like it had teeth and it was chewing. This could have been because of where I was sitting and the angle of my position to the fireplace, or the rift really could have been chewing on something, its movements rhythmic and predictable. Mrs. Slevensky, not an Oddist, said she didn't know the answer to Mr. Granell's question because she didn't finish the book. She said she wanted to burn the book. She said she burned the book actually. She was tired of trying to understand what the other side was thinking. That assumed what the other side thought was okay. It was not okay. "The reality is that we're living in a culturally diverse world, not a homogenous country," she said. Mr. Granell coughed. Someone pointed out that the rift looked mystical right now. Mr. Granell said, "What if my reality–the Oddist reality–is just a different reality than yours?" The rift chewed and twinkled. It was a tawny gold color, and while I don't think it necessarily increased in size as we sat around Mrs. Slevensky's family room talking about different realities, it did appear to pay attention to our discussion.

It did seem to take interest. My husband has accused me of transposing human emotions onto the rifts, while I think the rifts are capable of human emotion. This is a controversial issue.

Someone in the room pointed out that there can only technically be one reality, that the definition of "reality" necessitated a single reality. Mr. Granell said, "That's an outdated definition. Just because my reality is different from your reality does not make my reality unreal." Mrs. Slevensky's dog was lying at her feet. The dog got up. Mrs. Slevensky tried, half-heartedly, to prevent her dog from leaping onto the front of Mr. Granell's pants. Mr. Granell pushed Mrs. Slevensky's dog away. The book discussion descended from there into two, and occasionally three, separate but simultaneous lectures. When we had exhausted ourselves and accomplished very little or maybe nothing, it was suggested that our group avoid political books moving forward. The rift chewed and stuttered. I wanted to know what it was chewing on, though I was unsure how to casually find this out. I took several tentative steps forward. Before I could see anything clearly, my husband grabbed my arm and pulled me back to my seat. It was considered poor manners, I suppose, to stare too deeply into someone else's private rift. But it was okay to stare at each other. People were staring at me, as if I must have had something to say. "I'm also okay with the avoidance of political books," I said, and because I spoke first, it was determined I should choose the next book. "Look, here I am, facing reality," said Mr. Granell, opening his eyes wide and glancing around the room. Someone told Mr. Granell that we weren't talking about that anymore.

I ended up choosing a breezy thriller situated in a big city. The characters were wealthy and young, and the evil character was evil because she murdered people. The suggested discussion questions at the back of the book included "Did this book remind you of other books?" and "If you were making a movie of this book, who would you cast for the lead roles?"

That evening, Mr. Elliot said, "A great spirit of optimism is sweeping the nation." He said this into a microphone somewhere in Ohio.

Both presidents announced a series of dueling executive actions. They made opposing cabinet-level agency decisions and contradictory proposals for legislation. Mx. Jetrin expanded background checks for buying guns, proposed increased funding for Planned Parenthood, expanded tax credits for clean energy, talked about dismantling the school-to-prison pipeline, closed off public lands from natural-gas extraction, closed a tax loophole for hedge fund managers, required sexual education programs in secondary schools to cover consent and bystander intervention, nominated a pro-abortion judge to the Supreme Court, expanded the Affordable Care Act to encompass all families regardless of immigration status, created a national Office of Immigrant Affairs, proposed legislation that would end tax subsidies for oil and gas companies, and broadcast photographs taken on an odd day of a new wave of needy refugees, caravans of overcrowded migrant vessels stuck at the maritime border of our country. Mr. Elliot cut the number of refugees allowed into the country by two-thirds, implemented an extreme vetting system, approved the flow of surplus military vehicles, weapons, and equipment to local law enforcement, banned transgender Americans from serving in the military, cut funding to international NGOs that promoted abortions, removed methane emission reduction requirements from solid-waste landfills and oil and gas operations, nominated an anti-abortion judge to the Supreme Court, revoked residency permits for 200,000 Salvadorians, casually suggested we look at sterilization as a requirement for welfare benefits (although he said we wouldn't call it sterilization, we would call it something else), issued an executive order forcing federal agencies involved with welfare and public assistance to make that public assistance more difficult to access, and asked that the government sell off and/or open up for development a portion of land from our national monuments, our national forests, and certain underutilized national parks.

As this list morphed and expanded, disagreements between my neighbors over the environment, immigration, transgender rights, freedom of speech, and freedom of religion turned into polite arguments. Polite arguments morphed into impolite arguments. Impolite arguments intensified into screaming matches, which became embarrassingly physical, in particular during the transition time between 9:00 p.m. and 3:00 a.m., when odd and even evenings leaked into each other and the rifts seemed most alive, crackling with dark matter and wanton energy. I repeated the word *neutral* to myself often as a reminder or a warning.

There is no official naming convention for the rifts. Often rifts are named after the nearest road or intersection or structure, although other times the rifts may be given the name of a dead pet or missing child. A rift might have several names depending on who you're talking to. This can make communication about a particular rift difficult. Rifts that reach the arbitrary size of thirty-two inches must be registered with the county clerk's office via a two-page, double-sided form and twenty-dollar processing fee. Only three rifts have officially been registered.

According to my most recent walkthrough, my village appears to have twenty-seven major rifts, located mainly in the center of roads and in parkland, and forty-one minor rifts, generally found along property lines. This roughly equals one rift per twenty-five residents, an above-average ratio for New York. The Reed Street Rift began as a minor rift, but it is now a major rift undulating in the air outside of my home. It is not pleasant smelling, and many residents on my block have stopped opening their front windows. I have stopped opening my front windows. The Highland Cemetery Rift is currently a minor rift located twenty feet left of the cemetery entrance along the chain-link fence. It looks like something shiny lost in the grass. The openings of both major and minor rifts are generally ragged and uneven, as if such openings were ripped into being by an animal with carnivorous teeth. The temperature of the air surrounding rifts is generally twenty degrees Fahrenheit cooler than the ambient temperature. My data does not include the private rifts inside people's homes, so presumably these tallies should be higher. All the rifts I've mentioned belong to the Marcellus Basin Rift Zone, which is part of the Upstate New York Rift System. There are also rifts of note at the bottom of the retention pond on Highland Drive, below the surface of both Mud Ponds, and in a puddle outside of my son's school, while several newer rifts are advancing toward my home and my neighbors' homes. The newer rifts appear to be expanding more vigorously. We—meaning myself, Mr. Granell, Mrs. Slevensky, Mr. Slevensky, my husband, and my son under threat of consequences—attempted to shovel dirt into the mouth of these rifts to protect our property. "Mouth" is not the technical term but I am using it for lack of better jargon. No matter how much dirt we shovel, the rifts will not fill up. There does not seem to be an end to the newer rifts, and we worry we will run out of dirt.

The largest, deepest rift in the country circles the city of Detroit. Mild earthquakes have been reported there. Rifts do not appear to have crossed any U.S. borders, though this does not necessarily mean that rifts exist only in America, though this is a possibility. In time, the government task force believes water will fill then overflow all existing rifts, forming new ponds and lakes and eventually oceans, meaning our little town, along with many towns and cities across the country, will one day be washed away. The task force also points out that rifts have always existed in the spaces around us, but they were likely contained by some outdated sense of community and rigid social norms.

Mr. Rettig threw himself into the rift at the intersection of State Routes 174 and 175 after that rift grew large enough to envelop an adult body. He was the first local to enter a rift willingly, so his journey garnered much attention. He hasn't come back. Mrs. Rettig likes to tell religious-tinged fairy tales about the other world Mr. Rettig must now inhabit. I don't believe her stories. The wind that blows out of the center of the Route 174/175 Rift is the stinking wind of dead animals and rot. If you look into that rift directly, you can see nothing, not one light or a refraction of light.

The larger national protests were held on Sundays at the nation's capital. The issues people protested depended on whether that exact Sunday was an odd or even day. An odd-day protest had Oddists shouting about the bloated welfare system; an even-day protest featured Evenists screaming about eligibility restrictions to Medicaid. Mr. Deenen, having attended several even protests, assured me they were life-changing events. They wanted me to accompany them to the next one so I could split the cost of gas. I told them no, repeating my philosophy of noninvolvement in partisan projects, and that I hoped to remain a neutral force. “I don't think there's such a thing anymore,” said Mr. Deenen. The first dozen protests in DC were televised live. Each protest had a crowd, a stage, a celebrity, a microphone, bandanas, scarves, signs, sunglasses, water bottles, and weather, either raining or not. The presidents rarely, if ever, attended, and the news outlets soon lost interest. There was footage instead of Mr. Elliot boarding his private plane and flying to Florida, where he played two rounds of golf then calmly sipped Diet Coke through a clear plastic straw. Smaller protests occurred at the local level. Several may have even happened in Syracuse, although I didn't hear them happen. I just read about it. I read some of the local protests ended in violence, which is too bad. Certain people involved in the violent protests lacked the flexibility required for our new system of governance. The ability to shift one's definitions of right and wrong, good and bad, depending on the day—or to simply be above it all. Or not above but to the side of it all. To participate through the act of observation, as I am.

On which days were we happier? On which days were we better people? The data appeared inconclusive. On even days, it was said to rain more. On odd days, there was an unusual number of crows.

The curb separated from the street outside of my home. The reason the curb separated like that was the arrival of a new rift whose main characteristics were agitation and panting. Mr. Granell named it the Lightly Foaming Lucinda Rift, Lucinda being a woman he once knew. The neighborhood children wanted to leap across the Lucinda Rift like they once leapt across rain puddles, but that seemed a reckless thing to allow. When I peered inside this rift, I saw the furious churning of shadows. I couldn't tell what was making the shadows, and for the first time I felt unsafe. Mr. Granell and I lay down planks of wood so residents could cross the street if necessary. It took two days for the rift to widen and swallow the wood. One day the rift I am talking about will sever my side of the block from the other side. I'm not sure how my son will then get to school. I'm not sure how I will reach the public library. If the rift continues growing, eventually it will become difficult to leave my home or for anyone here to leave their homes.

My husband and I arrived late to the next book club meeting. We were late because it was difficult to reach Mrs. Slevensky's house due to the rifts that were widening at what seemed like an accelerated pace. A walk that would have once taken us several minutes took us half an hour. At times, I thought what we were doing—exiting the house, attempting to cross the bottomless rifts by taking a running start—was dangerous and foolish. We were not the only people late to the meeting. Mrs. Rettig texted her regrets that she was unable to attend. She could not find a way to reach the group without taking hours of detours. Perhaps this would be our final meeting. We talked about the breezy thriller I had chosen. To start the discussion, I asked, "Who's evil in this book?" Everybody in the room agreed it was the girl who murdered her friend and later murdered her boyfriend and most likely murdered another friend in the past. It felt good to all agree on the answer to a question. "How was the friend murdered?" asked Mr. Slevensky next. Again, we all agreed on the response: the friend's head was bashed in with a rock. "Were they ever really friends?" asked Miss Boersema. This question we went back and forth on for a while, which was stressful—can you be friends with someone you will later murder?—but my husband pointed out the evil girl may not have known at the beginning of the friendship that she would murder her friend, so he suggested the answer was yes, they were once real friends, and we all said yes. After that the meeting was over [illegible] to avoid [illegible] size [illegible] eve- [illegible]

[illegible] cramps [illegible] labori-ous pulses. It was hours still before dawn, too early to leave my bed, so I pulled up the local news on my phone to distract my mind from the physical discomfort. All the top news stories were related to the rifts, to new rifts or expanding rifts or deepening rifts or things that were disappearing into the rifts, and soon after I began browsing, I was gripped by an irrational or maybe it was a rational fear. A heavy emotion (or was it a suffocation?) prevented me from getting up that day and the succeeding day or days, and I found I could not leave my room let alone the house for a time. Many people in my neighborhood were venturing out of their homes less frequently. Oddists like Mrs. Granell and Mr. Granell emerged only on odd days. Likewise, Evenists such as Mx. Deenen went out only on the even days. This reduced the arguing and simplified our interactions with each other, though I supposed there would be consequences.

The portion of Route 20 that ran through the southern part of our town fell into the Route 20 Rift. A veterinary clinic and a quilt shop needed to be evacuated. The Blowfish Café should have been evacuated but the owners refused. First the café's parking lot then the entire building slipped into the growing rift. "This is not a joke, people," said our village leadership. That evening, Mr. Elliot spoke from a rally in Fort Myers. He spoke about his decision to withdraw American troops immediately from both Syria and Afghanistan and his impulse to increase tariffs on foreign goods coming from Mexico. He said, "Half of America doesn't believe in me. But you know what? Half of America does. Guess which half is the real half?" He left the stage. A portion of the stage was already covered by a rift, or maybe it was multiple rifts branching off from a single original rift. The rift (or rifts) swallowed the stage. This would be Mr. Elliot's last travel engagement for some time. In the future, we would see him sitting in a secure location behind an anchored desk, surrounded by scientists and radar displays.

In a high school gymnasium in Scranton, Pennsylvania, Mx. Jetrin spoke about their plan to establish a consistent national feed-in tariff for solar power as well as federal incentives for the construction of solar parks. They also spoke about the true versus the not-true America: "Half of America doesn't deserve to be in America. So let's just eliminate them from our thinking." At the side of the room a rift, practical, ragged, and probably nihilistic, cracked farther open, swallowing several rows of bleachers. Mx. Jetrin tried not to step backward away from this newfound destructiveness (or was it a hunger?), but the rift was broadening, and eventually she needed to step backward.

What does a healed rift look like? Is there an empty space, and if there is, what reaches across the empty space? Is it like a thin layer of skin over a scar, or is it more substantial, like the regrowth of bone? The idea of a shared reality sounds radical to me right now; it wasn't always radical.

I don't want to forget what I know to be true. This was what I said to myself later on in the car driving home from that day's errands.

It was late in the year for snow, and the flakes, small, individual, separated, hung in the air as if stuck. The next day the snow came again, but this time it was falling heavy like it used to. I stood by the window. I could see Mrs. Slevensky standing beside the window in the back of her house and Mr. Granell standing beside his window. Between us the snow twirled around itself, around an invisible center.

5. Conclusion

I've put off ending this report for some time now, hoping that something definitive would happen, such as that the rifts would be mended. They would mend themselves, or someone would mend them. Perhaps the young people in this country would find a way to do such mending, I had thought. But the young people of this country appear as susceptible to extremes as those of my generation. I can't wait any longer. Therefore, in conclusion, I believe the time has come for me to explore these newly rendered places and see what exists in the rifts other than the dark.

My decision has little to do with heroism or self-sacrifice. Partly

I am tired–it is tiring, existing in two realities! Partly I am bored. I hope you will, in time, follow my lead and consider making your own explorations.

For my initial expedition, I have chosen the rift located alongside Ninemile Creek. It's a smaller rift, for now at least it is smaller than the others and more approachable, less static coming out of it, less of a smell. It looks like an entrance to me. The wisps of brightness at the edge of it look like puckish flags beckoning in the wind. I asked my husband if he would like to accompany me and he said no, that such exploring of possible middle ground is surely, for lack of a better term, a woman's job. "Make sure to be back by dinnertime," he said.

A black walnut tree grows beside the creek's edge. I have tied one end of a rope around the furrowed trunk. The other end of rope I've knotted around my waist. Below me I can hear noises, not necessarily discordant. The scent of charcoal and residue. A faint pink light. I'll write more when I emerge.

LK-32-C

Two Moons

The quad of A[illegible] Academy was positioned on top of a hill too steep [illegible] on the eastern side of the school's campus. The spot offered [illegible] view. To the east one could see more hills, typical for the region, as well as a serene pond surrounded by red oaks and white [illegible], where one might imagine the boys pensively rowing [illegible] across the misty waters. While to the right stood a dozen charming buildings, the classrooms, the dorms, their wood weathered and authentic yet still structurally sound. Though no one there would have called such places a dorm. They would have used a word like "home," such as, *Do you want to stop at home after lunch?* or *Welcome home, boys.* A portion of an atmospheric barn could be spotted in the near distance, as well as the corral for the horses, since boys such as these were rumored to thrive if given the opportunity to care for larger mammals.

Today being the second Sunday of October, the boys' parents gathered on the quad, most of them exhausted, having driven great distances to be there, driving for hours or days. The boys gathered there as well, looking unfamiliar, wearing their unfamiliar expressions. Children are always changing, but they seem especially to change when they are sent away from home and not seen nor spoken to for three or four months. Several parents stood on the mowed grass with their hands at their sides, quiet, having forgotten the script. Or had the script changed again? It was useful with these children to follow scripts. A father jotted observations regarding his child's behavior into a steno pad, an old habit of his. Other parents asked their sons questions concerning topics that didn't matter to anyone, such as which variety of toast had been served at breakfast, or when was the last time they had a good dream. These inquiries went unanswered as the boys tended to be busy, twisting their hands around the pieces of silk sewn into the linings of their pockets, or they went off spinning in circles, or they counted the bricks that bordered the garden path.

The fathers in attendance tended to be dressed for golf, wearing khakis and visors and surprisingly colorful polos—all wishful thinking as there were no courses within one hundred miles, only farms—while the mothers walked around with bright distracting scarves knotted around their necks. "Look at me," instructed one mother, her scarf an electric turquoise slashed with orange. "Look at me. Come on, look at me. It's not like you've forgotten who I am. Look at me." Other parents took out their phones, though not Beth or Tom Corbett, who did not wish to bring any pictures of this place back—who would they show such pictures to?—but there were other parents who attempted to snap a few photographs, generally of their child in a spot of light, twisting away from them, as the light was everywhere that day. The annual Fall Jamboree was the only time, excepting emergencies, when families were allowed on campus.

The Corbetts stood apart from the other parents in a shaded spot beside a rock fountain. Their younger child Ruby—average, normal Ruby—was at home with a sitter. "I don't want to see my brother ever again," Ruby confided to Beth the afternoon before they were all to leave. Understandable, considering. So Beth had scrambled to find a last-minute grad student who asked for too much money. "Just feed my daughter a lot of ice cream, okay?" Beth told the sitter. They had been standing there beside the fountain for what felt like a long time. The sound of water trickling into a gray basin appeared to soothe their son Luke, who had been quizzing them, contentedly, ever since their arrival late that morning. Already Luke had cycled through the presidents—who died in office, who lived with their children in the White House, who owned pets, and what kind of pets—and he was now moving on to tsunamis, his head tipped back so he could track the flock of geese flying southward in a ragged formation across the sky.

"In what country did the tsunami of 2004 begin?" Luke asked. The boy wore a plain gray polo, gray socks, and a pair of gray shorts with sagging pockets. His hair had grown too long, covering his neck and now falling into his eyes. He looked hungry to Beth and a little hollow, like if she tapped him on his shoulder she would hear an empty thud. She would never tap him on the shoulder like that. If she tapped him on his shoulder, he would scream. The only touch he used to tolerate was her two fingers, her pointer and middle finger, pressed below the hairline of his neck. A neck hug, she had called it euphemistically, the skin there scaly from lack of wash but also tender, a child's skin still.

Tom guessed China. "I think it was New Zealand," said Beth, taking a tentative step, a very tiny step, toward Luke, who jerked backward onto a flower bed of wild-looking red daisies, as if she had shoved him back. It turned out they were both wrong. "Indonesia!" Luke shouted out as he crushed the flowers with his feet. "Indonesia! Indonesia! Indonesia!" In the center of the quad, a trio of grills billowed charcoal smoke in preparation for the afternoon barbecue, while a dozen staff in polos and khakis set out folding chairs under a wide white tent.

Beth said, "I have some questions for you too."

"It's not your turn," said Luke.

"You've asked us thirty-five questions, Luke. I think it's my turn to ask a question."

Tom laid a hand on her arm.

"It's not your turn," Luke repeated.

"What are you doing?" Tom asked her.

"One of my questions is how are you? What I mean is, how do you like it here at your new school? Are you happy?" She kept her voice soft, quiet, edgeless, like she had practiced, the voice of a patient mother, a kind mother. Instead of answering, Luke recited questions back at her. What's the highest speed a tsunami can travel? The tsunami wave from the Tohoku earthquake was how high? How many people died in the 1883 tsunami caused by the eruption of Krakatoa? Beth had to raise her voice to be heard. "Another question I have is who are your friends. Do you have friends? Tell me about two of your closest friends."

Luke's hands swatted at the air as if surrounded by biting flies.

On the drive to New Hampshire, Beth had read and reread the letter that the school therapist sent home the previous week. The letter was supposed to contain everything a parent needed to know for a successful visit. *Keep your personal devices in your pockets. Be forward looking. Stop dwelling in the past but start dwelling in the bright rooms of the future. Embrace change!* "Who was the first person to associate tsunamis with underwater earthquakes?" Luke shouted. "True or false: palm trees often survive tsunamis intact. True or false: only two large tsunamis are known to have struck

Europe." At the bottom of the letter, the therapist had scrawled, in hasty handwriting, four additional points. *If I may, Beth? 1. Meet Luke on his own new terms, please. 2. Wait for him to reach for you before you reach. 3. However small, celebrate the successes (and HAVE FUN)! 4. Also please do not bring up that planet he invented as I think he is ready to finally leave that place behind.*

"Knock it off," Tom whispered. "Whatever you're doing, you have to stop. I mean, look at him."

By the start of second grade at his old day school, Luke had exhausted the geography of Earth, having memorized all of the countries and the capitals, the rivers and lakes and mountain ranges, as well as the major economic industries of each region. He would have been content to continually reidentify the saltwater environments of Asia, but his teacher Ms. Beale hid the map work above the wardrobe, claiming repairs were needed. "The maps aren't broken," Luke insisted. "Yes they are," said Ms. Beale. "No they're not," said Luke. Pulling a worn encyclopedia of space from the class bookshelf, his teacher suggested that he spend the morning instead reading about the solar system, in particular Jupiter, with all those odd icy moons. Luke read about Jupiter, then he read about the other planets. He read through lunch, in fact, refusing to touch his sandwich or apple slices. At recess, there he was with that big book on his lap under the slide, and by the afternoon, ignoring Ms. Beale's lesson on the life stages of a butterfly, as well as the visiting Irish dancers, he had moved on to other aspects of the universe.

For a time he found comets fascinating, their timetables like a train schedule, only with the enticing possibility of a collision. Later, he focused on asteroids and supernovas, then it was black holes, eventually settling upon the exoplanets, specifically the ones that existed as far away as possible, on the edge of what is visible.

Many such planets are inhospitable and strange, like 55 Cancri e, likely made out of diamond and graphite, though a few appear similar enough to Earth to support the possibility of life. Luke's parents bought him two enormous atlases of the universe so he could compare the differences between the editions. Eventually his interest narrowed to an exoplanet he called LK-32-C. He must have come across it in a reference book, Beth assumed, or somewhere on the internet, though she could find no mention of the place. Eventually she realized he had made the planet up. Luke said if she didn't know what the name of his planet meant, he wasn't telling her. He spent afternoons in his bedroom, at his desk, pinpointing LK-32-C's precise location in the universe. Each of his drawings were exact, magnificent, as detailed as a blueprint.

"LK-32-C," Luke wrote in a research paper for school that should have been about amphibians, "is a gray land covered in crumbly sand. On top of the sand grows *Bulla crudus,* a knobby green plant that feels soft and warm if you touch it." A planet is not an amphibian, Beth pointed out. Luke handed in the report anyway. In fact, every class presentation, every project, he turned into a further investigation of LK-32-C. Such focused dedication to a made-up subject did not sit well with his teacher. Luke began lagging behind his peers at school.

To reignite the boy's interest in learning, Beth suggested that Ms. Beale use LK-32-C for motivation. "I think he's just bored," Beth said. Luke could graph the planet's monthly rainfall during math lessons or design a robot to carry out remote testing of the soil acidity.

"The only problem here is that planet of his isn't a real planet. You do realize that, don't you?" Ms. Beale asked Beth.

"There is no dirt on the ground," Luke wrote. "The ponds are salty. The green knobs can be eaten in an emergency. They are rich in potassium." The double moons cast down dueling shadows.

Some rare animal rolled through the sand on silver-wheeled feet. He called them *the figures*: two-legged, colored blue for some reason. They ate rocks and possibly once were human.

One afternoon, Luke showed Beth how those figures danced. His arms swung recklessly around his head as he jumped. It was a long dance. Beth lay back on his bed and watched him. He looked far away and glad. "Stop staring at me," he finally said. Outside, below Luke's window, a group of neighborhood boys crouched in the street near the sewer grate, believing they had seen a vibration of light down there that opened up like a long flume further into the darkness.

The incidents began that winter.

One: Luke slammed his chair against another student, pinning her to the snack table. He refused to move, even when the girl began sobbing.

Two: Luke threatened to shove a walnut into the mouth of a child who was allergic to walnuts. "Maybe he didn't understand she was allergic," Beth suggested. "Oh, he knew. That boy keeps a [illegible] every student," replied Ms. Beale.

Three: Luke drew a rifle on a student's forehead using a per[illegible]er.

Four: Luke told a classmate that somebody should go and shoot the president of the United States. "I don't think he's serious about that," Beth said. "You don't *think*?" questioned Ms. Beale.

"Hello again, Beth," Ms. Beale said tiredly. Five: a fight where Luke punched a boy's face after the boy insisted Luke's new haircut turned him into a girl.

Six: During recess, Luke threw a jacket over a student's head. Should he go get a rope, he asked the boy, cinching the jacket closed. Should he tie the rope around the boy's neck?

It was the school secretary who called. Could Beth and Tom

both come in at some point, such as this afternoon, let's say at two o'clock, to meet with Mrs. Moreau, the school counselor? Beth explained that Tom was out of town again. "He's away for business reasons," she explained. "Of course he is," said the secretary. They scheduled a meeting for Tuesday of the following week.

Beth snapped the ends off half a pound of green beans for dinner that night then threw the beans into boiling salted water. She seasoned several slabs of tofu and set them under the broiler until the edges blackened. This was the meal she usually made when Tom traveled. Ruby ate five bites before wandering into the living room to play with her rainbow ponies. The ponies were about to have an adventure in which they flew around the couches having fun. Luke remained at the table stabbing his fork into the tofu, which he refused to eat, claiming to tolerate at present only three foods: tomatoes, toast, yogurt.

"Luke," Beth began. "The members of this family do not throw coats on other people's heads, then hold the coats there."

"Well, I do," said Luke.

Stab. Stab. Stab.

"I do not want you to throw coats on other people's heads. I don't want you to use violent language either."

"Why?"

Stab stab.

Beth handed him one of the plastic frogs now scattered around every room of their house, a twelve-pack purchased some previous month in a spree of optimism. If you squeezed the frog's stomach hard enough, the creature's eyes popped out. This gesture was supposed to calm children like Luke. Luke squeezed the frog's stomach. Its eyes popped out.

"Because those actions, that sort of language, scare other people. It makes other people afraid of you."

"I want people to be afraid of me," Luke said.

A thick soft thud from outside interrupted them. "I didn't

see anything," Luke insisted, though he had been looking in the same direction as Beth, so he must have seen the bird, a robin—pregnant?—smash into their sliding glass door and plummet to the deck, mistaking the reflection of the trees for the trees themselves, a devastating error of perception. "Birds are so sturdy. I bet that bird's okay," she told Luke. Once a liar, always a liar. "I'm not stupid," Luke said. These kinds of avian accidents happened several times a year at their house. The birds generally didn't survive. But today, in the time it took for Beth to step outside, the robin had already vanished. Either it managed, despite the impact, to escape, or she couldn't find its body.

The following day, Beth drove to their neighborhood library and checked out *The Friendly Brontosaurus*, along with several other books about kindness that the librarian recommended. Luke glanced at the book's cover, featuring a gentle brontosaurus giving rides to his smaller friends, the jolly microraptors and the adorable bandicoots, before he hurled the book at the wall. "Dinosaurs never did that," he said. Beth retrieved the book, lifted Ruby onto her lap, and read the book loudly to the younger child while Luke drew at the kitchen table. His drawing showed an astronaut who had been jettisoned out of a rocket ship without his helmet. Surrounding the suffocating man was an exquisitely detailed map of a distant solar system, every planet uninhabitable and dark except for one, in the lower-right corner of the page, encircled with a silver marker as if throwing off a metallic halo.

The phone rang. Beth put the book aside. "No," Ruby moaned. They were at the part where the brontosaurus has to decide whether or not he will help his friends gather palm leaves for a surprise party. "Noooooooooo," Luke mimicked from the kitchen. Ruby's eyes widened as she took in one deep breath and wailed into Beth's ear. The child was exhausted, dark rings under her eyes. Luke chanted, "Crybaby. Crybaby!" He had begun creeping at night into his sister's bedroom, where he would wake her by pinching her arms. Ruby grabbed onto Beth's shirt to try and keep her there. "I'll be right back," Beth promised. She had to pry open Ruby's hands to reach the phone.

Mrs. Moreau, the school counselor, asked if now was a good time for a chat.

"It's not, really," Beth said.

Mrs. Moreau continued anyway. "I wanted you to know that the headmaster and I, along with your son's teachers, reviewed Luke's file at a meeting this morning. What a special kid you have! I'm seeing so many puzzles in him, so many locks and keys."

"That meeting was supposed to be put off until next week."

"This was a *different* meeting," explained Mrs. Moreau. At this different meeting, it had been recommended that Luke undergo both testing and therapy in order for him to remain enrolled at the school. So that everybody is kept as safe as can be. "I want to assure you that no one is trying to get rid of your son. Do you have any questions?"

Beth said, "Most of all I want to see that labyrinth again. The one next to your house. I mean, your home. I think on the east side of your home. The boy who showed me around before told me the labyrinth was his favorite place out of any place here because it gave his brain a rest. It guided him so he didn't have to think about where to go for once. He just followed the path. I've pictured you there every morning dropping a stone in the center before classes begin. Do you do that? Do you set a stone down there every morning before your classes?"

Luke did not take them to the labyrinth. In charge of escorting his parents around the school grounds until lunch, he led them in the opposite direction, to a woodpile in a clearing, where he turned his back toward them and proceeded to split wood with a red axe. His legs strained against the ground, the muscles of his back contracted, and with each swing the axe, balanced above his head, seemed to delay itself in the air, as if there were so many possibilities about what might happen next. Luke grunted, loud and low, every time he forced the blade to hit the log. Firewood already littered the clearing, enough to last anybody for months. Tom said, "Though this is sure nice, how about we move on, buddy?" He had to repeat himself four times before Luke finally threw the axe into the dirt. Beth reached for Tom's hand. For once, the day was glorious after weeks of steady rain, the sky above them archetypal, a rich blue, cloudless.

Only last year, she had brought up the idea of a separation. Luke's expanding needs had become this painful light in their house that never went away, an exhausting, demanding light that kept exposing everybody's worst parts. "We're like two miserable roommates living in a closet," she had said. "Doesn't something need to change?"

Tom assured her that she worried too much. "So things have to be different between us for a while. Fine! Eventually you and I will get back everything good that we used to have, okay? The dinner conversations. The Sunday mornings in bed. [illegible] Do you remember? We'll get back to where we were."

"But what if we can't get back there?" she had asked.

"Then we'll find something else to [illegible]," Tom had said, his hand lifting to touch her.

Next Luke brought them to the barn, a wind-blown structure that might as well have been haunted, a vinyl banner flapping from its eaves: WE WILL NOT GIVE UP ON YOU! "Do you get to take care of animals, Luke?" Beth asked. Beside the barn, a makeshift hutch housed rabbits, all white with floppy ears. Unhooking the latch, Luke scooped the smallest of the rabbits into his arms. Beth questioned whether he was supposed to be doing that. In response,

Luke threw the rabbit at her. Somehow she managed to catch the creature, though she had no idea how to hold it properly. She cradled it like a baby. The animal kicked its hind legs to get away from her. She felt its panicked heart beneath its fur. It was about to jump. "It's about to jump," Beth announced. The rabbit jumped, leaping from her arms into the dirt. "I don't think it wants to be held right now," she said. Luke grabbed a ratty toothbrush from beneath a bench, lifted the animal into his lap, and stroked the brush along its back. Under such steady and predictable motion, the rabbit stilled.

"They never yell," Luke said.

"Who, the rabbits?" Beth asked.

"Not even when I broke the window then threw the chair out of the window."

"Why did you throw a chair out of a window?" asked Tom.

Luke continued to smooth the rabbit's fur. Why had she not thought of buying him a rabbit? "They never hit me. They take away points but you get the points back. They think I'm doing a good job."

Dark patches were appearing around them in the woods. As if to say danger and concealment lie ahead.

"Are you doing a good job?" Beth asked.

"They don't ask me questions."

Luke's name was placed on a list at the university pediatric psychiatry clinic that Mrs. Moreau had recommended. "When will you be calling?" Beth asked. The intake counselor sighed. "Honey, it's a long list." During the wait, Luke's interest over LK-32-C only deepened. "This is what their music sounds like on that planet," he told Beth. "It isn't the actual music because that can't be written down, but I made this music up so I know what it sounds like." He composed the music on her tablet. Every song seemed the same, a choir of male voices repeating vowels into a space she pictured as cavelike and cramped. Luke listened incessantly to these songs. He listened to them in the morning during his breakfast of dry crustless toast and a tomato. He insisted on listening to them in the car every day on the drive to school. "No," Ruby would cry in protest. "No, no, no, no, no!" "We'll listen to *Annie* another time," Beth promised her daughter, though they never did. If she neglected to immediately plug the tablet into the car's speaker system, Luke kicked the driver's seat with all the force of his foot. Or he grabbed Ruby's hair, once yanking hard enough so that strands of her hair came out in his fist.

After all the songs were recorded, Luke moved on to mapping the planet itself, sketching the prominent landscape features, the mountain chain that ran along the ragged coastline, the splatter of shallow ponds. In particular, he drew numerous maps of a teardrop lake and the land surrounding that lake: the lake as seen from various angles, from the east, from the south-southwest. He drew diagrams of the transport ship that would bring him there and of the tent in which he would live, and of his supplies, and what was in his storage trunks. "I would like to go there with you. Is there room?" Beth asked. [illegible] [illegible] a joke. This ability to capture, in exquisite detail, a world he could never visit, a world nobody cared about but him. One of the constellations, the largest one, resembled a ship, and at the edge of its left rudder, he marked the sun, our sun, around which a minuscule Earth must have circled.

While documenting LK-32-C, Luke looked happy. Or if not happy, at least he looked content. He looked, at least, like he did not want, in that moment, to destroy something. Beth encouraged him to stay in his room beside his drawing supplies. She served dinner to him at his desk on a melamine tray. Most children believe in all sorts of ridiculous things. Why shouldn't their child be allowed to believe in this? Luke could finish off a sketch pad within days or in a day. Soon LK-32-C's supporting materials filled several cardboard boxes that the boy kept in his closet for easy access.

It was March, still frigid, the streets coated in black ice, when an intake counselor from the clinic called to say there had been a cancellation. "You can't imagine how lucky you are," the counselor said. The tests and interviews took up an entire Friday, and by the following week, Luke had a diagnosis, which his parents welcomed with a sense of relief, as an identified problem usually means identifiable solutions.

"Look, this is not some death sentence I'm handing you," the psychiatrist promised them at their final debriefing. "Many doctors, myself included, believe that what your son has can be managed and occasionally outgrown under the right conditions." The psychiatrist's office was located on the first floor of the clinic. The doors to the clinic, in fact most doors throughout the building, were kept locked. To get anywhere, a person had to be buzzed through. The doctor tapped the paper on his desk containing his concluding notes. He circled the box labeled SOCIAL. The box had four arrows coming out of it, connecting it to other boxes. Apparently more arrows were needed. The doctor drew several more. "I'm going to give you some important advice now, so I want you both to listen. The worst thing you can do is to let a child like yours retreat from the world and from everybody in the world. So don't do it. Okay? Because it's what these children long to do, to live in their own little universes where they exert total control and make up all the rules. You have to encourage your son to remain a social being. Your most important job moving forward, in my opinion, is to create those right conditions, the *social* conditions, in which your child will thrive."

Beth purchased every book on the psychiatrist's recommended reading list. She stacked the books neatly on her nightstand. At the bottom of the stack, she placed the more technical books that dealt with the neurology of the brain. Those she would save for later. At the top of the pile, she put the books she wanted to read first, books that contained 1,001 practical ideas, and the true stories of heroic parents, and the narratives of a cure. Here was what Beth learned from such books: that any parent of a child like Luke—any good parent, that is—must approach each idea, each therapy, with an open mind. You never know what might work for your exceptional son or daughter. In order to find something that works, you must be willing to try anything.

It was in the spirit of such open-mindedness that Beth and Tom embraced applied behavioral analysis; then behavioral observation, reinforcement, and prompting; then visual schedules; then nurturing the hearts; then checklists. They tried the diet change that many of these books recommended, though Luke shrieked when he was no longer allowed to eat his yogurt because the casein in it might be the cause of all their problems. They—or rather Beth, as Tom was usually working—[illegible] She attempted to organize play-dates, though the parents generally did not return her messages or their children were busy. She bought things, a weighted blanket, a plastic necklace Luke could chew if nervous, a cozy caterpillar sleeve, a vibrating pillow. For herself she purchased a notebook with cheerful yellow flowers exploding across the cover, in which to record daily observations of her son, as if she were a scientist, and this was her work, and it was all making sense.

Day eight of vitamin therapy. Had to shove pills down throat. He screamed until his voice went. Peed once in pants. Threw ball repeatedly at R.'s head. ~~XXXXXXXXXXXXXX~~. Slept.

Day nine of vitamin therapy. Screamed for half an hour then he broke rocking chair in his room ~~XXXXXXXXXXXXXXX~~. Shut the door to his room. His teacher asked what was wrong with his throat. Refused to go to sleep. Banged on my door until 2 a.m.

Beth's mom, who lived in Indiana, preferred not to visit, but wrote supportive texts.

Luke led them to the art annex, into an airy atrium illuminated by a row of skylights. "I can just smell the creativity going on in here!" Beth gushed. The room smelled like old paint. Luke gestured to an exposed beam where a hundred identical God's eyes dangled down like some kind of nest or infestation. "Are they yours?" she asked. Luke shrugged, nodded. "They're wonderful," she forced herself to say.

Not once that day had Luke brought up LK-32-C. Nor would he mention the planet after they departed from the annex and veered right into a different part of the woods, to where an iron gong hung suspended between a framework of logs. Luke grabbed a stout stick from the ground and banged the gong a dozen times, the sound reverberating uncomfortably through Beth's chest, like someone was shaking her chest. Of course that fictional planet had been a connection to him, the academy's therapist admitted in their last phone call—"My only connection," Beth corrected her—but now it was time to revel in reality and let such connections go.

"My turn," Beth said, intending to demonstrate how one could hit a gong delicately, creating a recognizable beauty, but Luke had already lost interest and went running off down the trail, not slowing until he reached a pond, the final stop of their tour. Eventually they caught up to him. Luke pointed to the algae, as if there was something meaningful hiding in its green folds, then settled himself into a squat in the mud. Beth crouched there too, pretending not to care about the muck ruining her shoes or the stink of the water. Tom stood somewhere behind them. A pair of empty canoes bobbed beside the dock.

"So how are you doing, Luke?" Beth asked. Luke continued staring at the surface of the pond. She tried to follow his gaze but all she could see, in the direction where he looked, was a jumble of dead logs in the shallows. What was she not seeing? She repeated her question again, this time more loudly.

"That is the stupidest question I have ever heard," Luke said, his fingers fidgeting as if his hands were trying to communicate something to him or about him. Were this a different type of story, a story in which magical things happened, he might, with such movements, have been casting a spell. The spell could have conjured forth a golden sphere hovering above their heads that radiated out light and warmth. The sphere could have been a physical manifestation of Beth's love, or else Luke's love—or both of their love—so if anyone ever questioned whether or not there was some love here, she could have pointed to that sphere.

The sphere vanished, it was never there, and Beth explained to Luke, her voice sharper than intended, that this is what mothers do: they ask questions when their sons go away. The questions poured out of her after that. Question after panicked question from that list in her head, a list that kept her awake at night, because it is impossible to get rid of a question if there is no one to ask that question to. She asked Luke about the ages of the other boys in his home, and whether he had been in a canoe yet. How often did they have campfires? It wasn't as if these were trick questions or difficult questions. Did he like campfires or did the smoke bother him? What was his favorite meal he had eaten so far? She found herself unable to stop, despite the fact that Luke was curling in on himself, shoulders hunching, his fingernails digging into his scalp. He would not look at her. "Beth," Tom said, as if the act of speaking her name would fix something. She asked Luke what he was staring at and whether he had any pictures up in his room—of her or Tom, she meant, though she did not say so specifically—and what was the best and worst thing about his new school, and the weather. Was the New Hampshire weather different from weather in New York? What did he miss most from home?

"You lied," Luke said.

There was a flash of movement in the pond, a frog leaping from its perch on one of the logs. It turned into a shadow. The shadow kicked away beneath the water. The water moved and rippled.

"Lied about what?" Tom asked.

Behind them, on the edge of a branch, a red bird swelled with what seemed like the ending to a song. There was a feeling of ridiculous loss in the air, though Beth did not care to examine the feeling closely enough to figure out who or what was losing whom. And whether it had already been lost long ago. Or was it in the process of being lost. *Silence is okay too*, she remembered a therapist—which one?—telling her. "Silence is also a valid connection," this kindhearted woman with the weepy eyes had insisted, not because the statement was true—it wasn't—but probably because they, Beth and the therapist, had been sitting in the silence of that suffocating room for such a long time, because Beth had not wanted to admit what she had begun to do to Luke when her temper flared. "I think I would be a better person if I was not given this child," she ended up saying. The therapist did not understand this was a confession. She told Beth, "You won't believe how many mothers think that."

By the spring of Luke's second-grade year, the people in distant orbit around Beth and Tom's life, such as Beth's old friends, or her two brothers who lived elsewhere, or her mother, also living elsewhere, believed Luke to be improved. What a quick recovery! Like magic. Like a miracle! How happy they were for her, they told Beth, praising the wonders of a little research and good therapists. Her mom texted, *Glad you are feeling better. I just want to give you a hug for all your hard work you are doing on behalf of L. He is lucky to have you! We are both at 46 degrees outside but I am cloudy here. You have the sun.*

Nothing had, in fact, gotten better. Beth had simply stopped telling others the sorts of things her son continued to do. How, during circle time, Luke told his class "I am thankful for my sister to be dead," or the comic strip he shoved under the bathroom door in which he had drawn Beth, lost in some galactic landscape, and then a wolflike animal lopes along and bites off her head. "Why is the wolf doing this?" she asked Luke, pointing to the final square where the animal was devouring her face. "He's going to get sick after eating your hair," Luke said. Too much energy was required to edit one's day into a story that could be spoken aloud, and besides, the stories one shared about parenthood were supposed to be funny, or at least lighthearted. If any confessions were made, they must be charming, like how you fed your baby a dessert when he was a day old. "That's just the terrible truth about what we do in my family," one mom confessed at the park, laughing as she recalled the ice cream given to her newborn, *cappuccino bliss*, of all the flavors. The mom turned to Beth. "What about you? What's your deep dark secret of motherhood?"

Somewhere there was a running list Beth had kept for their

family therapist, where she wrote down whenever Luke kicked his sister in the head while the younger child was napping. Or when he hissed to Ruby, thinking Beth out of earshot, "I can see your underwear." Or when he trapped a neighborhood girl in their garage. Glancing at the list's first page, Tom said, "You are making our son sound deranged." In fact there was too much to record and none of it made them look good. Luke was refusing to remain in his bed at night. "What are we supposed to do, strap him down?" Tom asked. "What do you use to strap a kid down, a belt?" Neither of them wished to be the sort of parents who used a belt in that way, but the moment the lights were switched off, Luke stormed around his room, letting whatever heavy objects, his books, his microscope, his rock collection, thud to the ground. He stood outside the door to the master bedroom and kicked their door, yelling, "Emergencies!"

Out of all this, their family therapist was trying to construct a narrative of hope. Which turned out to be an impossible task if Beth kept bringing along her glum unending list to their weekly sessions. Finally the therapist ordered Beth to throw that list away. "You're the one who told me to take notes," Beth reminded her. The therapist shook her head. "I want you to spend your energy on creating positive experiences with your son. Explore his interests. Make your child's interests your interests. Let's see if that improves things at home."

Luke's interest, as he had only one, was LK-32-C, though the planet had recently undergone a change. The place seemed to be dying, or at least the things inhabiting the planet seemed to be dying off, leaving behind a skeleton of a world devoid of recognizable shapes or color. Luke made a chart listing all the creatures of the water that once existed on his planet, in its ponds and its lakes. There were asterisks next to those creatures now extinct. Every name on the list was starred. He made another chart for the birds; every bird was gone also. "It sounds like a lonely place," Beth said. "Wrong," said Luke. The pictures he now drew consisted of three or four intersecting lines, alarming in their bleakness, especially if Beth tried to imagine herself or anyone living there between the lines or on top of the lines. Luke continued to roam the house at night. He turned on every faucet in every bathroom. She, or Tom, or sometimes the two of them, dragged Luke back to his room, and they would hold the door shut from the other side so Luke couldn't get out. Beth tried to stay awake as long as she could, to keep an eye on him, using those pills that the truck drivers swore by, the ones they sold at gas stations near thruway exits. The wood of Luke's bedroom door cracked from the boy's repeated kicks.

"Luke, where did all the living things on your planet go?" Beth asked one afternoon, *your interest is my interest*, barely able to keep her eyes open in the dimness of his bedroom. The blinds were drawn, only the green light of the closet turned on.

"They weren't supposed to be there," he said. His most recent drawing consisted of a paper colored entirely black.

"Does it look like this all the time now?" she asked, pointing to the drawing.

"Only to people like you," he said.

[illegible] animals or beings walking around. Happy animals. Happy beings! Can't we talk about one of those places?" Luke pulled his weighted blanket over his shoulders and faced the wall. The way he stared at the wall, it was like he was seeing something other than a wall. But what was he seeing? It was also like she was no longer there.

Hi Luke,
Can I quiz you?
Love, Mom

Hi again,
Can I quiz you now?
Love, guess who

Luke,
Can you open your door?
Mom

Hi Luke,
How are you?
What is the largest planet? (Please circle)
Venus
Uranus
Jupiter
your house
LK-32-C
Love,
Me

Luke,
What is 78 × 23 =

Hi Luke,
Are you getting my notes?
I slide them under the door and then they disappear.
Are you eating my notes!?!
Are you still in there?

Luke,

Apollo 12 landed where?

____

Love,

Mom

Luke,

Choose one. Then can you come out of your room?

LK-32-C is:

A. hot arid

B. rainy tropical

C. subarctic wet

D. dry tropical

From,

Your Mother

Luke,

Here are some fun definition questions.

What is the meaning of kell?

Also, what is a sward?

Mom

Luke,

If you don't respond to this note, I am going to open the door.

Luke,

Don't make me take the door off the hinges again.

Unlock it now

I'm going to kick the door down get away from the door

The cookout lunch was held back at the quad: platters of veggie burgers, corn, potato salad, and stewed peaches, with lemonade to drink. They sat at a picnic table in the sun with another boy and his parents. "Is this a friend?" Beth asked. Luke threw his corn onto the ground. "Pick up the corn, Luke," Beth said. He did not pick up the corn, so Beth did. It was covered in dirt. She wrapped the dirty corn up in a napkin. The men shook hands across the table, and soon they were comparing the sad facts of incompetent management while the two women discussed their upcoming travel plans. "It's been years since we've vacationed anywhere," the other mom confessed. "Too much unpredictability. And the planes. Whew! I said never again. But we're planning a grand tour in the spring, just the two of us. I want to visit every country in Europe, and during the trip, I intend to complain nonstop about other people's disabled children."

The boys did not look at each other. Luke studied the trajectory of his crumbs that he rolled along the curve of his plate. The other boy watched the trees that were doing nothing at the far end of the quad. The trees weren't even moving in the wind as there was no wind. The mother leaned toward her son, bringing her face in front of the child's face. "I like how you're using silverware today for lunch, Mark," she said, looking into her son's eyes. Mark wasn't exactly eating, though he did grasp his fork limply in his hand. "You're also doing a good job of listening. I can see you're working hard on your listening skills." Beth recognized this parenting approach; she had tried it, its unending praise, briefly, the previous year. In addition to making her sound ridiculous in public, it had also failed.

"Anyone in need of fruit?" she asked, rising from the table.

In line for dessert, Beth found herself standing behind the school's headmaster, a purposeful young man who had led Luke's intake interview the previous spring. Like an old friend, he greeted her with a kiss on her left cheek. He wore a T-shirt that read, in fiery orange letters, COMPLIANCE IS NOT MY GOAL!

"And how are you finding Luke? Amazing, right?"

"Actually," Beth said, "I thought he would be further along than he is."

The man raised his fingers to his lips as if to suppress a smile. Then he shrugged and smiled anyway. "I knew you were going to say that! You won't believe how many parents say that to me their first year. Everybody expects us to pull off this miracle in three months, right? Everyone expects us to be magicians! But we don't use magic here. We use hard work, and hard work takes a whole lot of time. Keep in mind, Beth—it's Beth, right?—that every day we have to choose so carefully what to put into our action baskets. Because the baskets we're given for these kids are only so big." He held his hands a foot apart as if he were holding an actual basket. The sun was high and obvious above them in the blue sky.

"I guess what I'm saying is, if I were the one choosing what to focus on, I'd like my child to be able to use silverware and respond to simple questions."

"I know this is hard for you. Nobody imagines their role as a parent to be so hands off." The headmaster was a tall man who had to look down to meet Beth's eyes. His eyes were careful and warm and caring, like he had the ability to care about anyone. "But I think certain children like your son are happier, how do I say this, without the active parental involvement. My god, you should hear Luke laugh on certain days. It seems to me like he's never really laughed before. It seems to me there's all this laughter and joy stuck in Luke behind this dam of concrete, and we have to break that dam down and let out the joy."

At the intake interview, the headmaster had wanted to know what they loved most about their son. "Of course I love him," Beth insisted. "That wasn't my question," said the headmaster. Now he reached out to squeeze Beth's hand. "Come on, it'll be okay. What a day, right? And let me tell you, you have one heck of a treat in store for you. Just you wait until you hear what Luke does at the afternoon performance. Just you wait."

The line jerked forward. In the middle of the folding table lay a pile of spotted bananas and the quarter of an apple alone on a plate, its cut flesh already browning. A woman in a hairnet bobbed her head and smiled apologetically. The headmaster grabbed the last apple, and he took a substantial bite.

The first dozen times Beth brought up the idea of a therapeutic boarding school, Luke swore he would never go. That he would lock himself permanently in his bedroom. "The locks are on the outside of your door now," Beth reminded him, a recent development. She showed him photographs of boys his age gathered around a campfire and sharpening their sticks with knives, smoke snaking into their eyes, and another photo of three boys in a canoe, the boy in front holding a fish. She told him about Abbot Academy's two ponds, and the farm with the horses and the pigs, and how the wild turkeys wandered through the surrounding woods. They watched a video where a current student explained, "This school has changed me into a different and better person." Beth had already sent in the paperwork and the deposit.

"Then I will lock you and Dad in my room," Luke said.

"Then Dad and I will climb out the window and slide down the gutters and come and find you." Tom had not wanted their son to be sent away, believing they could handle him, that it was their one job as parents to handle him, but that was because he was so rarely home. Beth noticed a wet spot spreading across the front of Luke's pants. "Did you just pee on yourself?"

"Then I will take my bike and ride down the train tracks in the direction of an oncoming train," Luke said.

Clearly a change in approach was needed.

"Now hear me out," said Beth a few days later. "What if I told you that you wouldn't be at this new school forever? What if this new school isn't your final destination? What if—" She had his attention now. He was looking at her, looking at her lips. "What if Abbot Academy is a gateway to reach LK-32-C?"

On the first of August, Beth loaded up their van with two trunks, three bags, and six boxes, and she and Luke headed out for New Hampshire. "It's going to be so nice once you get to that planet of yours," she said as they pulled off the toll road, her voice chipper and shrill. The only time Luke had spoken in the previous hour was to say he needed to change his pants again. The scenery soon grew repetitive. There were the trees. There were the impenetrable woods. Luke had jammed himself against the passenger door and was studying the seam of his right sock. "You'll get to finally dip your toes into that exotic pond water, right? You'll get to eat one of those green knobby plants, and if you look up, I bet you'll see the double moons. I hope you'll write me all about it, but I especially want to hear about those moons."

"What about the moons?"

"I don't know. How does it feel to have two of them above you? One day, I bet I can come visit you and see the moons for myself. We could live there together. Maybe I'll never come back either."

The six boxes in the trunk contained technical information Luke would need to survive on his planet once he arrived: the maps of the landing site where he would be set down by the transport mini; an inventory of necessary supplies; the binders of data, including graphs of the annual rainfall and charts that registered the rare hours of sunlight. It was against the rules of Luke's new school to bring such objects of the child's obsession into the territory of a fresh start, but those boxes seemed necessary for the boy's well-being. She had not imagined Luke's belongings would be searched.

The house which would soon become Luke's home sat on the south end of the school grounds, connected to the academy's other buildings by a path made out of crushed gray stone. From the porch, you could see one of the two ponds, along with a pier where a boy, splayed out on his stomach, dipped a fishing line into the water. Beth pointed out the boy, the pier, the pond. Luke asked, "Does the pond have shadows in it?" "What kind of shadows, like ghosts? Or like fish shadows?" Beth asked. Tom wasn't there, having offered to stay behind and look after Ruby. "No," Luke said. He did not want to walk down the hill to see the pond. The house had checkered curtains on all the windows, and recently the entire exterior, including the eaves and the shutters, had been painted a pristine white.

Beth was instructed to hand off her son's belongings to a young man dressed in a white polo who introduced himself to Luke as the house dad. "You can call me House Dad," explained the man, "or John, or Mr. John, or whatever you want. Whatever you're most comfortable with." He did not introduce himself to Beth, and when he walked her child up the stairs to what was now the boy's bedroom, Beth was not invited in past the front doorway. From what she could see of the interior, the house was uncluttered, some might have called it sterile, the main room furnished with a stiff blue couch and, in the other corner, an antique cabinet with burned black knobs whose drawers looked stuck.

"Now what is this?" Mr. John asked in the foyer about each of Luke's belongings before he allowed an assistant to carry the trunk, or the bag, or whatever it was, upstairs. "Socks," he would announce. "Underwear. Shoes! Pants. Very nice. What a nice hoodie." He moved on to the second bag. Eventually he reached the boxes that held LK-32-C's documents. For several minutes he sorted through the papers before asking, "Now what is this?"

Luke was still upstairs. Beth had no idea what he was doing up there. "They're papers my son needs," she said quietly. John allowed the lid of the box to fall shut. “They’re drawings about a place he made up. A planet that’s necessary to him.” She did not mention this was the first of several such boxes. The house dad pulled a handkerchief from his pocket and wiped his hands.

“You know what?” he told Beth. “Let me get someone to give you a tour of our school.”

While she was on the tour, led by a boy several years older than Luke who stared at his feet when he spoke—“Here are the stables where we keep the ponies, here is the labyrinth where we pick up and drop a stone, here are the canoes where we paddle across the lake”—the house dad loaded LK-32-C’s data, every box of it, back into Beth’s van.

Luke did not come downstairs to say goodbye. Instead, Beth said goodbye to Mr. John. “Do you need a hug?” John asked. She intended to say no, of course not, she needed no hug from a stranger poised so effortlessly to replace her, only she found herself opening her arms and crying against his chest, his polo already damp there, either from sweat, as it was a muggy day, or from the tears of the other mothers who had rested their heads in the identical place below his left shoulder. He patted her hair until she said she felt better.

A month into the first semester, Beth received an envelope addressed to her in her son’s precise handwriting. “Why does your face look like that?” Ruby asked, tugging the edge of Beth’s skirt. Ongoing communication from a child attending Abbot Academy was not to be expected. The school’s headmaster went as far as suggesting that parents imagine their children were leaving them for another world, a better world so distant that conversation would be sporadic or probably impossible. Yet here was this letter. Ignoring Ruby, she carried the envelope into the kitchen where she tore the thing open. Inside: a blank sheet of paper folded neatly into thirds. She called the school and the first woman she spoke to said, "It sounds to me as if your child wanted to send you a piece of paper."

"Could I talk to someone there other than you, please?" Beth demanded. She was transferred to the school therapist, who assured Beth that a sheet of paper was meaningful in its own way, like a coded message. Now she merely needed to figure out the code.

Dishes from the previous night's dinner had still filled the kitchen sink, an elaborate meal she cooked up for no reason at all—a seitan roast, herbed potatoes, a homemade gravy, the kind of meal one made for out-of-town dinner guests, though no guests had been present. Beth turned the faucet on with water hot enough to scald her fingers as she told the school therapist how, last summer, Luke's psychiatrist had recommended medication for the boy. "I keep wondering if I should have listened to that doctor instead of sending Luke away," she said.

The therapist laughed. "You know, I have never viewed a child as damaged goods that must be 'fixed' or 'cured,' or whatever those men think they're doing with their medicines. Children come to us, and of course they bring along their challenges. What child doesn't have challenges? But instead of shrinking that child and his challenges into a narrow and predetermined shape, we work with them and help them to build a life where they can thrive. Let me give you an example. Let's consider a child with a singular obsession. This may sound familiar to you, Beth. Luke wasn't the only one, you know. Practically every one of our students has their own fixation by the time they're sent to us, so focused that they're unable to interact properly with their own surroundings. That's no way to live."

Beth scrubbed the plates first. She was rough with the scrubbing, causing droplets of sudsy water to splash out onto the tile. When Ruby was a baby, Beth had placed her right there on the kitchen floor, on a clean blanket in a patch of sunlight, then she left the room to use the toilet. When she returned, Luke was standing beside his sister, and her first impulse was to think how sweet, as the boy so far had taken such little interest. Then she noticed his right leg pulled back as if he were about to kick her. Then he kicked his sister in the head. He was wearing his pointed dress shoes as if going out to a birthday party.

The therapist said, "You'd be surprised how many of these kids, with a little nudging, and in a different environment, will choose new and healthier interests on their own. I'm talking about a more diverse stable of interests. Of course, their attention might not run as deep, many instead of one, but we've found that deepness to be a form of isolation for our unique children."

Beth scrubbed at a porcelain tray next with the sponge's rough end, her fingers red and irritated from the heat of the water. Luke had kicked the baby twice more before she could reach him, yanking him away by the arm more roughly than necessary, as if she wished to hurt him in return. Afterward, howling and fussy, Ruby had spiked a fever, and Beth had to take her in to the doctor's, where she told the nurse exactly what her son had done. The nurse had given Beth an accusatory glare, and it was clear that Beth had told the wrong story.

"Sometimes it seems that the parents were as interested in that old obsession as the student was. Or, in certain cases, the parent more so, as an obsession can create this artificial platform for connection and communication." Up until this point, the therapist's voice had been amicable and pleasant, almost overly so, like here they were, two old friends chatting about their kids. But here her words took on an element of reproach. "Yet if you remove the parents from the setting. If you remove that encouragement—do you understand what I'm saying? The child can move on and find their appropriate place in this world. Your son is going to be fine, Beth. Trust me. You're by no means the only one who did this."

• • • •

The performance took place after lunch beneath a white tent. Beth and Tom sat in the final row of folding chairs, having arrived several minutes late, Beth needing to use the portable toilet, for which there had been a line. Along both sides of the tent, someone had strung up pale party streamers that twisted carelessly in the breeze.

The staff presented first. The school's history/drama teacher silently tapped the top of her left breast, beneath which must have been her large heart. The headmaster told a story using puppets about a wolf lost in the woods who went around destroying things and people, in particular destroying children. The wolf, he explained, was a metaphor for the kind of adults who did not understand these boys or accept their gifts. Additional teachers strummed guitars, juggled safety scissors, led the children in a silent meditation. Luke's house dad shouted from the podium, to rousing applause, "We have taken off our braces and our casts, and we have let ourselves loose, so we are free to grow magnificent into the people we were born to be!"

This went on for at least an hour.

"How much longer do you think this can last?" Beth whispered to Tom.

The student portion of the program followed, in which a boy read an acrostic poem about how he liked horses' manes. *H is for horses. O is for original. R is for real.* Another boy recited a list of affirmations detailing how much he was loved. A third boy instructed the audience to write down the Pledge of Allegiance, but they had to cross out every third word and write that word again, and each time the boy clapped his hands, they had to tap their pencil on the paper. This was followed by several minutes of break dancing, after which Luke stood up from his chair in the second row, turned toward the side of the tent, where no one sat, and he began to sing.

It was a song Beth didn't know, rhythmic and heavy, perhaps a fragment of music leftover from LK-32-C, and at first, as he was stumbling over almost every note, she hoped the song would end soon, for his sake. Only when he reached the refrain, where he repeated what sounded like the colors of a rising sun, did he find his pitch, and his voice turned out, surprisingly, to be beautiful, growing stronger until it filled the air and then all the available space of the tent. No one in the tent was moving, it seemed, or even breathing. As the song continued, several women began to cry. One man started clapping softly. Tom grabbed Beth's hand and held on to it. There is something affirming in watching one's child bring a gift into the world and to find that the gift is recognizable to other people. Luke's voice became that of a choir stained with the light of colored glass—full bodied, sweet, whole, rich with adult emotion, some sadness, yes, of course, but also hope. She worried the song would end if she did so much as shift her weight in her chair, so she sat very still.

Though at no point did Luke look up at her, she believed his voice to be seeking her out for the first time in a long while, his voice passing over the heads and shoulders of the other mothers, as if she alone possessed something fiery and necessary to him. When the sound of his voice found her, and enveloped her, it was like he was holding her, like he had thrown his arms around her neck, a gesture she couldn't remember him ever doing. Through his song, he seemed to be telling her that even without his planet, even without a bridge to her, he would be all right. So it was time to let the idea of a place she might share with him, where she was necessary to him, float away.

In the end, this is what she did. The idea of such a place bobbed like a soap bubble in the sun, iridescent and complex, near her for a moment more, near her face, hovering near her mouth like a kiss, then it moved away, floating oblivious above the bowed heads of the other mothers and fathers, eventually easing out of the tent where it drifted skyward and out of sight. Who knows where it went after that. Maybe to some other mother who would do a better job catching hold of it, and turning it into a reality, then offering that reality to her child. In Luke's voice, she felt the imagined pressure of his arms and the warmth of his skin one last time against the skin of her neck, as if she was no longer needed here and he was saying goodbye. Even with his hair grown out, he still resembled her. People always used to tell her that. *Your little "you,"* they would say, and she appreciated the possessive, though it wasn't true.

The headmaster, while in line at the dessert table, had assured her how every day Luke was improving in these small yet substantial ways. He had placed a hand upon Beth's arm. His hand felt like a warm and unwelcome weight. He said, "Let's you and I recognize right now that your child was headed down a wretched path with you. I think Luke could have, at some point, harmed someone or himself irreversibly. But you know what, you figured this out. You put him on a different path. That sort of clarity requires a lot of courage." The headmaster's voice was pitched low and it sounded thick with affection. Or love? At first she thought, ridiculously, it was love for her. *Is he hitting on me?* she wondered as his hand continued to press onto her arm. But then no, of course not, it was love for Luke, and once she recognized who that love was for, that unedited and easy love for her son, she wanted to wrestle it from this man—what right did he have to it?—and stuff it into her mouth and swallow it, because it should have been hers. No one had ever told her that she had loved her son too much.

The song Luke was singing had to have an end to it, because

that is what songs do, they end, but before it ended, a magnificent red bird soared in through the back entrance of the tent, its wings as red and open as an open wound—were any birds of this world actually this color?—followed a moment later by another bird, equally as vivid and as expansive, and then, just as quickly, both birds were gone.

After the group bow, Luke filed out of the tent following his classmates, all of whom, immediately after, turned around and walked back through the tent opening to cheers. Luke was the only boy who did not return, at least not immediately. Perhaps he needed to pick something up from his room, Tom offered. Something to give to them. A drawing? A craft? A gift? Around them the other parents were shaking their children's hands in farewell or dragging their protesting child into a hug. Certain mothers cried into their boys' hair. Beth was reminded of a wake. Then those other parents left while Tom and Beth continued to wait beside the podium, playing silly games to occupy themselves—how many chairs are in the room, how many windows are in the tent, how many crumpled pieces of paper are on the ground—until Luke's house dad finally appeared and reminded them that the event was over and it was time to go home. "Go on, get out of here! Go make out in your car or something. Go have *fun*!" Luke's house dad assured them that everything was fine, that this was his job after all, and he was perfectly capable of taking it from here.

"I wanted to tell Luke goodbye," Beth said. "Can't I tell my own son goodbye?"

"Don't you worry about that. There's an ice cream party going on at the main hall, and I don't think wild horses could drag your little guy away right now. Luke figured out thirty-seven unique topping combinations so far. He made a chart, and let me tell you, when the charts come out, you know it is going to get *wild*." The house dad grinned. He had such tiny and perfect teeth. He looked like the sort of man who would make a good father. "Look, I'll tell him goodbye for you, if you want. If that would help." Beth said how kind of him. That would be very nice. Thank you. "Hug?" he asked, opening his arms. "Of course," Beth replied, recognizing that somewhere along the way the script had changed, and this was her role to play now. The hug, this time, was brief. Luke's house dad smelled like Old Spice and sunscreen. She imagined she was hugging Luke though this man was nothing like her son. But he would have to do.

"Do you know what I've been thinking?" Beth asked as she and Tom strolled across the quad to their car, their shadows having grown distorted and long. Behind them they could hear the braying of horses and the occasional shout of a boy's laughter. Luke's? Would she recognize the sound? "I mean, this could be a sad moment. I mean, I could be crying right now."

"You are crying," Tom said.

"What I mean is I could be crying more than this. But it's about Luke, not us. I mean, I love him too. It's not like a contest. It's not like only one person can love a child and then, game over. And there are many different kinds of love, right, like useful love, or loving someone from a distance. You don't have to be standing in front of somebody to love them. Right? It's not like, in order for Luke's happiness to be real, we have to be there to witness it. Who are we to say what his happiness should look like anyway. We want him to be happy, right? And if we weren't the ones able to help him, so what. He's being helped. There's no rule saying he needs to know we're loving him for our love to be real."

She would have left with Luke, without a glance back at what they were leaving, had she found a way to go. Tom reached for her hand. "I adore you but you're not making any sense," he said. In his grip she felt the weight of his knuckles, of his wrist, his arm, the weight of his entire adult body, their shared decades, fixing her to the earth.

Ahead, on the other side of the field, something emerged from the woods, darting into the final light of the sun, oblivious, scratching frantically at the ground. It was brown, feral. Not even real. Before she could ask what it was, it disappeared back into the trees.

Dispatches

7043.2

The ship mom told me I had an hour to gather up my things then it was time to go. This was yesterday. "Are you ready for this?" she asked, like it mattered what I said. Last month I watched her get a guard's attention, then they dragged a kid away to his new habitat using some payload rope. The difference was, unlike him, I wanted to go. Ship Mom followed me to my room where I folded up my pants at the bottom of my duffel, then folded my shirts on top of my pants. My roommate was sleeping so I took his shoes from under his bed and placed them in my duffel as well. The reason I did that was so my bag didn't feel empty. Also I wanted to take something from him. While I was packing, Ship Mom stood humming in the hallway, guarding the door to my room like there was the chance I was going to run away to a different room. It was early, before any of the wake-up tones or the daylights, nobody else in the ho-hum hallways but us. Ship Mom led me to the second dock and boosted me into the transport mini, then she climbed in after me, showing me how to buckle the safety harnesses, then we left. Supply boxes filled the cargo area behind our two seats.

I can't answer the first question on your list because, during the ride to LK-32-C, I didn't feel like staring out the window. I stared instead at my hands. After we touched down and the brown dust settled around our landing gear, my ship mom, who never reminded me of you, said, "What a nice place to live, right? And you have it all to yourself. Wow, all this space. Lucky you." But she was frowning as she glanced around, like maybe she was expecting someplace less barren.

The whole time my ship mom was here she acted very busy, setting up camp, and opening the trunks and unwrapping the bags, and checking off each item on her packing list, 1,127 waters in the water trunk: check! 1,081 food packets in the food trunk: check! When my ship mom talked to me, she either looked at the trunks or at the tent, and the wind made her eyes water. "I hate this fucking job," she muttered, fussing with the tent's pulley system until the top of the tent looked taut and strong. In case I wasn't being a good listener, she went over each item with me twice, and she also read several pages of the handbook out loud, especially the parts about my courage and my isolation. Then she set up this recording machine on a low pedestal inside the tent. She told me if it's easier, if it would make me feel better, I could pretend I'm sending my audio journals back home to a certain someone. "Who actually reads these dispatches?" I asked. "Come on, don't ask questions like that," my ship mom said. After 14 days, the machine will stop transmitting—"Why?" I asked. She said, "I mean it, stop with the questions. The time for questions is over. It ended, I don't know, five years ago"—but after that I could continue talking into the machine if I wanted. If that, too, would make me feel better. Then the woman tried to hug me, then she said sorry she forgot, then she pressed the opalescent button on her belt. The ship moved into position above us like a hard cloud, then she left in the transport mini, then the ship also left.

Today nothing happened.

From,
Luke

7043.3

On a walk this morning, I saw a line of tracks on the other side of the lake leading to a spot of sandy dirt covered with indentations, as if a group of fretsome creatures had been burrowing all night. I'm supposed to be the only one here. I was always fine with that fact. When you used to believe I was lonely, I wasn't. Today I am breaking two rules. The lake water tastes like generic pro-drink (*rule #4, don't drink the water*) and I am no longer wearing my enclosure suit (*rule #7, keep your suit on*). The suit was hot and it made my skin sticky so I took it off and threw it into the lake where it sank. Gliding along the bottom of the lake were eleven wide gray shadows. They looked like the shadows of things I haven't seen before. At the lake's edge, mounds of shiny green knobs grow in clumps out of the rocks. On another day I'll touch them.

Remember how you gasped when you figured out LK-32-C was orbited by double moons? You promised that sleeping under moons like these would be a big deal event in my life. Guess what? It's not. The moons are small and dim. So they move across the sky like moons. So what. When I wake from my nap, there those two moons are, leaking their wimpy light like they're about to go out. I ate another food packet, both moons vanished behind a cloud, and in the new dark, I dug several paths in the sand with my favorite rock.

Sincerely,
Luke

7043.4

I don't use the tent anymore either. It doesn't rain at night, there aren't bugs, so I'm not using it, so what if that's rule #2. When it's time to sleep, I unroll my pack and lie on a sandy area to the right of the tent where, last night, I saw a silver animal in the moonslight running away from me. Or not running, as the animal didn't have any feet. It had circles on its legs. It had wheel-shaped legs. *Rolling?* I wanted to draw it only I don't have my colored pencils since you didn't allow me to bring them. As if there wasn't room on a ship for pencils. Were you afraid of what I would draw? Because there was room on the ship. One kid brought his dad's comforter which he dragged everywhere until I took it away from him and threw it down the chute. Another kid brought a bucket of figurines that looked like regular plastic people, only if you bent their limbs a certain way it turned out they were monsters on the inside with fangs.

The food packets are supposed to taste like *tempting high-pro casserole* or *finger-licking power patty*. Guess what? They don't. They taste like acorns, like trees, no matter the stated flavor. For breakfast today I ate half of a green knob. The knob tasted fine after I warmed it in the pot. Its insides softened like melted cheese.

Luke

7043.5

On the far side of the lake, I can hear them in the almost dark singing their music. I don't know what to call them. They have voices like low vowels and they repeat the same sound many times. I bet you would hate their singing. Because it repeats itself and you thought nothing should be repeated. A lot of kids cried when taken off the ship but I didn't because I knew I was finally going where I belonged. When the music stops, there is a silence in front of me and behind me which I can fall into, which is like falling into a pool of water I am keeping all to myself. In my old life, this never got to happen. Somebody, you, was always ahead of me, messing up the structure of the surface.

I am facing the lake now, whose ripples are patterning to the other side, four new ripples per second.

Now something else is moving over there.

Remember when all those ships were leaving home and I wouldn't come inside? A long time back I asked our ship mom, *Remember before when all those ships were leaving. Where did they go?*

Yours sincerely,
Luke

7043.6

There were four of them last night on the other side of the lake. Four figures, or whatever you want to call them, dragging themselves across the sand using their arms, and I don't think they were wearing clothes. Either they are an odd color or else they coated themselves in a blue substance and also they appeared to be eating rocks. Before they wandered away from the lake, they looked up in my direction, all four of them, all at once, and their throats made a single sharp clacking noise, loud enough to carry across the water.

Another question on your list is *Tell me whether there are seasons on LK-32-C.* Why does that matter? At home, everything kept changing, and you would not help me stop it. I'd wake up and the house would smell incompatible with the day before because you refused to make toast again for breakfast, you had to make eggs. My room looked divergent because someone—Ruby?—shifted my maps from the top of the dresser to the top of the bookshelf while I was in the closet. Outside, additional dandelions filled the yard, and I couldn't wear my blue socks because you said they were dirty. I had to wear the green ones. *Every day is a new day*, you kept reminding me, *so we have to do new things.*

That statement of yours is untrue.

There are no leaves to turn colors here. There are no trees. There are no birds either migrating across the sky to mess up the picture of the empty sky which is always in my head. In my head, the picture of the sky is clear without any clouds in it or birds. It's the same picture of sky that I will see if I open my eyes. So I don't even have to open my eyes.

Bye,

Luke

7043.7

If you were here, I bet you would go chasing after the figures on the other side of the lake, and if you caught them, I bet you'd make them act like you, or you would try to. They don't want to be chased, Mom. They don't want to be touched. They don't want to know anything about you or me and I don't want to know them. We don't care about each other in that way. When you used to care about me, it felt like your arms were ropes and you wanted to bind me to you. Nothing is binding me here. There are other ways to care about people, like not staring at them and never asking them one hundred questions.

You told me you would think about me all the time after I left. That's impossible. Do you think about me when you're asleep? Do you think about me when you're going to the bathroom?

From,
Luke

7043.8

Yesterday I wondered why the hatch of the ship had to open outward instead of in. After that, I studied the ripples as they repeated themselves across the lake. I did that for the rest of the day. Nobody tells me to stop thinking and go make some friends. This is the nicest place I've been.

The fifth question on your list is *How do you spend your time on LK-32-C (your new home!)?* Here is the correct answer: Every day I walk on the identical path along the lake, and when I get to the end of the path, I lie in the same spot of sand where I press my ear against the ground so the world can talk to me. I used to know its language, but then you made me forget it, so I have to learn it all over again. What you called my *nonsense.* "You are not some wild animal, so I will not let you talk like one," you had said, bringing that woman into the room who made me speak like you and everybody else.

Today I removed my clothes, stacked them into a pile, and placed the pile inside the tent next to the unopened sanitary kit. Then I made a new list of rules. Brushing my teeth is not on this list. Neither is putting on my clothes. The rules are private. This sky is yellow. It's only when the sun sets that the sky turns blue.

From,
Luke

7043.9

I wonder what this world would look like to you if you came. Would you travel all the way here and see an ugly desert, then would you yell at me to go finish my morning checklist, to go brush my teeth and put on my clothes? Like when you used to wrap your fingers around my arm until I stopped staring at my bedroom wall because all you ever saw was a wall. People don't stare at walls, you said. Later, I felt bad for you because you never will see what I get to see. If you had to come here, I would make you live on the far side of the lake. You could wave at me once in the morning, then you would have to go away like the other figures do. Tomorrow you would come back and, at the same time, we would wave at each other across the water. Then you would go away for good.

On day one, when my ship mom was still here, I picked up a rock. One of its sides was smooth. The other side was pockmarked but not random. The rock was amber or purple depending on how you tilted it, with lines of silver threading through it. There are thousands of rocks here. Would every one look the same to you? The ship mom had cleared her throat. She was standing behind me, and I wanted her to leave. "I'm going now," she finally said, and if you were here, you would have taken my rock away from me and forced me to look her in the eye. You would have made me say a line from the script, such as, *Thank you for having me goodbye.* But every rock is not the same. I don't miss anything about our home except the wall in my bedroom.

Luke

7043.10

At first, I didn't know what to do here. The handbook said do whatever you want. What does that even mean? I walked 100 steps in one direction, then I came back. Then I walked 100 steps in another direction. Then I drew a map in the sand that included the lake, my tent, and the spot where the transport mini had landed. The next day I walked 200 steps in those same directions. The ground is made out of a brownish sand and, far out, there looks to be some hills, or they could be mountains. When I stop moving, nothing is moving. There isn't even a breeze. All my life I've been attacked by other people's voices, then I had to smell how they smelled and act how they expected. Maybe my old life would have been okay if nobody said any words. People were always trying to touch my shoulder or look at my eyes.

Sincerely,
You Know Who

7043.11

My watch stopped working. The watch that you gave me before I climbed the ladder into the ship. It stopped telling time because I laid it on top of a rock, took another rock, then banged the rock I was holding onto its crystal face. Now there is no time. Instead of time, there are patterns. The water in the lake moves toward me then moves away. The sun is in the sky, the sun shines onto the rocks, the rocks encircle the lake, then the sun leaves the sky.

If I pick up a rock, I must replace that rock with another. I can also change the order of the rocks but only temporarily. I can put rock 10 into position 35 and move rock 35 to position 50. Then I have to find a rock to place in position 10. There is an order whirring beneath everything. At the end of the day, I make sure to return the rocks to their correct places.

Someday the food packets are going to run out. Nobody talked about what would happen after that. I checked the handbook and the pages under chapter 3, "Survival and Purpose," are full of errors, including 13 typos.

Luke

70-3[illegible]

Some people are just born at the wrong time or in the wrong place. I used to be one of those people. Thank you for sending me away to a world that wants me. Now you can finish the rock garden in the yard with all your extra time and teach Ruby to write her sevens correctly. Some kids (like Ruby) need their parents for a long while. Other kids only need you in the beginning. Or maybe not even then. Why do people think everyone requires a mother? You did what I wanted you to do, which was to let me go. In the evening, I lie on my back and stare up at the point in the sky where I think you are. The silence around me is like a parent finally giving me what I need. The silence puts its arms around me.

From,
Me

7043.13

I don't know if those figures on the other side of the lake were here from the beginning, or if they began as us and transformed into what they are now, but I can feel myself turning into something different, what I was always supposed to be, what you wouldn't have allowed me to be back home. There's no reason for me to keep holding on to those behaviors you used to call *a part of being human.* They felt like a costume, one that never fit. So I am letting those behaviors go. Everything you taught me is now drowning in the lake, and I think I am becoming clearer than the stars we used to watch from our deck after you blew the dinner candles out, clearer than the piece of broken glass you once picked up from the sidewalk and held in front of the sun.

There are 97 questions left on your list, including *How would you describe the weather? What is the best and the worst thing about your world? If you could have one thing or person from home suddenly appear beside you, what or who would it be?*

Luke

7043.14

What do you get when you cross a cow with a trampoline?

What do you get when you cross a cow and a lawn mower?

What do you get when you cross a lemon and a cat?
What do you get if you cross a cat with an elephant?
What do you call a cat crossed with a fish?
What do you get when you cross a fish with an elephant?
What do you get when you cross a frog with a rabbit?
What do you get when you cross a fish and drumsticks?

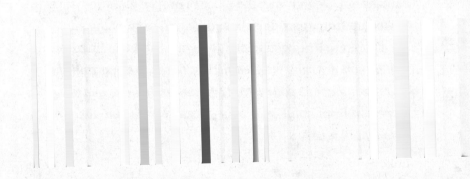

Bye (forever)!

Luke

Reflection

I used to dream my son was killing me. Though I don't think it was actually him. It only looked like him. I don't know where my actual son had gone. This other version of L. was stuck under a gate that was lowering down in my dream. The gate had spikes and L. kept calling out, using my son's voice, "Mom, help me. *Help me!*" My husband, T., waited in the shade. He asked, "So you're okay just standing there and watching our kid die?" If I moved to save L., I knew what would happen to me. That's why I wasn't moving. I don't know why T. didn't save our child himself. It was a dream. "So you're going to stand there and watch him die?" T. asked again. He repeated himself until that question broke me. I ran toward the gate and felt my rib break first, and then my shoulder blade, then something in my hand, each bone snapping until it no longer mattered what happened to me. I have always loved my son the best I could, despite what certain people have suggested. From beneath the spikes, I dragged L. out before any harm came to him, then his face turned gray, like I knew all along it would. His face cracked open with multiple crevices as he clawed at my cheeks. His hands were like hot ash. I don't know why T. didn't save me either.

Out of dreams like this, I awoke sweaty and exhausted. I would turn on my lamp and spend the remainder of the night skimming through the books stacked upon my bedside table about my son's condition. The books are still there. I was not halfway through the pile when L. went away. I flip through them from time to time, though not with the same urgency. My favorite books dealt with how to improve the minutiae of the day, instructing the parent on what toothbrush to use for their special child or how to whip up a batch of edible clay in the long afternoons. There are books concerning the management of one's own anger and how to live in the moment. Supposedly, not all moments can have pain in them. One of the books has a poorly taped spine. The spine ripped after my husband tried one evening to yank the book from my hands. He yanked hard enough to tear the book in two. It was a book written by a mother who cured her son. I asked T. whether he thought this mother cured her son by spending her evenings in bed fucking her husband. At the bottom of the pile is a book of Raymond Carver's poetry. He wears, in the book jacket photo, a collared shirt, as if he is this civilized man. His fingernails are meticulously clean, cleaner than mine, for sure. I wanted to read some of Carver's poems after I heard rumors about how he hit his first wife and wanted his son dead.

I do not think I look like a terrible person. If you were to see me today on the street, most likely walking alone and in the opposite direction, you might think, *There goes a competent librarian, or someone who, in the very least, likes her books.* My acquaintances will tell you I don't seem the [illegible] lose my temper or raise my voice, or, God forbid, take [illegible]. I make donations every December to three charities the[illegible] as my husband and I used to support when we [illegible], Greenpeace, Doctors Without Borders, and And [illegible] Children. In return, I receive personalized holiday ca[illegible] each organization, signed by their respective presidents. "Honestly, honey, you are the calmest person I know," my old hairdresser used to say, and in return I had to explain to him how my son was special, that he had special needs, or whatever you wanted to call it, special abilities, and really, I was just tired. I believe I used the language *I was blessed with*, as that was how people expected you to talk if you had a child like mine.

The house where my husband and I raised our kids for a time is on a dead-end street, a cul-de-sac would be the more optimistic term, a split-level ranch painted a dull sage with monstrous lilacs out front blocking the windows. I hadn't known the lilacs would grow so tall or I wouldn't have planted them. I imagined them more as waist-high bushes of a fragrant purple bloom, but whenever I hoped to cut them back, to allow for more natural light to enter our house, my husband told me now was not the right time of year. "Then when is the correct time?" I asked. I think he intended for our home one day to dissipate into the landscaping, and good riddance. In the backyard, we anchored a cedar swing set the kids never used, because they didn't want to play outside unless I dragged them out. There was a deck. There was a rusted gas grill beside two ceramic pots.

That was the outside of the house. The interior was, I'll be honest, a mess, cluttered with every item we had been told would help our son. We owned so many timers back then, some with these oozing bubbles of color, others with flashing lights, one so complicated we never figured out how to make it work. Also, the knobby fidget balls on the dinner table. The stress balls on the stairs (both the squeezing kind and the twisting kind). Stacks of the collaborative board games our second therapist recommended, which my son refused to play, because what is the point if no one loses. The No More Meltdown card game my son also refused to play, so I played it with my daughter, R., hoping L. would join in once he saw the fun we were having, but he did not join in. The game was not much fun anyway. Upstairs, the tranquil turtle, the tranquil starfish, the soothing rain tube, and the mini Hoberman sphere. The posters on the walls in which a cartoon frog proselytized about making good choices. "I am not listening to an amphibian," L. hollered. Another frog, this one made out of a flexible plastic that you could squeeze if angry, forcing its exaggerated eyes to pop out of its head. An actual frog in a terrarium, because one book promised that boys like my son responded well to pets, though this was not the case with my particular son, or else the definition of a pet did not include cold-blooded animals. The books scattered on the coffee table, nonfiction for me, fiction for L. Graphic novels about children I thought my son might relate to, children who got teased because of their differences. Or animals, a lone rabbit in a world of otters, for instance. L. never read such books willingly. He preferred almanacs and accounts of disasters.

Our house did not always look like this. We used to have a wooden arts-and-crafts table with four small chairs. On top of the table, there used to be several clean brushes and a stack of watercolor paper. We used to have a piano in the corner with an adjustable-height bench. My husband and I used to lie in bed upstairs, my head on his shoulder, me reading aloud from *Prevention*. My mom used to get me a gift subscription every year. I used to read about "The 10 Superpowers of Hemp Seeds" or "The Hazards of Eyelash Extensions." T. used to wrestle the magazine away from me and take off my underwear.

[illegible] these types of kids is going to be easy," he said, "only that it will be possible. A large portion of your life right now may be devoted to learning how to help your son. Remember that's not your whole life." T. drove straight to the library after the meeting, where I assumed he was researching our son's disorder. He returned home with a stack of fantasy DVDs featuring grand vistas of impossible worlds on the covers. T. watched the movies in the basement after the kids went to bed. The sounds of imaginary warfare floated through our heating vents. I heard a lot of horses, for a time, being slaughtered.

One particularly loud battle ended up waking L. He stumbled into my room, squinting at the bedside light. I think elves must have been massacring a herd of dragons.

"Why is there a war in our basement?"

"It's not a real war. Your dad is watching a movie."

"Was the *Hindenburg* disaster history's deadliest airship accident?"

"I don't know."

"Out of the ninety-seven passengers and crew aboard the *Hindenburg*, how many survived?"

"Go to sleep, L."

Certain days my son talked incessantly to me. He was a stream of trivia that followed me from room to room. Other days he would not tell me anything or say anything. For several days, or a week, he might refuse to smile. Instead of smiling, he would scream for an hour or longer, especially if we expected something of him. I don't know why he acted one way or the other. It could have been how I wore my hair or the fact it rained. Once he screamed until he ruined his voice, and the next day, he left the lights on in my car so the battery would die. He closed the laundry basket at the bottom of the chute so dirty clothes spilled out all over the wet basement. The week before Halloween, he ate the candy meant for the neighborhood children, stashing the wrappers in boxes of pasta in the pantry so I wouldn't know. I had to hand out pennies to the trick-or-treaters. "I'm so sorry," I said when the little ghosts cried. Such small things on their own.

For a long time, I didn't know it was him. I just thought these things happened. L. lied often but I think it was more complicated than that. I think he believed if he said something out loud, it became true, which made conversation, when we did speak, very confusing. Where in the indexes of my books should I have looked for help? *Anger*? *Animals*? *Answer keys*? *Answering*? *Antonyms*? *Anxiety*? *Appearance*? *Applesauce*? There was the possibility I was looking in the wrong books. When L. was in a certain mood, he wanted me to lie in bed beside him, not touching him, or even close to him, and pretend his stuffed animals could talk to each other. Often he made me be the meerkat and he was the snake. "What do you do all day?" the meerkat asked. The snake replied, "I think about how to open the window without hands so I can escape." The meerkat asked, "Escape to where?" The snake said, "Somewhere you don't know." *You are only given the child who needs you*, my mom used to text me before I sent my son away, after which she did not text that saying to me anymore. She also wrote, *God will give you what you can handle and no more.* When I was pregnant with L. and she assumed I was harboring a typical baby, the kind of baby you expect, she declared, *You'll know what to do. Once you hold your child, you'll know what to do.* After my son went away, she texted, *Remember, L. has only one real mother, and that mother will always be you.* [illegible]

[illegible] a psychopath. He had begun to inflict pain upon his sister—a pinch, a flick, a scrape—then he would step back to study her reaction. The therapist said sure, that is one possibility, psychopathology, but before anyone gets carried away, let's see what our subconscious can tell us about what's going on, as the subconscious already knows all of our secrets. "I don't have any secrets," my husband announced. We sat on a plaid couch in the corner room of a dilapidated mansion,

L. sandwiched between the two of us, my husband and I trying our best not to touch our son, which was difficult because of how the couch sagged. The therapist set out a box of markers and a stack of butcher paper. We were told to draw pictures of our three favorite animals while she, in her swivel chair, her fingers stroking the armrest, watched us draw. L. took his time, sketching every detail of a bird's gray wings until it looked like a real bird.

T. drew a wood thrush, a wolverine, and a frog.

I sketched a penguin, a unicorn, and a grizzly bear.

L. drew the gray bird, an armadillo, and a red panda.

Our therapist nodded to herself as she collected our drawings. "Amazing. Just amazing. Already this explains so much about you guys."

The next step was for us to name a positive and negative trait about each of our animals. I was told to go first. "Well, a grizzly bear kills people," I began.

"While this is fascinating," T. interrupted, "we had an unfortunate incident this morning between L. and his sister that I wanted to talk about. It happened after breakfast. He was playing robbers—"

Our therapist made a rolling motion with her hand. "We'll get to such issues eventually, I promise," she said. Right now, however, it was time for discovery. She instructed us to each pick a new marker. In this activity, we would create a group picture of a boat in a storm. One of us was to draw the lighthouse. Another would draw the boat. The last person was to draw the storm itself. We had to draw the picture together on the same piece of paper but without gestures or talking out loud. L. drew the boat because he liked modes of transportation. T. drew the lighthouse, which made sense, as he considered himself to be the savior to our family, the shining beacon who kept it all together. Which was somewhat comical as he was rarely home. I was left to draw the enormous waves that would destroy everything.

"You guys are naturals at this," said our therapist. "I'm getting a real sense for how you interrelate.” She promised to share her insights with us the following week but we never went back. On the drive home, T. turned each exercise into a joke, asking if I was going to eat both of their hearts, or tear off their scalps, or whatever grizzlies did to their prey.

Our second therapist told me to stop researching psychopaths on the internet and suggested, instead, that we get L. evaluated. My husband acted indignant, disliking the idea of doctors permanently attaching a label to our child. The second therapist said, “Your child happens to have a locked door in his chest. He was born that way, so the door is there, whether you want it to be or not. You may be wondering, if I open this door, what am I going to find, and what will that say about me? And will I get to close the door again once it’s been opened? An evaluation is only knowledge. The knowledge an evaluation gives you is the key to your child’s door.”

“Can we quit with the metaphors?” T. asked.

[illegible]

[illegible]

[illegible] Jobs.”

“Jobs was an asshole.”

“There are a lot worse things to be than what your son is. Trust me. You need to start celebrating his strengths. You need to start doing this right now. I think L. is going to be one of those people who have the ability to extract a great beauty from reality. I think he’s going to see reality so differently than us that he can dream up questions we would never think of asking. Those questions will be his gift to the world, and to us, even if he doesn't like this particular world that much. He is bringing us his gifts anyway. It'd be a shame to push such an offering away."

We took L. to a pediatric psychiatry clinic for the evaluation. For three consecutive mornings, my husband and I sat in waiting rooms or in the various offices, filling out stapled packets of surveys and other paperwork, while my son played diagnostic games with the psychiatrists. There were so many potted plants in those rooms. I was asked questions such as "Is your child easily scared?" and "What does he worry about?" and "Does he care about other children?" I didn't know the answers to all the questions. "He doesn't really talk to me in that way," I had to explain.

Dr. Brieman was about my age, unmarried, soft-spoken. He wore the same checkered shirt each day, brown and white. We were not to call him by his first name. He called my husband T., and he called me Beth. He had acted excited to meet L., though I don't think he was acting. He spoke to my son, to us, with this searching curiosity, as if he were looking for something in L. that only he could see. What did it look like, that thing he was hunting for? I tried to believe it was beautiful, whatever he thought my son might have, a dark glitter under L.'s eyelid, or an unbearable concentration of light gathering behind his ear.

Dr. Brieman referred us to our third therapist, who, at the initial session, handed me an essay that's all over the internet about how having a special child, a child with a diagnosis, is like going on a trip, only you end up in Northern Europe instead of the more temperate country (Italy?) where you had planned to go. Still a vacation, claimed the essay's writer, but a different one. I found the piece deeply offensive.

"You know what, I hate this fucking essay," I said too loudly, crumpling the paper. I threw the crumpled paper at the window, like it could have broken a window. Guess what, it didn't. Our third therapist, who had, up until this point, appeared preoccupied and bored, leaned forward in her chair.

It had been such a lousy string of days. That morning, L. had refused, again, to go to school. I had to drag him out to the car. He was getting too big to be dragged like that. I couldn't find the ear protection I usually wore if he was screaming. A neighbor happened to be outside at the time, hanging up a new flag from her collection of seasonal flags. Last month's flag had portrayed the sun, and this month her flag had what looked to be a fir tree on it. This must have meant something. *Forever green*, or something. When L. began shrieking, this neighbor of mine hurried across the street, her face troubled and urgent. I had finally managed to lock L. in the car. He was banging his fists, then his feet, against the window. "Are you in control of this situation?" my neighbor asked me. The only thing this woman was responsible for was a small and obedient dog.

The third therapist said to us, "Now I find the author of this essay is suggesting how, even if we didn't choose our lives, or our [illegible]

A picture of a tree is not a tree. A story is not always what happened. A child is never a guarantee of love. The third therapist reached out and put her hand on my arm. It felt strange to be touched by someone. "I worry that the two of you are spending all your time looking into the gutter, into the streams of—whatever you want to call it, the crap running past your feet—but there are a lot of other things going on around you, right above your shoulders, in the air. Like birds. Like there are butterflies. All you need to do is look up. It strikes me as ironic and sad that you want to escape from this place so badly without knowing where you are."

The fourth therapist was less hopeful, which was a relief in many ways, as it was becoming obvious to me that my family was not part of some optimistic allegory, and I resented people asking me to pretend otherwise. This therapist wanted T. and me to talk about our marriage. I am going to tell what happened one session, but I am going to tell you in the third person. This way, it can be like a story about somebody else.

"Why are you still in this marriage?" he asked his wife.

"Because we're married," the wife said.

"That wasn't a real answer," he said.

"Because I love you. Okay?" she said.

"What does she even mean by that?" he asked the fourth therapist.

"I'm sorry but you're asking me a ridiculous question," the wife said.

The fourth therapist interrupted. The question *Why is so-and-so in this marriage?* was a fair one. Therefore it would be useful if she, the wife, answered the question more specifically.

"I don't expect a marriage to be everything to me. I used to, but I don't anymore. Actually, I don't want to be here," the wife said.

"Where is *here*?" asked the fourth therapist. "In this room? In this world? In this life?"

"Here. Your office. With my husband."

"Why don't you want to be here?"

"She doesn't want to be here because this is a space where it isn't all about her," the husband said.

"Nothing is about me right now."

"Do you see that as a problem?"

Her husband had begun bellowing from the shower if the kids, or she, entered the upstairs bathroom before school. "This is the only time I have to myself," he would bellow, "and I want you out!"

"No," she had finally said that morning.

"You go have your conference with the kids in the hallway. Get out of here!" he had roared. She was discussing tooth brushing, specifically whether one of the children could brush their teeth in the upstairs bathroom while the other child used the bathroom downstairs, as their son had begun throwing his sister's toothbrush into the toilet, which was often left unflushed.

"No," she said again to her husband.

"Do I have to get out of this shower and make you leave?" He stepped out of the shower. He was dripping, wet and naked and tall. It was a relief, in a way, to witness someone other than her drowning in anger. She waited to see what he would do or what she would do. The kids were miserable.

"I do not think this is the right time in my life for reinvention," she told their therapist.

"What does that even mean?" the husband asked.

"You must have heard how the divorce rate of families with a [illegible]

[illegible] idea?" asked the therapist.

"Those weren't my exact words. What I said was 'Your father will turn into a monster.' That 'he is turning into a monster.'"

"And you are what," he said, "metamorphosing into a butterfly over there?"

• • • •

When L. was nine, he tried to teach himself to ride a Razor scooter. What happened was he began falling on a daily basis. The wheels of the scooter kept catching in the cracks of the sidewalks and he would tumble on down. In the beginning I rushed toward him, like any mother would, and scooped him up, and wrapped my arms protectively around him.

"It will be okay," I murmured. "You're okay. I'm here."

But I couldn't soothe him. Nothing I did soothed him. In fact, my presence seemed to make his pain worse. Either he would push me away, hard enough that I might fall myself, or he screamed into my ear. His screams were lengthy pointed needles thrust straight into my brain. Sometimes he did both, the screaming and the pushing both. So I began to leave him there on the ground, howling, a little blood dripping from his elbow or his chin. At first this felt uncomfortable. I became used to it. Eventually I didn't care. He seemed always to be in some kind of pain, physical or otherwise. If I cared, my life would have turned unsustainable.

After one particularly nasty spill near the park, a mother glared at me then rushed over to crouch in the gravel beside my son, where she made a show of handing him three green lollipops, which he sucked greedily between his screams, all three at once. As if I hadn't tried lollipops before. Sometimes I wondered if my son realized who I was, or if any middle-aged woman of medium height wearing a coat and glasses would be a suitable replacement.

This is what L. used to talk about with me when he felt like talking.

"What is the capital of Botswana?"

"What is the largest freshwater lake in the world?"

"What class is the sugar glider? Classes are mammals, reptiles, amphibians, birds, fish."

"Proboscis monkeys have three stomachs. Do we have one trillion backward stomachs?"

"Oh my god, there's someone richer than Bill Gates."

"Oh my god, the sinking of the *Sultana*, 1865, had more deaths than the *Titanic*."

"Oh my god, 9/11 had three parts to it. Part one happened when two planes went into the World Trade Center, killing 2,752 people. Part two was when a plane went into the Pentagon, killing 184. In part three, a plane went into a field in Pennsylvania, killing 40. That makes the total 2,976, which is almost twice as many dead people as the *Titanic*."

"In the 1839 Indian cyclone, three hundred thousand people died. Twenty thousand ships were lost at sea. That cyclone wasn't the deadliest cyclone. The deadliest cyclone was in 1970 in East Pakistan, where five hundred thousand people died in floods. Those weren't the worst floods. The worst floods were the 1931 China floods, where either one million or four million peopl[illegible] di[illegible]

"T[illegible]e [illegible] o[illegible] [illegible]2 va[illegible] al[illegible] t[illegible] [illegible]s [illegible]26 [illegible] [illegible]s."

"W[illegible] e[illegible] e th[illegible] Ko[illegible] n W[illegible] [illegible] n le[illegible] s [illegible] al [illegible] We lost [illegible]3 [illegible]d[illegible] r[illegible]."

"T[illegible]e [illegible] a[illegible] Wa[illegible] w[illegible] a le[illegible] [illegible] 4[illegible]34 [illegible] di[illegible] w[illegible]ch is m[illegible] th[illegible] h[illegible] K[illegible] r[illegible] a[illegible] a[illegible] d[illegible] f [illegible] bi[illegible]."

"Wow, World War Two we won. We lost 291,557 soldiers, more than the War of 1812, the Korean War, the Vietnam War, and the Gulf War combined."

"The Gulf War we won. We lost 148 soldiers."

"The war in Northwest Pakistan didn't end yet."

"The Afghanistan War didn't end yet. It says 2001 dash nothing."

• • • •

"Look! Do you think this one is going to fly the best?"

"Do you think this one is going to fly the best?"

"Do you think this one is going to fly better or worse than the last one?"

"Will this one fly better or worse than the one before?"

"This one has a secret message on it. Do you think it's going to hit the wall?"

"Is this one going to fly the best, Mom? Are you watching?"

"Black goes first."

"Red goes now."

"Black goes now."

"Next goes red."

"Next goes black."

"Then red."

"Then black."

"Gliese 667 Cc is an exoplanet that might have life on it."

"Kepler-442 b is another exoplanet that might have life on it."

"So is Kepler-452 b."

"Wolf 1061 c."

"Kepler-1229 b."

"Kepler-186 f."

"K2-3 d."

"LK-32-C."

"My perfect exoplanet is LK-32-C and you and Dad aren't on it, it's just me and some bodies of water. R. isn't there either. Nobody's there except the figures who leave me alone. They're blue. They eat rocks. I'm going there."

We were in the yard, my son and I lying on our backs on top of an old blanket. I lay on one corner of the blanket and my son lay as far from me as he could. The night was cloudless, the moon dark, the stars clearer than usual. L. pointed to a bright star in the west. That, he said, was LK-32-C's sun. It looked far away as well. My husband was inside taking a nap. My daughter was dancing in her bedroom by herself.

"They take you there on a ship," L. explained. "Then the ship leaves. You can't come back."

"What if you want to come back?" I asked.

"You don't want to do that."

The following day, L. sketched his planet in a notebook. He had always showed some aptitude for drawing, in particular drawing modes of transport, though in the past he had tried to keep his artwork private. I had to sneak into his room if I wanted to see his work. He used to draw a lot of rockets. Sometimes the rockets would be hurtling toward surprised people. These new drawings were different. He was eager to show them to me. Often he demanded I trace, with my finger, certain lines across the page. [illegible] rocks, and the indentations of sand caused by the blowing wind. The second drawing was of LK-32-C's night sky, which he covered with strange constellations. "What is that?" I asked, pointing to a jumble of connected stars. "I'm never telling you," he said. In the center of the sky, he placed two reflective moons.

• • • •

If one morning I forgot to mention it was my son's turn to set the dinner table, or that there was a doctor's appointment in the afternoon, or that it was going to rain, L. would collapse, hysterical, on the couch, acting as if the world he expected to find around him that day was crumbling apart, which, in his eyes, I suppose it was. "Stupid mom, stupid mom, stupid mom," he would holler. If I forgot to buy mild salsa the night we had tacos, either I would need to run out to the store or else he would hurl his plate onto the floor. Or if his taco shell broke. Or if the restaurant we had planned on going to for dinner closed early that Monday. *Flexibility, lack of.* Or if I accidentally put his lunch in the incorrect containers, using the containers that were rectangular instead of round.

My books advised better preparation for the upcoming day. Such as every morning, tell the child what will be happening to him that day using the most vivid words you can. *The dirty blue sedan. The red school. The little brown library.* Or you can write out a daily schedule. Late evening, I found myself at the kitchen table drafting frantic lists about what my son needed to know. By morning, those lists were no longer true. Sometimes the weathermen were wrong. I tried to keep everything in the day from changing but I don't think anyone can do that. Also I made a lot of mistakes. Once I forgot to tell L. I put mustard on his sandwich. Once we were having a violent evening because L. no longer liked orange cheese.

My son had never been an enthusiastic eater, but at one point, he began hating foods that he previously tolerated. At first I kept serving these foods to him, thinking it was a phase. It was not a phase. He suddenly despised the texture of a carrot. If a carrot appeared in his lunch, he would toss it into a neighbor's yard on the walk to school. Then it was yogurt. Then hard-boiled eggs. Food is not a battleground, my books advised. One book told the story of a famous scientist who ate only legs of mutton for every meal. Guess what, he turned out fine. In fact, he discovered hydrogen.

"You used to eat a hard-boiled egg each day," I reminded L. Then it was hummus, then cucumbers. Dinners became miserable affairs. He stopped liking milk. He no longer ate tomatoes. Then his specificness spread to other parts of his life. He listened only to songs by Liz Phair, a singer-songwriter from Chicago that I had liked in high school. When I told L., "We need to listen to something else right now," he would scream. He would not stop screaming until I put on one of Liz Phair's CDs, preferably *Exile in Guyville*. Also, he would only wear gray athletic clothes made from synthetic fibers. I had to buy him multiple gray outfits or else he refused to change his clothes and he would start to smell. The only subject he would quiz me on was LK-32-C. "What kind of sound do the blue figures make?" "What kind of legs are on the silver animals?" "What do the shiny green knobs taste like if you heat them for long enough?"

I informed our therapist at the time about L.'s demands for repetition. "All in the realm of normal!" she said brightly while I watched my son's world constrict around him until he could barely take a breath. Actually that is inaccurate. It was our world doing the constricting. L.'s world, where he was supposed to be, remained [illegible]

[illegible]

"That's offensive thinking," T. said.

"I would rather he be one of those sweet Down syndrome kids who hug everybody. I would rather he be in a wheelchair so I could help him by pushing him around in the wheelchair."

"Stop it. I'm not going to listen to this."

"If he had Down syndrome, he would let me touch him, and maybe he would look me in the eye."

The behavior charts should have worked, you know. If they didn't, the collaborative problem-solving should have improved our situation. When that didn't work, a complicated system of rewards and punishments should have made a difference. Or else the natural consequences and the excessive praise. The manipulation of the environment, the lists, the negotiations, the forced enthusiasm, the constant coaching. The lowering of expectations. The positive discipline. The absence of discipline. "Perhaps you didn't implement your techniques consistently," one mother at a group session suggested to me, not unkindly. "Perhaps you should give it another try, only this time try harder."

Autumn came. This was the autumn in which everybody acted entitled and disappointed because the maples caught some blight, meaning the leaves turned brown instead of their usual burning color—it was this huge deal—and L. quit sleeping. He did not want to talk to me or anyone. He would only willingly leave his room if the entire house was dark and the blinds closed. Getting him off to school, or getting him to do anything, like getting him to come downstairs to sing "Happy Birthday" to his sister, or getting him to take a bath, or getting him to change his underwear, required the use of physical force. I sat in the hallway every night outside his room, chewing ice to stay awake. If I fell asleep, L. would climb over me, and I would be woken up by the escalation of R.'s whimpering as he dragged her out of bed. This was before we put a lock on the outside of his door. The only time he appeared reasonable was at his drafting table in his bedroom, where he continued to develop LK-32-C through his sketches. His repertoire of drawings had expanded. There were drawings now of the planet's salty ponds and viridian lakes, and maps of the northern mountains and the coastline. His drawings made me think, *My son has something worthwhile inside of him. He has an entire world inside of him.*

I wanted to look at the drawings instead of him. I wanted him to stay away from me.

My books recommended *task reductions* and *the deprivation of a favored reinforcer*. My husband's solution was to wear foam earplugs when he slept. He left a pair on my nightstand. I refused to wear them. Other times L. kicked his closed door until I thought he broke the door. One night, he broke the door. This went on for a week, then two weeks, then three. Our therapist at the time called it a stage and promised it would pass. There was a technical term she used for such stages that I can't remember. An explosion burst? An extinction blast? Something fiery and violent, in any case. Each day felt covered in dread. "I don't want to be here!" L. screamed and I wanted to scream with him. My husband had to peel the comforter off of me in the morning and push me out of our bedroom. I nodded off in inopportune places, such as in my car while driving across the city, or in the waiting room of my dentist's office. My tiredness took on a physical presence, a surreal sheen that oscillated in front of my life, making it impossible to focus on what was real. *Model emotional expression. Avoid ultim*[illegible] many books to [illegible] L. stalking aro[illegible] to twitch. Every[illegible] out of porcelain[illegible]

The first time I hit L., I wondered if there would be a bruise, so I filled a plastic bag with ice, wrapping a dish towel around the bag, then I brought the compress upstairs. I couldn't get into L.'s bedroom. He must have pushed something heavy in front of the door. My books were of little help on such matters, the entries on anger and violence dealing only with the child's rage, and the subject had not come up in any of my parent groups. I guess there are certain topics no one wishes to discuss. If there was a bruise, what did you do? Keep your child home from school, I suppose. Or send a note explaining there had been an accident, that old story: he walked into a door. This couldn't be my life. I'm pretty sure this was somebody else's life. "I'm so sorry. I should not have done that. I will never do that again," I told L. through the door.

"You hit L.," R. said in the kitchen after it happened a second time in an almost identical fashion, after L. lunged at me, shoving his mouth against my ear. He screamed into my ear as loud as he could. My reaction was more a reflex than a conscious choice. Or is that what every parent tells themselves after. I had not planned to be this kind of mother. As before, L. fled upstairs. I could feel the leftover violence in the house, like spikes pointing out from the walls. I went down the basement stairs to start a load of laundry, as L. had peed through all of his underwear, and when I returned to the kitchen, I found the remaining marshmallow Peeps from Easter had been taken out of the pantry. My daughter was lining them up in a row on the kitchen floor, the yellow ones alternating with the pink ones, all of them facing in the direction of the back door. "They are getting ready to escape," R. said, not looking up.

Upstairs, all the lights were off in L.'s room. I found him in bed, watching the blue blobs of his timer drip alongside the pink blobs. Though it was not yet four in the afternoon, he was wearing his favorite pajamas, the ones splattered with constellations. (L. had once complained they were inaccurate: many constellations appeared twice and not in the correct place. If Orion was on his shoulder, then Orion should not also be on his elbow.) The stick-on stars were glowing on the ceiling of his bedroom because the blinds were down, though L. had recently rearranged the stars into new formations, what you might see in the sky from another solar system. "I'm sorry," I said again. He acted like he couldn't hear me, like he was already gone. There were other times. Another dream I used to have was a dream in which I cured my son. The way I cured him was that I held him underwater for the entire length of the dream, keeping him down there with the heel of my boot, so that some cured look-alike could rush up to me and throw his look-alike arms around my waist, as I had always wanted my own son to do, and he would press his look-alike face into my stomach while I let L. drown.

We discussed the possibility of medication with L.'s doctor. My husband said absolutely not, but that was only because he was so rarely home, having found other activities to occupy his evenings, so he had no idea what was going on. Glancing at my unshowered hair, at the shadows beneath my eyes, the doctor wondered if I would consider taking something myself. I told him no. "I just need some sleep," I said.

Everybody used to say he looked like me. People used to call him "little you" when they were talking about him to me. I wonder what they would say now that he has grown his hair so long. The [illegible] become lost in that kind of light.

The day before L. left, I went into his room where he was resting in bed. Either he smelled like pee or it was his sheets. Maybe it was both. I should probably have changed the sheets, but we had changed them the day before, and the new sheets weren't yet dry. I should probably have bought more sheets. L. was agitated, his face to the wall, his legs jerking across the mattress. As always, the blinds were drawn. He did not tell me to go away so I lay down next to him. Lying beside my son, I felt such an absence of need. I suppose some people could find relief in that, in not being needed.

"What's happening on LK-32-C today?" I asked. He shrugged. He was lying inches away from me. I listened to his breathing. Eventually, I told him not everybody belonged here. Some people were meant to be elsewhere. That it's okay to belong somewhere else.

There was a lot to do after L. left. Like what to do about his bedroom. I decided to dump whatever remained of his belongings into black contractor bags. There was no reason to keep the room set up like a shrine. He was not coming back anytime soon, despite some people's insistences that my situation need not be a permanent one. "This is a world of action and not one for moping and droning in!" a mother in my group advised. I wrote this down. Others acted as if L. never existed. "Your son?" they said, as if I'd imagined him. L.'s drawers had surprisingly little in them. The four black T-shirts he refused to pack. A pair of dress pants he never wore, the tags still attached. Underwear, the kind featuring cartoon dinosaurs, pushed to the back of the drawer on the top left. A rubber killer whale, adrift under his bed. The sketchbooks containing LK-32-C sat in rows on the shelves above his desk. I thought he would have taken those sketchbooks with him.

I wanted to send L. to a therapeutic boarding school. There was a boarding school in New Hampshire where boys like him spent their time canoeing across ponds and camping in pine groves. I knew he could be happy there. I thought my husband's parents would cover the costs, as they certainly had the means, so I wrote them a letter and included the glossy school brochure. They called me a week later on their way to the airport. They were flying to Bermuda, where they would enjoy the ideal weather and pink sand beaches for several weeks. They wanted to help L., my mother-in-law explained, they truly did, only not this way, as they didn't believe in the diagnosis. "He's just a boy," insisted my mother-in-law. "Please don't turn him into something he's not."

I told L., "Guess where you're headed? You won a ticket. The ticket is to LK-32-C!" Of course this idea was ludicrous, but I thought we could pretend to believe in it. Having a story like that to believe in could have made what was to come easier. L. didn't believe me. It would have been better if he believed me. It would have been better, actually, had I built a rocket and sent him off into space, to a planet circling one of those stars. *There he is*, I could have told myself at night every time I looked up. *A small part of the light, finally content.* I think about him all the time. I think about him when I'm going to the bathroom and when I'm waiting in line at the bank, a withdrawal slip in my hand.

The house [illegible] is freshly painted with [illegible] shutters [illegible] bedroom is probably [illegible] yard. There is a garden [illegible] flourishing [illegible] Several other [illegible] children, all boys, [illegible] [illegible] so they know what they're doing. Unless it's raining, or winter, I imagine every window in the house is kept open, letting in the sounds of playing children and the crying of birds. It is a good place to live.

The man who owns the house looks like a professor. I imagine he is always urging leatherbound classics into the boys' hands. The woman is younger than me and competent. She has learned how to successfully bake her own sourdough bread. They eat their home-cooked meals together like a family in the dining room, on top of an antique table they aren't fussy about protecting. I don't believe they would require the children to eat on place mats, as I did. *Don't worry about the wood. All this furniture? It's meant to be used!* I imagine the woman might say. In the summer, I imagine the man will grill up burgers on the back patio, and the woman will bring out a Frisbee, and everybody will remain outside until it grows dark, fireflies clustering around their heads. My son used to be a vegetarian, but I don't think he is anymore. That was another thing I forced on him. Maybe he enjoys eating the flesh of animals now. All the boys who live in the house are troubled in their own way, prone to fits of anger or seclusion. The adults watch for the warning signs. They know how to gently coax a child out of his private basement, or his dark cellar, or wherever such children go, and bring him back. In L.'s room, a twin bed is likely pushed against the wall, a blue plaid comforter tucked around the mattress. On the desk, near the window, is a jar of colored pencils and a notebook where he has sketched and labeled the various perennials found in the back garden. I'm guessing about most of this.

On the day I was scheduled to visit L., I stayed outside, in my car, on the street, for a long time. The freshly painted house might as well have belonged to another world. I wished it were in another world and I was watching it from afar on a screen. "Experience is simply the name we give our mistakes," said the mothers in my support group the day before. They had become my chorus. I wrote down whatever they said. If my husband were with me—if I still had a husband, if he had not moved in with another woman and her pleasant child—I might have been able to ring the doorbell. All I managed to do was creep up to the side door and glance into the yard—I saw the garden, I saw the trampoline—and slide a sealed envelope addressed to L. into the mail slot. A coded message without a code. The story, let's say, of a mother who, because she loved her son, allowed him to travel without her to another world, a world that she made for him. Then I returned to my car, pulled the visor down, and drove away.

Almost all my pictures of L. I have taken down by this point. To fill the resulting blank spots on the walls, I've hung up posters of mountains, not the stout New England sort but the kind of mountains people die climbing. R. says the new pictures scare her. I tell her not to look at them. The only portrait of L. I left up is from when he was two. It hangs in the hallway that leads to what used to be his bedroom. The photographer, after the portrait session, recommended that I talk to a child modeling agency—a ridiculous suggestion, as child models are usually smiling, aren't they? "But the way he looks at you!" exclaimed the photographer. L., in that picture, is staring into the camera with an expression I have yet to witness on another child's face. I can't see anyone reflected in his eyes. His eyes look darker in the picture than they actually were, and his hair is wispy and yellow and already savage. He looks worried and scared. I often find myself standing in the hallway in front of that photograph. I [illegible] to imagine what L. was thinking. I wondered if he was glimpsing the future and he knew what kind of mother I would turn into? Did he know what kind of child he would become? The following month we cut off his hair, his baby curls. I saved several locks in a plastic bag that I've since misplaced. "You know, a child's hair is never the same, never as soft, after you cut it." That was what my mom had said. For once, she was right.

When my son was about to go away, I said to him, "I bet on your trip out there to LK-32-C, you'll get to see some pretty amazing things. Like how about an asteroid belt, or an exploding star!" I held out my phone to L., having pulled up a photograph of a star in such a state, only he refused to look in my direction, so I found myself reaching around him to wave the screen in front of his face. He shut his eyes but before he did, I think he caught a glimpse. When a star explodes, it does so with such vivid and violent energy, and while I know the star is dying, it still looks like a birth to me, or at least an expansion.

A FEW PERSONAL OBSERVATIONS ON PORTALS

The first portal had appeared in our town [illegible] Mr. Hogan. It showed up on one of his bathroom [illegible] and proceeded to block a good deal of his vanity mirror, resulting in several shaving accidents. I don't know why a portal appeared to him first. It's not like he was the best at attracting otherworldly things. Benny and I walked over to the Hogans' house a few days after the rumors began. I carried a Ziploc baggie of homemade gingersnaps, intending to drop by for a chat. Before leaving the Hogan residence, I planned to ask to use their bathroom, the one with the portal in it. I assumed that having a portal would be a private matter, like having trouble with one's digestion. They might not initiate the sharing of it. We would have brought along our son and daughter, only it was Saturday, so they had their own activities, basketball and figure skating, respectively.

The Hogans resided on the other side of the park in an older and tree-lined neighborhood. Because of the crowd spilling across the sidewalk and into the street, I thought there must be some kind of festival that day, like the Hometown Homemade festival. Most people would find a portal's appearance either suspect or ridiculous, I presumed, so they would stay away. There was no festival. The crowd consisted of some neighbors I recognized and others I didn't know, attempting to form themselves into a resemblance of a line that led to the Hogans' house. At the front of the line, in the driveway, sat Mrs. Hogan behind a folding table, collecting money. The various admission options were posted on a sign taped to the garage door. We could have chosen a day or weekly pass or a season pass that lasted through the end of October. I hadn't brought my wallet with me. Neither had Benny. When we reached the folding table, Mrs. Hogan said she'd vouch for us, and we could drop off the cash later that day. "Trust me, this is going to be worth the wait and the expense!" she promised as she wrote our receipt. By this point, Benny and I had eaten most of the gingersnaps. We offered the final cookie to Mrs. Hogan, who claimed she wasn't hungry.

The Hogans' bathroom, located on the first floor opposite the living room, was neither spacious nor modern. It was a half bath, a powder room I believe it's called, and in desperate need of updating. At least they should have taken down the golden wallpaper. A lot of people were crammed inside that tiny room. The atmosphere felt festive and celebratory and also uncomfortable. Everyone was taking pictures, not only of the portal itself but also of the bathroom ceiling, and the contents of Mr. Hogan's medicine cabinet, and the plunger, and the pair of identical toothbrushes set upon the vanity. Every item in that room radiated importance, including Mr. Hogan himself, who, dressed in an ill-fitting blazer and tie, knelt on the toilet, a few fresh scabs on his chin. Probably that blazer had been borrowed. Every few minutes, he recited a speech to whoever was in the room. “I think each of us might belong to a different world,” he said.

The portal itself looked spectacular hovering there above the sink. I still have a picture of it on my phone: a luminescent sheet that wavered as if caught in a crosswind. It smelled of mouthwash and lavender. I stayed in the bathroom for as long as I could manage. Through Mr. Hogan’s portal, I saw a sky like ours, only the sky was filled impractically with many suns, so bright it was hard to look at. Mr. Hogan said he saw something very different. He wouldn’t tell us what he saw. At the close of his speech, he demonstrated how he could push his fingers through. Once, to much applause and hooting, he shoved through his entire arm. That must have hurt, judging from the way he cradled his elbow afterward, carefully kneading his skin. He promised us he had no plans to cross the threshold completely. “I don’t think I’d fit,” he said, laughing. He seemed to be suggesting the portal might not entirely [illegible] him. This turned out to be true, of course; a po[illegible] ple they want [illegible] know a l[illegible] back then, [illegible] knew [illegible]

W[illegible] thro[illegible] me a [illegible]certain [illegible] once we emerged from the house. “Lucky guy,” [illegible] said to me on the way home.

The following week, Ms. Bauer found a portal under her basement stairs. Her portal looked different from Mr. Hogan’s. This came as a surprise to a lot of people, myself included. Previously I assumed portals could only look one way, that they had to resemble a shining rectangle, like in the movies. Ms. Bauer's portal was an odd shape with thirty-two sides–what is a shape like that even called?–and in addition it was short and squat. If you wanted to peer through it, you had to get down on your knees on the basement floor, which I don't think had ever been swept.

Ms. Bauer charged an entrance fee as well. We brought the children and chose the family admission option. Despite her charging half as much as Mr. Hogan, there were only three others in line when we arrived. My children acted uninterested as we waited our turn. They said they had already seen numerous portals on their screens. "But this portal is *real*," I told them. "Those other portals you saw might have looked real but they weren't. They were made up for a movie."

Billy said, "No, they were real."

I said, "They weren't real."

Billy said, "They were real."

I said, "Let's go into the basement."

In the basement, I made each child ask a question. "Can we touch it?" Billy asked, reaching out his arm. "No, you may not," snapped Ms. Bauer. She had strung a nylon rope in front of her portal and ordered us to stay behind the rope. Jeanie asked if there was any milk to drink. To be honest, this was not a pleasant place to be. The basement was neither refinished nor upbeat. The portal, trapped under the stairs, resembled a dreary and many-sided rain cloud that produced its own atmosphere of dread. Benny was already on his knees in the center of the room. I made the children get down on the floor with me. "What do you see?" I asked them, struggling to breathe deeply.

"I see a little hill," Jeanie said.

"Is this all it does?" Billy asked.

I stood up and dusted the filth from my knees.

"Too bad it's not busier today," I told Ms. Bauer.

"Oh, don't you worry. They'll come running later on," she explained, so confident that her portal would remain special.

Our town's third portal appeared to Mrs. Juliet Luna, who lived with her wife in a two-story bungalow across the street. They never shut their blinds for some reason so I always knew what they were up to. A week after Mr. Hogan's portal appeared, I knew they had begun looking for portals of their own. Every evening I watched them. Mrs. Ada Luna carried a clipboard. Usually they searched the rooms together, but Mrs. Ada Luna was in the attic for some reason when Mrs. Juliet Luna peeked into the linen closet and found her portal, a circle the color of a sapphire and infused with light. She cried when she found it. For a long while, she, crying, stared at it pulsating beside the pile of folded towels, her face messed up with tears. Then she shut the closet door and went into the bathroom. I watched her splash water onto her face. She didn't show the portal to the other Mrs. Luna until the following day.

After Mrs. Juliet Luna's discovery, many people, including my children's friends, began searching for their own portals.

"Are we getting portals too?" Jeanie asked me.

"I thought you weren't interested in portals," I reminded her.

"I like them now."

"We aren't getting a portal," I said with such confidence I didn't know what I was talking about. Back then it seemed to me that portals appeared only to unhappy people. For example, it was a well-known fact that Mrs. Hogan desired to have sex while Mr. Hogan didn't. She thought something was medically wrong with her husband. She kept dragging him to specialists and complaining in online forums about her "dead bedroom." And

Ms. Bauer had needed her stomach pumped twice in the emergency room. And Mrs. Juliet Luna could not find employment, having spent decades honing her skills as a switchboard operator. Nobody needed switchboard operators anymore. I see now how I was simplifying the situation: I wished to find a pattern, because I wished for the appearance of the portals to make a rational sense. What if portals weren't rational? What if they were angry instead? Or vindictive? Or greedy? Or wrong? I believed my family was different from our unhappy neighbors. I loved my children. If children were loved as much as mine were, I believed they would want to stay where they are, rooted by my love. Likewise, I loved my husband. He was so familiar to me. We were experiencing our share of difficulties, sure, but such difficulties, I still believe, fall within the cyclical nature of a marriage. I have always considered familiarity to be the most stable form of love.

Portals turned up all over town. Many of the newer portals materialized to children. Though not only to children, and not everyone with a portal had been unhappy. Honestly it was difficult to distinguish the rules, if there were any rules. One Wednesday, a portal appeared to the Riccis' squinty-eyed newborn who could barely make out his mother's face, let alone notice his own wispy portal stretching, like a web, across the corner of the hospital room. Nobody noticed the infant's portal for hours in the chaos after birth. My neighbor Ms. Li, a night nurse, was the one to bring the baby's portal to Mrs. Ricci's attention. "Why on Earth would my baby need a portal? I think it's actually *my* portal," challenged the new mother. But there are certain feelings surrounding a portal, a certain force of feeling, which generally makes clear who the portal wants. When it isn't yours, you experience a violence restlessly pushing against the inside of your chest. Maybe *violence* is too strong a word. But that's what it felt like. A hard shove back. Eventually Mrs. Ricci asked that she and her child be moved to a different room. The baby cried all night and the night after that.

On Thursday, a dark portal appeared to Mr. Underwood, who is deaf in one ear and widowed.

My husband and I talked at night about the portals of other people. Here's an observation: a person's portal generally reflects some aspect of their personality. By studying people's portals, it was like we were learning each other's secrets or gaining confirmation of our suspicions. "Did you hear about Mrs. Sikora's portal?" I asked Benny. Mrs. Sikora, a frequent visitor to the library where I worked, did not allow her children to read fairy tales or check out DVDs, even the educational ones. I found her overbearing and small-minded. The previous year, she campaigned to remove computers from the elementary school. "Her portal is the size of a quarter," I told my husband. "I hear you can barely see anything through it, and what you can see looks like a dead end. Which is just about what I'd expect from her." It seemed, at the time, like the portals were going to be okay, like the appearance of portals in our town would ultimately help us to understand each other. Also it gave Benny and me something to talk about in the evenings. Evidently your portal could appear anywhere, in the upper branches of a tree, or in the children's section of a library beside the audiobooks. But in all the excitement and newness, I think we forgot what portals actually are: a gateway to somewhere else. Meaning an *exit*. Do you get what I'm saying? It's like we thought they were static works of art, these harmless and fascinating compositions that would not take people away.

Mrs. Roszak's portal appeared one afternoon on our porch. Hers was large and thick, thicker than most, and as tall as a person, making it impossible to enter our home through the front door. To enter our home now, we had to use either the back door or the garage. Also her portal smelled like dying roses, so our house smelled like that too. At night, it moaned. Despite the moaning and the funeral smell, this particular portal interested my children more than any other portal. They wanted to be near it, to poke their fingers at it, or toss stones through it. When the portal, in protest, flashed its freaky yellow light, all they did was laugh. They both must have become immune to the discomfort one felt when standing near another's portal. Or else they didn't care about such discomfort anymore.

I asked Mrs. Roszak if she could move her portal, please, as it was becoming a distraction to my family. "I can't," she claimed. I had never thought of her as miserable. She was married to a self-sufficient husband. She had a grown daughter who made a lot of money in banking, and her two grandchildren were cared for by a professional nanny. Maybe nobody needed her. If nobody needs you, maybe you can get a portal. There I go again, trying to make up a rule. I have no idea whether anyone needed her or whether her portal cared.

Mrs. Roszak brought her lawn chair over and set the chair down in the center of our front lawn. Here's another observation: people like to stare at their own portals. At first they might show some restraint, an hour or two hours of watching in a day, but such restraint always vanishes.

Soon Mrs. Roszak stopped showing up for her shift at the Mediterranean diner. She stopped sleeping in her bed. Instead of going to work or sleeping in her bed, she sat in her lawn chair in front of our house and stared at her portal. Even I could see how her actual life was becoming a boring story compared to the potential narrative that the portal offered.

A week after Mrs. Roszak's portal appeared, my daughter stumbled into our bedroom. It was the middle of the night. She was crying. I couldn't understand her. It took me a while to calm her down. My husband, a deep sleeper, remained sprawled out across the far side of the bed. Jeanie had snot on her face and in her hair.

"Why don't I have a portal?" she sobbed. Several of Jeanie's friends had discovered their portals within the past week. "What's wrong with me?" Jeanie lay between my husband and me, her head in the space between our pillows. I stroked her hair until she stopped crying. I could hear Mrs. Roszak's portal outside our house moaning softly. I think it was trying to tell me something. I didn't understand what it was telling me.

"Not everybody needs a portal," I whispered.

"You're only saying that because you hate portals. You hate them and that's why they won't come here. I need one. I need one right now."

"You don't," I whispered back, but what did I know? I think it's any parent's instinct to try and keep our children away from things that might take them to other worlds where we aren't allowed to follow.

The gawkers arrived in the beginning of August after hearing about our town's portals on some news special. They came in RVs, or by bike, or on deluxe buses, the first stop on a grand tour which would carry them as far west as Buffalo and south to Binghamton, to the handful of other towns in the region that received one portal or at most two. Aimlessly they wandered around in packs through the downtown, peeking under benches or pawing through garbage cans. I felt sorry for them. It was obvious to me they would never find what they were looking for.

Mr. Roszak drew up a map that he sold at his gas station to any gawker with ten dollars to spare. He made some good money.

Updated weekly, then daily, the map detailed the location of every known portal in the area, as well as marking where visitors could find a clean restroom or a cup of coffee. Later, he sold a laminated keepsake version for twenty dollars.

Everywhere they went, the gawkers constructed shrines. In front of the more public portals, they piled fruit and stuffed animals and photographs of themselves. On people's front lawns, including my own front lawn, they tossed wildflowers and notes, which gave many lawns a messy appearance. The notes sounded like unanswered prayers. They wanted to know how it felt to live among so many gateways to other worlds. "It's not as exciting as you think," I told anyone who asked. I didn't want them to get the wrong idea or to start believing that because a portal appears near you, everybody's life is going to become a fairy tale.

Around the time the portals began appearing in our town, my husband told me that he wanted to start having sex with other people, as he was tired of having sex with only me. Had he felt this way for a while, I asked him. Or did he start feeling this way only after the portals appeared? He claimed his feelings had nothing to do with openings to other worlds. He still loved me, he said, though he labeled my feelings about our marriage, about there being an exclusivity to each other's bodies and affections, as outdated and wrong. "I can love you and I can love other people. I promise," he said. His face was flushed. He got aroused just talking about it. Already he had opened accounts on several dating sites. So far no one had responded to him. In his profile, he wasn't yet lying about being married. "All I want is something different right now," he said. "Like someone who isn't you. In addition to you."

I had always considered our sex life to be sufficient. To be honest, I was never that interested. It wasn't something I needed, that kind of mess, but at the same time it was a requirement, so twice a week, after the kids fell asleep, I got into bed and Benny removed my clothes.

"I mean, God, I've known you for decades. You're the person I know best out of everybody. It's like we might as well be the same person. Do you know what I mean? I'm not asking for a divorce," he said.

My husband grew out his hair and began wearing contacts. The contacts made him blink a lot. I missed his glasses. He had worn glasses ever since I'd met him. He was very nearsighted so his glasses shrunk his eyes down to a reasonable size. Without his glasses, his eyes looked enormous, like they might eat me up. Because of his longer hair, one of the gawkers mistook him for a soap opera star and stopped him on the sidewalk for his autograph. It was like he was trying to become attractive to a group of people I wasn't a part of, a group in which everyone had long hair. I found a condom in the suitcase he used for work trips. He told me he had never used this condom, which was obvious, as it was still in its packaging. He told me he merely carried it around with him.

"What if I tried other things in bed?" I suggested.

"What kinds of things?" Benny replied. "Could you become another person? Could you become several people at once?"

"I don't know. I don't think so."

"Wanting something different does not have to be this huge deal," he said.

My husband's portal, when it came, appeared in our laundry room, in the dusty space between the washer and the dryer. "It sure is an attractive one, isn't it?" said Benny proudly. Even if he was right, even if his portal was, in fact, attractive looking, I did not want the people in my family to have portals. "Other people might need portals but we don't," I reminded him. He asked what I was afraid of. Why was I so scared about other possibilities for our lives? These aren't the kinds of questions a person answers. Around his portal, I felt ill at ease and unsteady. I felt the floor shifting under me. "Look at me," I said. Benny dragged a chair into the laundry room so he could sit down. There was not really space in that room for a chair.

His portal was made out of a fine peach powder. It kept crumpling in on itself and then rebuilding. It smelled like the sea. It's not the portal I would have picked for my husband. I had imagined his as more utilitarian, like something carved out of rock.

I asked my husband if he thought he didn't belong in our family and our marriage anymore. If that was why he had a portal now. "Do you think there isn't a place for you here?" I asked. I was just making guesses. I didn't know.

Benny began spending an excessive amount of time in our laundry room. So did my son and my daughter, Jeanie scrunched onto Benny's lap every morning before school, Billy crammed, standing, into the corner. The portal collapsed in front of them then blew upward into a whirlwind or several whirlwinds. It collapsed in front of them. It blew into a whirlwind. Then, guess what, it collapsed. "It's doing the exact same thing over and over again," I pointed out. Our clean clothes now smelled like oysters, as did the entire first floor of our house. It was not this really great smell. There was no space for me in that room. At night I had to drag the children upstairs to their beds. I had less success in drawing my husband away from his portal. He preferred to sleep on the family room couch, which was closer to the laundry room than to our bedroom. He slept without a sheet, leaving drool marks on the cushion.

"Tell me what your other world looks like," I begged Benny. So far I had avoided looking through his portal. I was waiting for an invitation from him to do so. It seemed like that would have been an intimacy. For the first time, he shut the laundry room door. The door had no lock because that would be stupid, to have a locked laundry room in your house, so Benny posted a sign: *KEEP OUT PLEASE.* Jeanie cried when she saw it. "I don't think he means you," I said. He did. He meant all of us.

That evening I found Jeanie in the upstairs bathroom looking for her own portal. She was peering into the toilet when I found her. "Get your head out of there," I said. Later, I found her checking the kitchen oven and the hostas in the yard. "You aren't getting a portal," I told her. She looked under our basement sink and behind the boxes that contained my husband's record collection.

One night, when Benny was snoring deeply on the couch, I crept past him into the laundry room. I hadn't been in that room for a week. I had been taking our dirty clothes to the laundromat in town. A towel, an old one, stained, hung in front of the washing machine. I pulled the towel down, and there was my husband's portal, pale and awake. Previously I had only glimpsed it when he was in the room with me, and that was from several feet away. Often he was blocking my view. It felt so private, what I saw now. Looking at it was like watching someone I loved sleep. It was like listening to my husband's heart while he dreamed. If I leaned close enough to the portal, I could make out the world on the other side. The dark cliffs, the wind, a current. I didn't recognize such a place. Was this what was inside of him? It looked like a world where I might not belong. I have never liked the wind. I didn't stay in that room for much longer. I couldn't. I could barely breathe. There seemed to be an intentional lack of air.

• • • •

Eventually people began stepping through their portals. The children too. This was, most likely, inevitable. Still, it took me by surprise, the disappearances. I think it surprised a lot of people. After Mr. Hogan went through, the portal in his powder room became difficult to see. In another day, it was gone. A new observation: portals can go away. Pretty soon a lot of people had left. They did not tell anyone they were going. They did not leave notes. Mrs. Roszak left. She walked through her portal on our porch while I worked the morning shift at the library. By the afternoon, her portal had faded to a shadow. It vanished within three days. We now could enter our house via the traditional front entry. This was neither as exciting nor convenient as I remembered. For weeks, I left Mrs. Roszak's lawn chair in our front yard, thinking her chair might act as a locator to help her find her way back. Then Mr. Roszak came by and said he needed the chair.

Here was when the portals got a little creepy. We had no idea where our neighbors were going. People assumed the best but for stupid reasons. "Come on, her portal smelled like oranges!" Benny said of Mrs. Tamm, but an orange-smelling portal is not proof there will be pleasant amounts of citrus in the other world. Portals could be crafty and deceptive too, I was sure of it, and full of inappropriate longings, like us. Before long, most of my children's friends were gone as well. My own kids, feeling abandoned, because they were in a way, wasted hours looking for portals under their beds, and in the woods behind our house, and in our cellar, and under my bed too, and in the garage. "Why don't you go do something childlike?" I told them. It was a brisk fall day, blue sky, yellow leaves, the kind of day where children used to play outside with a ball. Billy remembered he hadn't checked one of the second-floor closets. He raced past me and up the stairs.

I pulled Benny aside later that evening and told him I didn't want his portal hanging around our house anymore.

"Well, I don't know how to get rid of it." He chewed his thumbnail. He was lying. We had been married for twenty-one years. That seemed a long time to me, long enough that neither of us should have considered leaving the other person by stepping into a different world. I told this to him. I told him, "Let's weather this storm."

"I want an open marriage," he said.

I tried to reimagine my husband's love, which used to be like a light that surrounded me. I had thought it was a spotlight. I imagined the same light still on me yet widening to illuminate other people, other stages, other houses, entire blocks of people and their belongings, entire worlds, flooded by this new version of his love, as if love were now, like any light, a light one shared. I couldn't get the image right in my head. I kept imagining an explosion.

Whenever someone, a gawker, or one of my children, asked me what I thought my portal would look like, I used to tell them it would look exactly like this world, a series of ordinary moments in time—which was probably why I didn't have a portal yet, because what's the point of walking through a magical doorway and ending up with this exact body, this exact family, this house? It has always been important to me to know that I'd choose the life I already had. I had hoped my family would say the same in return, that this was the life they wanted, the life I helped make for them.

The following week, my children found theirs.

My daughter's portal seemed spun out of glass. I'm not sure how long she had known about it. I was emptying her hamper when I spotted a glint of something foreign behind her desk. There was a humming in the air, a nervousness. Jeanie had thrown a pillowcase over it. The pillowcase wasn't large enough. I guess she was trying to hide it from me. Through her portal I saw a marshy world constructed out of water and trees. Trees growing out of trees. All the trees looked like oaks. It didn't make sense to me. We had trees in this world. Why would a child need more trees? My son did not bother trying to hide his. It appeared a few days later in the yard, billowing from beside the fence. It was made out of feathers, slender and brown feathers. Anyway, it was too large to hide. When the feathers lifted in the breeze, I saw fragments of cold blue light.

"You know when people go through portals, they have to do it alone," I lectured both children. I had been told this from multiple neighbors. "Your dad and I can't go with you."

"Fine," Billy said.

"It's okay, Mom," said Jeanie.

Over a family dinner of spaghetti topped with jarred tomato sauce, I suggested to Benny that maybe portals for children are understandable, given the circumstances–the fact that children, in general, are so prone to fantasy–but something is probably lacking in those adults who hold on to portals of their own. The ability to grow up, perhaps. Or to give things up? The things they think they want. Or maybe it is farsightedness, a problem with seeing clearly what is right in front of them. "Tell me, what exactly is lacking in my life?" Benny asked. I told him I was speaking theoretically and in general terms but I was so angry. These portals were an insult to all the work I had done to create a stable home. Benny, in return, suggested certain people, certain adults, will never have a portal because of who they are. If a certain person wanted to have a portal, they would need to become someone different, someone who didn't need to control other people's lives. "And who should I become exactly?" I asked. I really wanted to know. The kids picked miserably at their pasta which refused to stay twisted around their forks. When Benny left the table, I followed him to the garage, where he was loading up his backpack with camping gear. I had already imagined what the rest of my life would look like. I did not have the energy to reimagine it. Here's an observation: when a husband plans to go through a portal, he will want to bring along many supplies. It's not like we can count on other worlds to be stocked with practical provisions, I guess. In his pack, he may put matches, a small blue tarp, a water bottle, an inflatable pillow, a rain jacket, binoculars, and a Sibley's field guide to trees.

Because Jeanie was the youngest in our family, I assumed her portal would be the weakest, so I tried to get rid of hers first. She wasn't in her room. She was, that night, at a sleepover, at a friend's house. I had planned to load each of their portals into my car somehow, tugging or dragging them, using a rope if necessary, then I would drive them all to the dump and bury them for good beneath the expired car seats and the blown tires, and when I returned home, I would be returning to a safe and secure home, where my children would act like children, and my husband would act like the man I married.

Jeanie's portal was impossible for me to lift. I took a hammer to it. Its surface tinged orange then reverted to glass. I used to know everything that was going to happen to me for the rest of my life. There had been a common trajectory in place, a form. I hammered for a long time with no results. Nor did I have any luck with Billy's portal. With his, I tried to use a handsaw from the shed. I didn't know anymore. I used to know who I was. I was who my family was. Billy's portal shuddered once, after which I vomited on the compost pile. I thought I had a family. I thought that meant I would never be alone. Several feathers fluttered to the ground. Two feathers, or maybe three. That was all.

I did not bring the hammer into the laundry room, nor did I bring the saw. My anger toward these portals had, all night, been sharpening into ammunition. I wanted to use my hands. It must have been 2 a.m. The moon was either gone or covered by the clouds. This house did not feel like mine anymore. When I entered the laundry room through the back door, my husband's portal lit up with a welcoming and infantile glow. Perhaps it mistook me for my husband. Perhaps it thought here my husband was, finally ready to go.

The glow faltered.

All I did was touch it. I touched such a small part of it, and despite its powdery appearance, it shattered like it had been a window, but silently. Yes, it hurt. Like grabbing the sharp edge of a straight razor. My hand bled and needed bandaging. Afterward, I swept up the mess and dumped the pieces in the garbage can outside.

Benny burst into our bedroom early the next morning. He must have intended to go through his portal before I woke. He yanked the covers off me, off of the bed. I said, "We will get through this." He left our room and stomped down the stairs, still screaming, and out into the yard. I watched from our bedroom window as he threw himself, in desperate fashion, upon my son's portal that would not accept him, no matter how hard he charged. It was difficult to watch. He kept doing this. I imagine his body was becoming bruised. Here's something to know about portals: when you attempt to go through someone else's, it is like trying to push your way through a field of tensed muscle. At least, that's how it felt to me just before my husband's portal broke. I was able to get only the tip of my fingernail through.

A neighbor called after half an hour of this. "It is six o'clock in the morning, and it appears somebody is dying in your backyard," Ms. Li informed me. "Must I alert the authorities?"

I went outside and grabbed Benny's arms. Or I attempted to. At first I couldn't. He hit me in the neck, my right ear. He was flailing. I hoped Billy wasn't watching. He might have been. His blinds were open. Eventually my husband settled down. I led him into the house, to our room, where I put him to bed and pulled the sheet over his shoulders. He was shaking. I left the room to make him a cup of chamomile tea. When I returned, he was either pretending to sleep or he was sleeping. I set the mug on the nightstand. "I love you," I whispered.

My children became nervous around me after that. When I was home, Jeanie refused to leave her room. Billy slept in the backyard beneath his portal, attempting not to sleep, keeping guard with a flashlight and his clarinet. Without my children or my husband to hold on to, I felt as if I might very well float away. Or a version of myself might. Though that was just a feeling I had. I didn't go anywhere or leave anyone behind.

I said to Benny, "Go ahead and have sex with other people."

I said to him, "It's okay."

I said, "This is only one part of our much longer story."

My husband avoided looking in my direction.

I knew eventually he would look at me.

You can't not look at somebody forever.

Portals may appear to be made out of feathers, or sand, or clouds, or glass, or cobwebs, or ice, or velvet. Once I saw a portal that appeared to be made from butterfly wings. But portals are not actually made out of these substances. It's only an outer appearance, a shell. I'm not sure what portals are made from. When sweeping up my husband's portal, I'd held a piece of it. It felt like I was holding a bullet. I hid that piece in my sock drawer. A few days later, it was gone. I don't know whether it faded away or if Benny found it. He once thought portals were made out of stars, which makes no sense, but it was a surprisingly poetic image coming from him.

• • • •

On the day my children left, a colossal wind blew through our house. The wind knocked over a vase of daisies I was arranging in the kitchen and it tore the calendar off the wall. The calendar that featured, for September, a trio of adorable lions, as harmless as housecats. The gust was sudden, brief, a few seconds, after which an exaggerated quietness settled upon our home. Or was it more a shift in the air? A drop in pressure? It felt like some alarming thing had begun to tiptoe around the rooms. In any case, it became difficult to breathe. I left the smashed vase where it was on the tile floor and hurried into the yard to check on my son.

Perhaps, instead, I should have gone upstairs.

I didn't. I ran outside.

It was too late. Already Billy was standing so close, leaning closer than I had ever seen him get, bracing himself against the portal's frame. I could not catch his attention. There is the chance he didn't hear me. This is what I saw: his portal brightening, quickening somehow, then it opened so wide, the feathers multiplying and lifting. He walked away from me as casually as if he was headed off to school and would be home in the afternoon. The portal swallowed him. That cold blue light swallowed him up. I rushed to the garden shed, grabbed a crowbar, and tried to break open his portal. I tried until my arms were exhausted and useless, then I put the crowbar away, on its hook, and went upstairs to my daughter's room. I did not run. I should have ran. My children left within minutes of each other. They must have been planning it for days, whispering in the hallway, in the dark. I had assumed Jeanie was too attached to me to leave.

My daughter appeared to be wading into a lake, delicate ripples radiating out from where her body intersected with the portal's surface. The branches of trees curled gently around her legs. I yelled her name. She turned and held out her arm toward me, her left arm. I reached for her but it was like reaching for a picture. There was nothing to hold on to. She smiled at me. It was the kind of smile she used when somebody was taking her photo. "Please," I said. This must have been the wrong thing to say. What should I have said? She dove the rest of the way through, her orange elephant backpack hanging off one shoulder.

Eventually Benny came home from work. He must have heard me thrashing around in Jeanie's room. I guess I was hysterical. I guess I was destroying things, furniture. He held on to me until I quieted. "What did you think was going to happen?" he later asked. We were talking again, you see. We were trading facts. Here's one: all children must leave their parents someday. It has always been a matter of time ever since their births. Here's another fact: there are a lot of ways to leave somebody. It's not like there is only one correct way or one correct time. Here's one more: two people can still be in love even if it feels like they aren't.

Portals do not disappear instantly after your children go through them, but they do become less vibrant, as if any light and mystery they contained has been transferred to the other side. It is like looking at the back of a closed door. I sat in front of my children's portals for days, at times in the yard, other times in the glider in my daughter's bedroom, nibbling on saltines to relieve the nausea that washed over me. I took photos. Every hour their portals grew incrementally harder to see. We never look at those photos. Benny, beside me, drank mugs of warm ginger tea. We held each other's hands. His hands were rougher than I remembered. Occasionally, through a crack that flickered into being, we caught glimpses. My daughter appeared to be skipping through the shade. She has never skipped, as far as I know, in this world. While my son, in his separate universe, was singing lightly about birds of prey.

Here's something else I know: people who go through portals do not send messages home. They also do not come back.

Benny took up golf and also crossword puzzles. It turned out he had the patience for deciphering esoteric clues. *Rigoletto's forte* (four letters). *Leaflet-base appendage* (five letters). Occasionally he asked for help. "What's five letters for *Annuli*?" he said. "I don't care," I told him. On certain evenings he went out with a friend, I didn't ask her name, while I enjoyed my alone time in the kitchen cooking complicated dishes from countries not known for their cuisine, the kind of food we hadn't eaten for years because of the kids. Along with most of the businesses downtown, our neighborhood grocery store had been boarded up, but a Quik Mart with a thorough ethnic foods aisle was open late in the next town over.

"What were you planning on doing over there?" I asked my husband during yet another quiet dinner, this one featuring rice noodles from Burma alongside pickled tea leaves. "Were you going to ride horses all over the land? Did you plan on starting a new family?" These were just guesses. I didn't know. We tried some role-playing for a time. Benny said there was a difference between another world being real and us pretending to be in another world. Other nights we scavenged in our neighbors' homes, whose back doors were generally unlocked or smashed in. It's not the worst thing to live in an almost deserted town. Our neighbors' pantries were surprisingly well stocked. Who would have thought Mrs. Roszak would keep jimbu in her spice drawer? I believe these evenings brought us closer. My husband and I ripped the walnut doors off Mrs. Sikora's custom cabinets and set them on fire in her backyard. The mail was delivered infrequently by substitutes. A team of county workers drove a truck in every third week to pick up our trash. There was talk of our town eventually shutting down for good. It was only talk for now.

We took long walks together, Benny and I. On such walks, we claimed to be seeking out birds. Neither of us had expressed interest in bird-watching before. “What a nice evening,” I told Benny on one such walk. It was cold for that time of year, and I was underdressed. Honestly, I think we were both looking for portals. I told myself I was searching for my husband’s portal, but really I was searching for my own. I only wanted to see that I was capable of having one. I wasn’t the only person in our town without a portal but there weren’t many of us left. Mrs. Ada Luna had hanged herself in her garage. Several others climbed into their cars and drove out of state. Only a dozen of us stayed. Occasionally on our walks, I spotted them. Their panicked, embarrassed faces. It may have been easier for us, for me, had there been a clear reason. Sometimes you don’t get what other people have, I guess. I wish we were seen as heroes. It takes a certain courage to be left behind.

There was no need to wait at the red lights anymore. The roads were vacant that evening and clean. The only people we saw out were a trio of le[illegible] [illegible]kers poking around a drugstore dumpster. I th[illegible] [illegible] might appear as a gold bracelet I could f[illegible]n a[illegible] [illegible] as a piece of frosted glass.

“I’ve b[illegible] th[illegible] [illegible] about moving to a larger city,” Benny told me. We [illegible] cr[illegible] [illegible] main thoroughfare without bothering to look both [illegible]ys. “A[illegible] with more people in it.” We held hands. He dragged his nails across my skin. We hadn’t had sex since the children left. Or was it before then? I was no longer keeping track. Perhaps intercourse isn’t as necessary as I originally thought. At the same time, I had been taught it was a requirement. Lately, before bed, I might lay my head on my husband’s chest and listen to his heart. He might stroke my hair before easing out of bed. I might hear him turn the shower on as hot as it could go before he jerked off in the bathroom. Then he would clean himself up. I reminded Benny if anyone did come back, they would most likely emerge here, from the places their portals once were. I knew very well no one was coming back.

The sun shone directly into our eyes because it was setting right there in front of us. I have always wondered how certain sources of light can be so devoid of warmth. When I was growing up, all the lightbulbs in my childhood home were too hot to touch. "God, how peaceful this is," I said, turning my face away from that monstrous sun. Even the birds appeared to have left, disillusioned by so many empty feeders, so there wasn't that noise anymore. This would have been a problem were we still pretending to look for birds. Behind Mr. Roszak's boarded-up gas station, we found the remnant of a portal near the air pumps. I don't know whose it was. A few days old, a faint and exhausted copy surrounded by a suggestion of unease. My husband tried to pick it up.

"You can't pick portals up," I reminded him.

"I know that," he said.

"Then what are you doing?"

We continued our walk up the hill toward the old elementary school that our children had once attended—our usual spot to turn around. To reach the now vacant school, we needed to cross beneath the highway, and it was there, below the overpass, that I saw another portal, a bright one, still functional—the last portal I would ever see, though I didn't know this then. It cowered along the concrete wall near a pile of ragged towels. I thought it was mine at first. I felt my heart loosening in my chest when I thought it was mine. We took a few steps forward. It wasn't mine. I knew whose it was. It was made out of sand. The sand was shifting all the time in a desperate and unsettled fashion. In many ways it resembled my husband's earlier portal, though this one was smaller and less confident. I walked along as if I'd seen nothing, pointing out some broken glass on the road ahead in an attempt to divert my husband's attention.

But there is the possibility that he looked away from that portal knowingly. What I mean is, there is the possibility that he chose me.

THE DIRTY GOLDEN YELLOW HOUSE

On the first floor of a Colonial-style house constructed last century out of planks of old-growth cedar, a monster is dragging a woman's husband from room to room. The specific path this monster takes will be evident the next morning from the gashes in the wood floors and the splattering of the husband's innards upon the plaster walls. Blood on the ceiling. The woman herself is hiding in the upstairs bedroom in her closet, face buried in the nylon hems of her patterned dresses, hands to her ears, a washcloth between her teeth so she can bite down hard on something that isn't her tongue. It's her fault this is happening, certainly, she would not deny it, though I think she was justified. The husband's screams are muffled yet still audible, as if his face has been swaddled by a tentacle. He is about to be eaten. Due to the monster's narrow mouth opening, the act of eating him will be protracted and noisy and will take all night. The woman hiding in the closet amid the dresses is not a bad person, though she is not a good person either. She had asked for this to happen, but at the same time, in the dark, in the night, with a monster scavenging the first floor, it is difficult for her to exude confidence about her decision. She is aware, were this the opening scene of a story, that her choice regarding her husband's end would look indecent. But what is she supposed to do about that? Directly before sunrise, in the morning twilight, she creeps to the window and watches the summoned creature, whatever it is, burst through the screen door and escape, something limp and husband-shaped and dead dangling from its murderous jaws–

Wait, I'm getting ahead of myself. Let me back up.

He, being of the husband persuasion, never called what happened between them r— but favored alternate terminology such as *making love* or *pokey poke*. Part of being a fundamental human being, he explained, is to have intercourse where an orifice is penetrated on a regular basis, minimum once a week, by another human being, in this (his) case a husband, on a comfortable natural latex pillowtop mattress, penetrating an orifice of his legal wife, although he allowed for other combinations and other mattress types. I realize this is not the most fun paragraph to read but try and stick with me here. This is important. He has said this is important. The husband (such as he) cannot himself be guilty of an actual r— or r—-like behaviors upon the wife (such as she) on account of the matrimonial consent *which she has given and which she cannot retract*. He has said, "Everybody appears to know this except for you." It's not that r— doesn't exist, he argued. Of course it does. Unfortunately! But it exists only outside of their bedroom, in, for example, the industrial park on the far side of the city, or in the back alleys of the downtown, or in other foreign nations. In addition, he has faced real consequences to his health whenever the minimum conjugal responsibility wasn't met. His heart muscle has hurt. He has felt his blood pressure skyrocket and his risk increase for depression as well as prostate cancer which, he further explains, can cause discomfort in the pelvic area. He talks a lot. I think he is entitled. It can be difficult, in the chronically turned-on shadow of his monologues, to spot what is naked and face down on the pillow. "A wife," he says, "wants her husband to explore her inside and out with his fingers and make it an adventure for the two of them." He is quoting somebody. "Shut up," I say. He continues: "If you are not making love, you are not in love." I temporarily tape his mouth. He breathes through his nose and doesn't care–

Let me try this again. This is to be a horror story, in case that isn't clear. A husband and a wife of many years live together in a home that is metaphorically dim and cavernous. What I mean is–there is the feeling of caverns in the corners of the rooms and dimness matted in the composite crown molding that borders the doorways. The lights are all allegorically broken: lamps appear to blaze on in the morning and turn off at dusk. Along the floorboards, it is as if wild rodents have smeared their urine in dust while the feral children swing symbolically in the closets from the high-quality magic pants hangers that guarantee the multiplication of space by 80 percent. I haven't even mentioned the master bedroom, which might as well be draped in light abrasions and cheap matador curtains. The curtains which go *flap flap flap* in the cross breeze: they'll be proverbially ripped to pieces within the year. As for the wife's bathrobe, it has been confiscated again, hung in the attic rafters, out of reach. As long as she allows her husband whenever he wants, everything is fine for him. Remember that horror is relative and will depend on who is being scared. What scares her most is a room in the house. For him: a monosyllabic word. For me: domestic realism–

Too vague. Let me try this again. There have been conversations, though she, the wife, would call them *monologues* or *ultimatums*. She remains in charge of the picky children, the production of whole-grain meals, and the house. There is palladium light throughout the house, partly her doing. He is in charge of leaving for work in the morning and coming home in the dark. When he comes home at dark, he cocks his finger at her. The children are in the bedroom closet playing *What Happens Next*. "They'll hear us," she says, mistaking this for a choice. "I'll shut the closet door," he says. There are some funny jokes about r—. I am saving them for later. It's not a choice. He shuts and latches the closet door. "I love you," he says and, hold on, hold *on*, this is beginning to sound a little too familiar, like a part of my life I thought I had buried hundreds of feet below ground, beneath a concrete cap and a clay buffer and some dirt. Which I had buried multiple times, by the way, always at night, under a new moon, using a shovel and occasionally a backhoe, without artificial light of any kind, knowing what such a scene would look like to the neighbors if I turned on a light. Though no matter how deeply I dug, how deep I dig, my past each time has clawed her way out using her jackhammer elbows and her yellow teeth, this time emerging backlit to an industrial soundtrack, bloodworms in her hair, a straight razor in her hands.

I try my best to make small talk with her—what a dreary day, why won't my neighbors' dogs stop barking, they are always barking, let's go poison the dogs, shall we—though conversation falters, as it always does, whenever she appears like this, holding a razor with accusation in her eyes.

I was joking about the dogs, I have to explain.

She rummages in her roomy pockets anyway for a pint of antifreeze.

The gray clouds lower. I'm not sure whether she intends for me to drink the antifreeze or if it's for the dogs.

I wonder, I say, using my gentlest voice, the voice reserved for my children when they're hysterical, whether it might be time for me, for us, to move on?

Certain reviewers and readers have already started complaining about my recent stories, both their thematic similarities and their very specific view of relationships. I have examples. From one reviewer: *Other than the overt political addition to the obvious social metaphors which helps extend this to novelette length, this* [one of my stories] *is exactly like the same author's* [another one of my stories] *in being an overlong underplotted offputtingly narrated story of a repugnant asexual wife and a repugnant husband and their repugnant relationship.* From another reviewer: *It* [one of my stories] *is probably sending a message about something—menopause maybe? . . . I have no clue what the ending is supposed to mean.* From a reader: *My takeaway is that the story* [one of my stories] *was an exercise in catharsis for the author, and has no real value as a morality tale beyond—*

My past self slams her (our?) body against the window glass. Has she not been clear enough. Here is what she expects in my writing: revenge, on me, on him, on them, on the structure of the story itself, and if I ever consider not placing her at the bloody heart of whatever I write, she will do this to me. She acts out what she will do to me. There is so much blood. In case I don't understand her point, she smears my attic window with our blood, so our blood is dripping off the window onto the unfinished deck, onto my children who are trying to read library copies of graphic novels on the deck, who look up, I would rather them not see this, not to mention the neighbors—

I clean up the mess. I get the point. I'll keep writing this story despite the similarities to my other stories. Though I would like a break. The wife in this story needs a break. We need some good advice and a break! "I need a road trip," she tells her husband, who approves her request, so the next morning she drives herself and her kids to Indiana to her childhood home whose windows are painted shut, making the interior stuffy and recirculating. In the family room, in the evening, her mother delivers a lecture: "You can't change people. You can only change your reaction to them. Just like people can't change you. Only you can change you. People can make their own happiness by looking at things in a different way. Haven't you made love before with your husband? Your husband is a heterosexual who needs and wants to make love with his wife. How is this situation different now than before?" The woman requests her mother replace the term *making love* with the term *vaginal intercourse.* "Why would I do that?" her mother replies. The woman's husband texts hourly. Just checking in. She deletes his texts. At night in her childhood bedroom, the children bounce on the mattress and bite the furniture. Nobody sleeps. A study by a sociologist–a sociologist who, let me note, is also a woman–has proved it is more difficult to leave one's husband after marital r— when one is economically dependent on him. The economically dependent wife in this story would like to replace the phrase *more difficult* with the phrase *impossible.* Statistics are interesting. "Don't think of it as a choice, dear," says her mother in parting after a breakfast of multigrain toast and weak coffee.

The wife loads her children into the family vehicle and drives back along I-90 eastbound, past the lake and the bird sanctuary and the county park with the water features while the kids play the memory game in the rear seat and gobble generic Pringles. "Various factors may temporarily impede this solution [of leaving a husband after r—], particularly the problem of where she is to live, and how she is to finance the breakup and her own life afterward," agrees a legal scholar. She takes Exit 34A and pays her toll, which is exorbitant. The stomata open. While she was away, the neighbors staked colorful rainbow signs into their front yard: WE BELIEVE LOVE IS LOVE AND KINDNESS IS EVERYTHING. "Did you get my texts?" asks the husband. "No," she lies outright. Her husband believes her. He thinks she wouldn't lie about something. *Oh my, all the trouble, it's in your head, isn't it, dear? All we need to do is fix that dear little head.* That last bit of dialogue is the world talking.

I'd like to provide you with some background and statistics on marital r— now. Please skip the next two paragraphs, resuming your reading with the phrase *Later that month*, if any of the following apply:

- You consider interruptions like these an affront to your personal fictional escapism.
- You think marital r— in a story is stupid because why doesn't she just get a divorce so we can stop talking about it.
- You are a marital r— expert.

In the U.S., between 10 percent and 14 percent of married women experience marital r—, according to the National Coalition Against Domestic Violence. Yet I will bet my buttons that 10 to 14 percent of American literature does not contain marital r— scenes. Does even 5 percent? 1 percent? The only novel I can think of with a marital r— scene right now is *Gone with the Wind*; that was supposed to be romantic. Only in 1993 did marital r— become a crime in all fifty states. The reason it took so long: certain people, some of them lawmakers, didn't believe marital r— was possible. Or, if it was possible, they believed the state certainly shouldn't get involved ("*These are personal things* . . ."). Outside of the U.S., in forty-nine other countries, r—ing one's wife is still not considered a criminal act. There are only 195 countries. In addition, there are "r—-like behaviors" (see researcher and sociologist Diana E. H. Russell's *R— in Marriage*) as well as Andrea Medea and Kathleen Thompson's idea of "little r—s," none of which are technically illegal but still contribute to an atmosphere of compulsory and/or coercive sex in relationships and should be cause for concern.

Legally, for a sexual encounter to be r—, there must be physical force or threat of force, or else the victim must be unable to give consent, such as she is sleeping or unconscious. The proper term for what happened in the previous pages is more likely to be called, by the authorities, *sexual coercion* (defined by the Office on Women's Health as "unwanted sexual activity that happens when you are pressured, tricked, threatened, or forced in a nonphysical way. Coercion can make you think you owe sex to someone."). Though this also depends on who is defining the words *r—* and *sexual coercion* and *consent*. Advocates like author Louise McOrmond-Plummer have argued that sexual coercion is a form of r—, and r— should be redefined as any sexual act without consent. "Submission is not consent," McOrmand-Plummer writes. The boundaries of where consent ends and r— begins are still under debate and still broadening.

Later that month, the woman we are following enrolls in nursing school. She never wanted to be a nurse. There are blogs where stay-at-home mothers such as herself in marriages such as hers attend nursing school then finish nursing school then become independent and employable.

Her name is Lacey Balan. That isn't her real name. I'm trying to protect her identity. She carries the nursing textbook in her arms. Whenever the phrase *situational influences* is used in the textbook, she highlights that sentence. The textbook is heavy. "I need to study," she tells her husband, highlighting *situational influences*, this time on page 127. She does not complete her assignments. Her husband says there is a difference between want and need. I'm going to offer Lacey some advice now which was once offered to me: focus on his love which will radiate green out of his eye sockets, yellow out the pores of his shoulders, pink out of his chest brightly at that moment, like everybody says it should.

"What if I hate those colors?" Lacey asks. Don't be a picky bitch, Lacey. Here's that joke I promised. The husband says, "If you can't r— your wife, who can you r—?" The wife says, "But you can r— your wife." The husband says the joke again. It's funnier the second time around. Other funny r— jokes can be found by googling *funny r— jokes.* A less successful search is *funny marital r— jokes.* Only two jokes came up. There is a definite comedic need. If we can't laugh about it, then it's not real. If it's not real, then what is Lacey's problem? This is the end of the humor section.

She is kicked out of nursing school. In their king-size Logan industrial rough-hewn bed, beside the velvet brushstroke decorative pillows in storm/silver that she chose, and they weren't even on sale, all bought using her husband's income, she pretends to be someone else. But she doesn't pretend to be anybody bad. For example, she doesn't pretend to be a murderer–a woman who murders–in a suspense novel, also called a thriller, who is about to kill her husband out of either sociopathic tendencies or else revenge. She pretends, instead, to be a woman in a story (not this story, another story). While he pretends to be Humphrey Bogart, sad-eyed and dead. He tells her to take her clothes off. Gazing upon one's naked spouse is a legitimate form of love, correct? He tilts his head, holds her hands, mimes lighting a cigarette. "Come on, I'll be quick," he says. "Sweetheart, I promise. Lacey, you used to." He drops the act. "Here," he says, "if you do not right now open your pretty leggy-legs, these are your consequences, which are legal to the best of my ability." There is a relevant stack of documentation. Her consequences may include dissolution, dissolvement, disintegration, disappearance, impoverishment, and dispersedness. The man who is her husband considers himself a feminist in most if not all situations so he has offered other positions, so it is okay. "Oh, why doesn't she want to have sex with him, why why why?" chants a chorus of women lurking in the background. "Is it a medical condition? A hormonal imbalance? A species classification error? Why why why why why?"

If you are as confused as the chorus because you have never felt like Lacey feels in bed, and you can only relate to what you yourself have felt, let's get down on the bed with her, so that you can better understand! If you already understand, please skip the below paragraph and resume your reading with *Women, whether they be.*

We Are on the Bed with Her

Do as I say. Smell the sheets. The sheets smell of night sweats and lavender spray. Look at the sheets. The sheets are the color of ash and will not wrinkle no matter what is done upon them. Touch the sheets. The sheets are a satin weave for maximum softness. An embroidered hem adds poise. On top of the satin ashy sheets, a man is mounting her (us) from behind. The man is her (our) husband. To him, this fact that he is her (our) husband makes a difference. To her (us), he can be her (our) husband, or a stranger, or a distant acquaintance, or a relative. It would feel the same and as unwanted. As I am trying to explain how it felt to her (us), not him, let's forget that he is her (our) husband. The important detail here: a man is mounting her (us) from behind and she (we) does (do) not want it to be happening. It should feel as if he has fur and fangs. It should feel as if he has fur and fangs and a rope. With a rope in his hands, he would have a few options. Those options should help us understand how the woman on the bed is feeling. It should feel like someone, anyone, is shoving something, anything, unwanted into her (our) orifice. It should hurt and not for any multisyllabic medical reason with a pharmaceutical cure either. It should hurt because it hurts when someone, anyone, is shoving something, anything, into one's orifice that one does not want there. I am using words I hope you can relate to. "I love you," the man whispers in her (our) ear under these frantic and suspicious circumstances.

• • • •

Women, whether they be mothers, friends, or couples therapists, have always wanted to be helpful to other women throughout the twenty-first century. One of these women asks Lacey, "Have you, as a child, ever been sexually molested?" Lacey says no, never. It would have been easier, let's be honest, had Lacey been sexually molested because then everyone could understand her. Another woman asks, "What's the worst thing that would happen if you let your husband enjoy your body?" "The worst thing that might happen is I'll kill myself," says Lacey. The woman clarifies: "I meant your husband. What is the worst thing that would happen to him." "Oh. The worst thing that might happen to him is he would be happy," Lacey replies. A third woman asks Lacey if she understands the phrase *don't wash dirty linen in public.* Together these women form the chorus of women I previously mentioned, linking arms, now stage left under the bad fluorescent lighting, lecturing in singsong about the importance of the male gaze love touch hormones lubrication love sensate masters johnson arousal pretend disorder one two three four five la la la. They're entranced by their own definitions of feminism, intimacy, and liberation; their chitchat sounds like the territorial noises of the squirrels. Oh Lacey, Lacey, you're picking fights with everybody, aren't you. Remember what my mother told me: *bear in mind that at night every home is a potential spotlight in a field of darkness.* At night, after Lacey's husband r—s her (not legally but using that alternate definition I mentioned above, "tell me if I'm hurting you," he says), he falls asleep deeply, his hot love arm draped heavily over her beloved shoulder. The air in the room smells not of her but of him. He smells of crawl spaces and storage onions.

This cannot go on.

Or rather, this can only go on for so long.

Lacey considers the red nylon rope hidden in her underwear drawer.

Should she finally hang herself in the bathroom?

She reads in bed for the next hour.

This seems like a good time to check your reading comprehension thus far.

Keeping in mind the last few pages, what would you have Lacey do next?

A She should go to the doctor and get her hormones checked, then she should get her hormones adjusted, then she should start antidepressants. Then she should go to another doctor and sign up for therapy with vaginal dilators, which are (according to the Cleveland Clinic) *tube-shaped devices that come in various sizes. Their primary purpose is to stretch the vagina. People with vaginismus use dilators to become more comfortable with, and less sensitive to, vaginal penetration*, then everything will probably be fine for the husband.

B She should take the kids and put the kids in the family car, and she should drive west to the next state over, which is Ohio, and her husband will cancel the credit cards and she has no money.

C She should leave the kids and take the family car, and she should drive the car north, without a map or destination, and her husband again cancels the credit cards, and she has no money and is alone.

D This is a ridiculous story and Lacey should act like you would act, meaning she would act *very believably*.

I don't care which decision you chose.

The question I asked wasn't a real question.

I only wanted to remind you of what it feels like to be asked a question that isn't a real question.

Other examples of questions that, in my experience, aren't real questions: "Is this okay?" And "Do you want to do this?"

But enough about me! I will do my best, from this point on, to be a proper narrator and stay out of my own story.

Lately Lacey has been reading thrillers that involve a murder.

She likes the thrillers because the murderer is rarely who the reader has expected.

In one thriller, the narrator (a woman) was the murderer. In another, the narrator's cousin (a woman) was the murderer, though she had some help from a male cousin. In that book the woman was sociopathic, though other times women murderers are not sociopathic. In another book, the crime is never solved.

These books offer her an idea: In this unbearable situation, why must she be the one to go?

She dreams of floods, wakes sweating. Her husband insists on knowing what she dreamed. "In my dream I went on a vacation in the mountains, then a bird flew down to me, a brown bird with an orange beak, and pecked my shoulder until it bled," she lies. He believes her again, biting the skin of her shoulder playfully. "Like this?" he asks. He does what he did. Let's repeat that exercise. Get on the bed with her. Lie on your stomach. Remember the fangs, the fur, the rope. There were men looking down from the sky, men in the moon and men's faces in the sun. A lot of people were looking at her. Not, like, literally. But that's how it felt. "I feel so loved right now," the husband says, having always hated that word *coercive*. She had one twenty-dollar bill in her wallet. The credit cards, the bank account were in his name. "Is there something wrong with me?" Lacey asks the chorus during the space between one act and the next. "Yes, but that's understandable," the chorus replies, any one of them with sympathetic eyes. Lacey would have rather murdered the institution of marriage or at least its grammar but there were concrete difficulties with that plan. Please know that up until recently she had been very good, "good" being defined as allowing her husband to do what he wanted to her and not murdering him.

Before Lacey's husband wakes, she slips out of the master bed and down the stairs and out the front door. Walking east, she pretends she is on a morning stroll, passing by abandoned tricycles and sidewalk chalk and lawns covered in the reproduction of broadleaf plantain. These residential blocks are long and shaded from the sun; it takes an hour to get anywhere. When she finally arrives at the house where Ms. Imogen Shea lives, she feigns surprise to have ever arrived there, though all along this had been her intent. Beyond the house is the woods, both allegorical and actual. There aren't paths in the woods, there are wolves. We'll save the woods for another day. The house is ominous enough: yellow, looming, dirty yet golden, covered in pollen and other sticky particles and overshadowed by semiprecious trees. Emotional women are known to wander in and out of Ms. Shea's foyer at all hours, tissues to their noses, heads down, weeping about marital problems, their eyes crusty with inflammation. At night, stubby wax candles burn like fire hazards in the upper windows.

Lacey knocks on the old-world-style front door.

A breeze kicks up. The silver and ruby leaves bang against the silver and ruby branches. The noise wakes the neighborhood attack dogs who begin to salivate.

Lacey knocks again, louder and harder.

The door blows open.

Ms. Shea is an older woman, gray hair, crow's feet, a lack of collagen in her lips, loose wrinkled pockets in her calico dress. She does not call herself a witch, though every year of late she has accumulated a new and witchy quality, so what else would she be? Last year, the smell of cedar resin on her skin. This year, an iris freckle. Before that a white hair that curled from her chin. She is in menopause, in case that isn't obvious, has been for decades, a state of being caused, in her case, by a ceremony of her own doing, her power based not on fertility or mothering or lactation but on the opposites: aridity, conclusions, and destruction. This brief mention of menopause does not, metaphorically or otherwise, make this story about menopause. I am saying this to clear things up for that male reviewer and any others who thought a previous story of mine, also about a sex-repulsed asexual wife/mother, was metaphorically about menopause. "Come in," whispers Ms. Shea, motioning with urgency, her fingernails flickering with reflections of orange-red flame.

The interior of the dirty golden yellow house is dusty and cluttered, bottles of supplements stacked on the windowsills, succulents on the countertops, luminescent jars of nonperishables lined up on the shelves. In between stockpiling expeditions into town, Ms. Shea spends her time helping married women untraditionally with their intimacy problems. She leads Lacey to the living room, which is her helping room. They sit on matching armchairs. The room smells of autumn harvest air freshener though it is not yet that spicy cinnamon time of year. Lacey describes her ongoing bedroom situation. "I want you to kill my husband," she says.

Ms. Shea offers an embarrassed chuckle. "Oh my! There are much nicer ways to say that." She suggests *neutralized*, *deleted*, *erased*, or *snuffed out*—"Let's go with deleted"—but wonders aloud if Lacey can afford her help, as these acts are never cheap. Though a bucket of uncut sapphires might suffice. Or a diamond pickaxe. A pair of portals? Or hurricane-force winds—

Lacey does not have access to such items.

"Then your daughter."

"What?"

"Give her to me."

Lacey laughs.

"Give your daughter to me, and I will delete your husband," Ms. Shea says.

"No."

"Now don't be stupid, dear."

Lacey tastes bile in her mouth. Even if I did not get around to explaining this earlier, Lacey loves her daughter deeply. They take walks together. They read books to each other.

"What kind of woman are you?" Lacey asks.

"I'm not going to eat her."

"No, wait. What kind of monster are you? Are you a monster that eats other people's children?"

"I can give her a different life."

"No!"

"I can give your daughter a better life."

"No no no no no no no!"

Ms. Shea rises from the chair. She is taller than she was before, at least seven inches taller. Perhaps she has grown or perhaps she is now hovering off the ground. Lacey is afraid to look beneath Ms. Shea's feet to see what is going on. "You are not the first woman," accuses Ms. Shea, "to presume I work for the sole benefit of my heart." She shoves the front door open. Already, in the haze of early morning, a dozen other needy women wait on the sidewalk. They glimpse Lacey through the doorway; they clench and unclench their hands. "Time for you to go home, make love to your husband, then take your own life," says Ms. Shea, motioning to the door.

A flock of crows settles at the edge of the woods, filling the trees with an animalistic energy and feathers.

When the crows scream, the sidewalk women scream back although at a higher frequency.

"Go," says Ms. Shea, pointing.

The minute hand of the floor clock ticks forward.

Lacey shakes her head.

She gets down on her knees and shakes her head.

"Oh my god, get up," orders Ms. Shea.

Lacey does not get up. On her knees, she asks, "Different from who? From what?"

"What are you talking about?"

"You can give my daughter a life different from what?"

"I think you know."

The gray fingerprints of invisible and histrionic women color the crown molding of the doorway. The minute hand of the clock ticks forward again.

"I am not judging," informs Ms. Shea. "Although if you can't, on your own, for yourself, put your own affairs in order, if you cannot control what happens in the bedroom, your bedroom, to your own body, to your private internal areas–how do you plan to give your daughter what is of worth?"

In the intimate dimness of the foyer, Lacey begins to cry.

Mothers' tears are worthless and commonplace, and generally, Ms. Shea would have ignored them, only today's transaction, she realizes, will go more smoothly should Lacey feel valued and productive. So she goes through the ritual motions of tear collection, the choosing of the crystal vial, the sampling, the stoppering, and the labeling. After which the two women return to the helping room, where a tea tray has been set on a low table between the armchairs, petite ladyfingers arranged on a doily on a plate.

"I don't want my daughter to have a life like mine," whispers Lacey.

"Of course you don't."

Ms. Shea offers the plate of cookies; it is like eating a child's finger.

Unfortunately the tea tastes like tannin and gore.

Lacey stares down at the coagulating liquid in her porcelain cup. She hopes she is dreaming.

"You're not dreaming," clarifies Ms. Shea.

"How will you raise her?" asks Lacey.

"I will raise her to be angry," promises Ms. Shea.

"Will you raise her to be powerful as well?"

"I will raise her to be angry and powerful and towering and untouchable."

"And violent?"

"Violent, oh yes."

"And vengeful."

"Of course."

"And if anyone asks her to do something she doesn't want to do, something that feels wrong, or feels worse, if anyone pressures her or threatens her or threatens to withhold–"

"I will teach her to say no."

"You will teach her to destroy whoever is asking?"

"I will teach her to destroy whoever is asking."

"So if she is ever in my situation–"

"I promise she will never be in your situation."

"But if she is?"

"I promise."

"And you will get rid of my husband?"

Ms. Shea sips her thickened tea. "I will solve the problem of your husband."

"Because I cannot seem to solve that problem myself."

"I know, dear."

There is no need to turn over the daughter now. Later is fine. The promissory note is a quick prick of a ring finger, a smear of Lacey's blood on Ms. Shea's dress. "That blood will stain," Lacey warns. "Well, that's where the power comes from. Bring a photograph of your husband tomorrow," Ms. Shea instructs. Lacey shows herself out. She is blinded by the light of the sun, which has risen.

The women lined up and waiting in the increasing heat look tired and crazy, like they are about to play with fire.

The next morning, Lacey rises early, before her husband or daughter or son wakes, and she walks again to the edge of the city and knocks on the door to the dirty golden yellow house. Ms. Shea opens the door wearing the same dress, spotted at the hem with Lacey's delicate rust-colored blood. "I brought the picture," says Lacey, though she does not hand the picture over, as she is having second thoughts. She is having a new idea! Like what about turning her husband into a different animal, like a bird! If he was a bird, he could perch, no problem, on her shoulder during the dinner hour. She could clip his wings every one to three months, avoiding the blood feathers.

"I'm not that kind of witch," explains Ms. Shea.

"I don't believe you," says Lacey. After all, Ms. Shea has semiprecious trees all over her yard, like in a made-up story where a woman with semiprecious trees has special powers such as, for starters, the power to turn a man into a winged–

"Enough," mutters Ms. Shea, and the clouds surround the sun. She snatches the photograph out of Lacey's pocket and strides into the kitchen. Really, she should be wearing her yellow neoprene gloves. Such pictures, in such situations, have been known to dissolve into acid. She puts on the gloves and busies herself filling pots, adjusting the gas stove, turning on the fan. Ms. Shea is going to need a proper name for him. His name will be Arlo Balan. That is not his real name but it will do. In the photo, Arlo Balan poses in front of their automatic garage door, left eye larger than his right. "I don't want this," whimpers Lacey, who has followed Ms. Shea into the kitchen, which is frightening, jars of pickled skin, and preserved hearts, and braided smoke, and bloody shirts, and a child's left shoe alone on the linoleum floor. "Yes, you do," says Ms. Shea. She's probably right. After that, the older woman ignores her. There are fewer women waiting outside today. Only one woman, in fact, on her stomach, asleep beneath a silver maple, not that urban species of tree notorious for brittle splintering after storms, but a maple hammered out of silver metal. Silver bark, silver roots, silver cambium, silver branches. The heavy silver leaves fall upon the sleeping woman until she is covered. Covered and suffocated. Unable to claw her way out. What a strange and exhausting act this is, to arrange the disappearance of someone we love or loved or could have loved! What a loss of appetite.

Over breakfast the following morning, Lacey claims a sudden contagious sickness so she cannot, for the rest of the day, take care of anyone or any living thing.

"Wait. I'm sick too," Arlo says.

"Why don't you lie down on the couch and get some rest?" suggests Lacey.

He seizes her wrist. "Why don't you lie down with me and we won't rest?"

She forces herself to cough until she coughs up something red. A piece of her heart or lung.

"Jesus," he says, for once letting her go, though he is unhappy about it, unsatisfied, his chest hurts, [illegible].

[illegible] counts the orange [illegible] in front of her. There are twenty-seven. She counts them again. There are twenty-seven. She counts them again. There are twenty-seven. She counts them again. There are twenty-six. That has never happened before. A mockingbird lands on the skylight above her head. That has never happened before either. Two mockingbirds. They fight over a fat red berry. She practices her expressions in the attic mirror. Look surprised! She looks surprised. Look shocked! She looks shocked. Look sad. She looks sad. Not that far away, Ms. Shea is talking to herself in her kitchen in that singsong voice. The medium stockpot boils vigorously, its ingredients rising to the surface and bobbing in the turbulent water, the songbird feather, the moth wing, the paper scrap, the mouth cut from a photograph, the ear, the hand, the eye.

"Why do you think your husband wants to see you naked?" the chorus women ask in passing on the way from the attic to the tip-top of the pointed roof. They would like Lacey to understand her husband's urges before they jump. If she can understand her husband's urges, tragedies can be averted! "Oh, I think we're well past that point," Lacey replies.

"Okay, what exactly is going on downstairs?" asks Arlo Balan. It is late in the evening, and Arlo and Lacey are in the second-floor bedroom together because Lacey had to leave the attic because Arlo made her, despite the fake coughing, because they are married and married people sleep naked together in the same bed every night so he can rub whatever parts of her he wants. This is normal behavior. Arlo is naked, Lacey wearing only her blue-green panties, which will have to come off, which is not unreasonable. She is on her back, under the satin-weave bedsheet, which will also have to come off. There are noises downstairs. The noise of a window or patio door smashing. The noise of a heavy wide mass moving deliberately across the kitchen floor. Such noises are probably what Ms. Shea meant when she talked of solving Lacey's husband problem. "I have no idea what's going on down there," she replies convincingly. She practiced that line too, practiced looking honest and inquisitive. She tells Arlo she loves him. This declaration of love will hopefully negate whatever she is about to do. That's how love works. Generally she is not one for violence. "Neither am I," Arlo would say if they, together, were discussing a propensity for violence. The low tonality of the wind. Something breaks. A bone cracks. A wet weight continues to be dragged—or drag itself?—across the ceramic tile. "You should get downstairs and make sure we're safe," Lacey suggests. She has an overactive imagination. "It's probably the fridge," Arlo argues. Instead of going downstairs, he tugs the bedsheet from Lacey's body then removes her panties, tossing them onto the floor with pleasure. He rolls heavily on top of her. He weighs fifteen stone. "I love you too," he says. Lots of women want this done to them. The patio door will need to be repaired.

The next night the noises begin again, this time insistent and closer, not in the kitchen but in the foyer and on the stairs. Lacey repeats herself: Is it not the husband's job to leave the bedroom, thereby ensuring the family's primal safety? The beating of insect wings, the rattle of a metal cart or carts—it is more difficult to attribute that evening's performance to a kitchen appliance. "I'll be back soon," Arlo says softly, kissing her cheek with his chapped lips, his fingertips sliding across the skin on her neck. He leaves the room. There is, obviously, a monster in the house. The children are deeply sleeping, sound machines jacked up on *rainfall*, beach towels stuffed under the doors, so they don't hear what happens, what is happening. Each sound intensifies. Not wings but claws, thuds. Arlo is screaming in his own unique way. Lacey, in the closet now, closes her eyes and sees patterns of light. Gray, gold.

"My heart is broken," repeats Lacey to whatever neighbor or relative comes to sit with her outside in the deck chairs in the coming days. That is not necessarily a lie. It's not like this is a joyous occasion for her either. She, too, had imagined a different definition of love. Now she is not going to get that definition. Instead, she is going to become haunted. It's only a matter of time. "I hope Arlo is happy, wherever he is," Lacey repeats to whomever. This is the lie. She would not mind him suffering a little. If there are monsters, she would not mind them holding him down from time to time and toying with his kidneys or declaring enthusiastic love for his urethra. She might not really mean that. "Oh, I do," says Lacey. "I do mean it." There is no body. She exfoliates daily. The chorus of women dance grimly through the hallway. The neighbors deliver plastic containers of soups that are tasty and freeze well. Her skin has never looked so good.

Her husband's parents are comforting and sad. They send a series of sympathy cards, all of them containing the same message: *He will always be with you. He'll forever be a part of you.* This sounds like a threat. She burns the cards, scatters the ashes. "He'll come back," insists Lacey's mother. Another threat? She sells her husband's business, a lawyer deals with the paperwork, and Arlo's parents, who have the means to send monthly checks, send monthly checks. She opens a savings account in her name. At night, she can hear him, Arlo, in the bedroom, the absence of him breathing. It is difficult to get back to sleep after that. "I'm sorry," she announces to the dark; this isn't how she imagined marriage either. At the same time, there are improvements. Ghosts generally (85 percent of the time, according to a 1975 British study) do not touch a human being's body, not in the same way that humans touch each other at least. When Arlo's ghost approaches her at night, it is more of a temperature change mixed with the scent of burning charcoal.

"I'm fine," Lacey says to her neighbors, to her mother, not lying, only leaving certain pieces out. Arlo used to tell Lacey, "I know you're scared." Her fear tasted like a fancy French salt, according to him. She feels a pressure on her trapezius. He used to lick her. He said it felt every time like he was making love to a virgin, which he did not mind. After multiple washings involving vinegar and Borax, the sheets still smell like him. She washes the sheets again. Before she falls asleep, she feels his deadweight pressing onto the mattress. The next morning she washes the sheets again and, in addition, hangs circular mirrors from the doorways, burns sage, sprinkles salt, rings a bell. Part of the problem may be that Arlo's hair still clogs the shower drain. She buys a bottle of Drano Max Gel from the hardware store, and though this product has been noted to contain potentially significant hazards to health and/or the local watershed, she dumps all eighty fluid ounces down the shower. His hair dissolves in a wash of sulfurous chemicals.

Still, she hears a light tapping beneath her bed, a scrape behind the wall, a bit of disembodied laughter that escapes in the evening from the corner of the closet. The chorus of women chide her for worrying. Worry is the stupidest emotion. Lacey is tired of being followed by a smarty-pants chorus. Let's get rid of the chorus. She would like to know what happened. Is her husband in pain or not, is his body somewhere or not. Will she always be haunted. The woman in the dirty golden yellow house probably knows but she will not answer the door. The days are wonderful. She takes whatever the neighbors give her, piles of black tourmaline, a used bicycle, casseroles. Her daughter brushes her lips against Lacey's skin in an animalistic nuzzle, and if there are occasional unexplained shifts in the house interior, it is easy enough to return the displaced chairs to the breakfast nook or straighten the fireplace tools after they topple over. Water ripples in a glass from unexplained vibrations. "Hello, Arlo," Lacey whispers, swallowing the water. Their relationship is complicated. Her daughter climbs into bed with her. She will not sleep unless Lacey's arms are wrapped around the girl's body, and the girl's little arms are wrapped around Lacey's body, and the girl's breath is on her face. They breathe together, the same air, in and out and in and out and in and out. *I love your knees. I love your shoulder. I love your nose. I love your ear. I love your fingers. I love your elbow. I love your teeth. I love you!* Her son creeps into the bedroom and vacuums the dust off Arlo's suits, and this would be a happy enough ending should I stop the story here, only this is not the ending. When Lacey lifts the sheet to remake the bed, the rectangle of fabric holds suspended above the mattress, and her daughter laughs and laughs. "We are witches!" her daughter laughs. Lacey slaps the girl's face. Not yet. Too soon. The sheet deflates. That night the girl is back to sleeping in Lacey's arms, a child again, impotent and dependent, and Lacey thinks, incorrectly, that she will have more time.

A letter from Ms. Shea arrives in a gory envelope which Lacey incinerates in the fireplace. It wasn't a letter but a bill. The bill becomes due. Past due. Dead birds rain down like fleshy stones upon the deck. Lacey sweeps them up before either child wakes. There are contractor bags of dead birds in the garage. The neighbor Carol complains. The smell is driving her dogs crazy. Plus other signs, the flaming comets, the hail, locusts, drownings, war, bloodshed, murder, looting, tyranny. Lacey barely notices her husband's ghost anymore, she is so busy cataloging the harbingers and the portents. She finds a needle and an eggshell under her daughter's sheets. She finds a water basin on her daughter's shelf meant to hold the power of the moon. "What are you doing?" Lacey asks her. The girl, unemotional and curious, watches the sky in the east with clear gray eyes. Her eyes used to be brown. On the bathroom window, the words CONTRACTUAL OBLIGATION appear as barbed lettering in the shower steam. Lacey rubs the words away. There are threats made of blood. I WILL KILL HER AND HIM AND spells the new words on the glass and these don't erase.

"We're going on an adventure!" Lacey tells her daughter, best always to do these things in the morning at dawn, when the sky is red and threatening.

"Where?" the girl asks sleepily, her eyes like silver coins, her lips like bloodflowers.

"To a witch's house," Lacey replies. The girl startles awake and runs into her room to dress. Lacey follows. From the doorway, she studies her daughter's body for what will be the last time. *I am giving her a gift*, Lacey reminds herself. *This is an act of love. Anything done for love is good.* "What do you bring to a witch's house?" asks the girl. "I don't think you need to bring anything," Lacey says, assembling a bag for the girl anyway, a set of polka dot underwear, leggings, shirts, a plush penguin stuffie, a photograph of the two of them in June. The wind stops blowing on the walk over. In the stillness they talk about starlight, growing up, losing teeth, double digits, and love.

"Were you in love once?" asks the girl.

"Oh, once or twice before," says Lacey.

"Will you be in love again?"

"I don't think so. Not after today."

They arrive at the dirty golden yellow house. "This is it?" asks the daughter with obvious disappointment, having expected something like a cottage built at the very center of the forest with a wishing well and a thatched roof. "But wait until you see inside," says Lacey. They walk, holding hands, up the crumbling pathway. The door opens before Lacey can knock. "You got my messages," says Ms. Shea. "What messages?" asks the girl. "I got your messages," says Lacey. "I can take it from here," says Ms. Shea. "I would like to come inside," says Lacey, trying to get inside. Ms. Shea blocks her way. "You can't come inside anymore," she says. The girl tugs on her mother's arm. "Let's go, Mom," the girl says. "I'm talking about your mother, not you. I'm glad you're here," says Ms. Shea. "Let's go home," says the girl. "You must be hungry," says Ms. Shea. "Let's go now," says the girl. "I have porridge inside with a pitcher of cream," says Ms. Shea. "Or scones. Do you like scones? And strawberries in crystalized sugar. And all sorts of mushrooms and eggs." The house smells like soil and berries today. It smells like a burial. The girl tugs harder on Lacey's arm and turns to go. Ms. Shea grabs the girl's shoulders. "Mom?" asks the girl. Already Lacey has taken a step backward. She takes another step. This second step is harder than the first. The third step will be harder than the second, and so on. Ms. Shea keeps her arms secured around the girl's chest. "Mom!" The girl is screaming. Ms. Shea holds a crystal vial to the girl's cheek and catches every tear. The tears of a girl whose mother is leaving her are so valuable. "Mom! Mom! Mom! Mom! Mom!" Lacey turns and runs. The morning newspapers are delivered into the neighbors' driveways as if this is typical. *Thump thump thump thump.*

The first night after Lacey loses her daughter, she doesn't wash the sheets. Her bed smells like her daughter's hair. Then, as before, she washes the sheets multiple times in hot water, using more than the recommended amount of bleach. In the fireplace, she burns the puberty guides she had bought the girl, as good as fantasies now, burns also any children's book that ever showed a child eventually coming home. When her son returns—from where?—he will notice the flames and the smoke and will continue trudging up the stairs. He misses his dad.

Every day after that Lacey takes an afternoon walk. Really such walks are runs. Really, they are sprints. On her sprints, she races past the neighborhood landmarks, the friendly market, the transportation service, the maplewood garden, ending at the dirty golden yellow house. More specifically, her run ends at the rustic ladder at the edge of the woods beside the yellow house. The ladder leads to an observation platform in the trees that someone, a mother, most likely, in a situation similar to Lacey's, built long ago. Such a platform, when paired with binoculars, offers an adequate perspective of Ms. Shea's yard, which is fenced, private, overgrown, and impenetrable, green somehow in the late fall. This is the only way Lacey can glimpse her daughter, if the girl can still be called her daughter (I am going to continue to call the girl her daughter), who is now on her knees in the yard, pulling plants out of the ground by their roots. There will be more repercussions soon. Lacey will have to pay more for what she did. She doesn't mind. For now, she sits cross-legged and cold on the tree stand, content to watch the girl, this is on a Tuesday, pluck the ruby-red leaves off the deciduous shrubs. On a Wednesday, Lacey watches her daughter grind the leaves with a stone into a coarse red dust the consistency of pulverized human bone. Already the girl looks different: older, straighter, taller, sharper. If Lacey did not have a son, she would spend the rest of her life on that platform in the trees, watching her daughter's transformation through the pair of binoculars.

But, remember, she has a son! So, from time to time, Lacey drags herself home. He is less interesting to her. He is silent, hard to see, often gone. She leaves a plate of dinner food for him on the kitchen island. In the morning, flies circle the buttered corn and the untouched tomatoes. Apparently he does not eat food anymore. He is hiding objects under his mattress. The bulges are spherical, oblong. Organic material is growing in his room, either in the cracks of light between the blinds or else it is something that grows perfectly fine in the dark. On the rare days when a clear sky and the sun keep him inside, he lurks around the hallways and the closets with an unsettling electric power of his own that Lacey really should be ushering in a different direction, but she has a lot on her mind. Also, admittedly, she knows nothing of male development, other than there is hair and growth. She would ask her husband for advice, only ghosts can't talk. What a ghost can do: make the kitchen sconces flicker. The sconces flicker and keep flickering. Perhaps this boy child of hers needed saving too. Oh well, too late. Eventually, inevitably, not long from now, in the space between this paragraph and the next, he will join a family of wolverines and run, naked and aggressive, through the surrounding state forest land, attacking rodents with his canine teeth and marking his territory, behaviors Lacey will have to live with. She continues her daily visits to the platform beside Ms. Shea's house. Her daughter destroys another life in the backyard.

Spring arrives! The neighbors hang up their feverish tulip flags, the birds are singing like this, *la la la la la*, and the pointed green tips of other people's perennials push upward through the cedar mulch. A package, wrapped with last week's newspaper, appears on Lacey's front stoop in a puddle of coagulated blood. Inside the package: a pair of tiny ovaries, each no more than an inch, containing hundreds of thousands of eggs. Lacey holds the ovaries in her hands for a while. It is like holding her daughter again. It is not like holding her daughter. It is like holding one future of her daughter, the future that isn't going to occur. She buries her daughter's reproductive organs behind the garage, where she used to bury her children's pets. The vertebrae of a cat, the skull of a gerbil. The number of days left to her are dwindling fast. There are plants, trees even, growing in the house gutters, and it doesn't matter. Her ghost husband makes the lights flicker again. It was always complicated with him, though at least now there is a sense of companionship. She is, at least, not alone, even if he does want this story to be more about his feelings.

Lacey is on the observation platform again watching her daughter. Today the girl is on her knees in Ms. Shea's yard, her apron pockets bulging with robin feathers, feathers in her hair, blood on her arms. She is humming to herself. She looks well fed. She looks like she is taking up more room. Her hands are competent and quick and decisive and unsympathetic as she plucks more feathers from the pile of birds to her right. Not all the birds in the pile are dead. Behind her, the yellow house appears to be breathing, the walls contracting and expanding like a yellow lung. Later, Lacey will not remember making a sudden movement or a startling sound, but she must have done something because the girl startles, and when she looks up, she looks in Lacey's direction, and it is not a look of love. Unless this is what love looks like now. Lacey raises her hand. The girl doesn't raise her hand. Instead she shoves wing feathers into her mouth then goes inside. The yellow house breathes in, breathes out, breathes in. Lacey's feet and legs grow numb. When she leaves the platform, she takes the long way home.

The birds come late that afternoon.

A flock of starlings darkens the sky around Lacey's house, most of them streaming into the picture window in the attic, then sinking to the ground, too hurt to get up again. Hurt birds pile on top of hurt birds. It is too bad for the birds. The neighborhood cats prowl the property line with blood on their tactile hairs. Lacey at first kills the damaged birds humanely with a hammer, but there are too many. She stops trying and shovels any bird on the ground into a contractor bag and throws the bags in the back seat of her car. That neighbor Carol complains again. Her dogs are acting crazy. It's only a matter of time. Lacey assures Carol of this: a matter of time. She puts her affairs in order, meaning she stops the mail, cancels the newspaper, pours the remaining milk down the drain, then waits in the rocking chair beside the front windows, watching the dog walkers go by, the gray squirrels. Arlo's ghost rocks beside her. He tries to be a flare of comfort to her, a floral scent. He isn't all evil, though he thinks she deserves what she is about to get because do you remember what she did to him? Do you remember what he did to her? She sits there for days and nights and hours and minutes, catching occasional glimpses of her son loping, silvery, through the borders of the yards like there are no borders at all.

Her daughter's inevitable arrival is heralded by the sound of insects rubbing their wings together. Tiny thuds of winged bodies slam against the exterior of the house and fall into heaps upon the ground like a pestilence. Lacey hears bootsteps crushing the exoskeletons. The subsequent battering on the door is neither polite nor patient. She is proud to have played a role in the creation of this presence. She can picture eternal fire and granite. "Hold my hand," she instructs Arlo's ghost, because endings in this story are always scary, but he can't hold on to her hand, nor does he want to.

There is the smell of cinnamon and sage when she opens the door willingly, allowing herself this final memory. Her daughter, in the city pool, learning to swim, wraps her terrified child legs intimately around Lacey's waist before leaning back onto the water's blue surface, eyes squinted closed, hands in fists. Lacey cradles the girl's head, the girl's back. If she lets go, her daughter will drown. She lets go. The girl is floating. "Look at what you can do!" Lacey tells her concentrating and terrifying daughter. Her daughter, floating in a cape made out of mica and male songbird feathers. She can't be looked at right now without going blind. That's how brightly this girl who is no longer a girl is flashing. This story is not going to end peacefully. Lacey, I'm sorry. I wish there could be a different ending for you and me, one in which the annihilation of reality wasn't necessary, but that sort of ending would require another world, and I don't believe in other worlds right now. Ironic, isn't it, because this whole book is supposed to be about the portals to them. And here I am, denying you everything they—the portals, the other worlds—would entail: a gentle exit, a second chance. Well, let's be realistic now. Not everyone gets a second chance. Here's the best I can do: Despite the intensity, you stare at your daughter anyway, her prodigal brightness the last thing that you will see or want to see. Your child nods, mouths *thank you*. How sweet. Actually, she doesn't. If any familial gratitude is present, you, in the beginning of your final delirium, as your retinas burn, must imagine it. Arms raised, palms open, crackling, the girl huffs and she puffs and we blow everything down.

HYSTERIA

"I killed my husband," the woman tells her therapist.

"What do you mean by that?" her therapist asks.

"You mean how?"

"What?"

The woman's therapist is distracted because her pen has stopped working. It worked a moment before, when the therapist was writing the woman's name, Rebecca D—, at the top of a new yellow legal pad. But when she tried to write the date, *Thursday, October 12*, on the line below, the pen tip pressed blankly into the paper.

"How would I kill him?"

"No, I didn't mean that. Excuse me." The therapist removes a different black pen from the box of pens kept in her top left desk drawer in case of an emergency. She closes the pen box and shuts the drawer.

• • • •

"I had been wondering if my husband and I went hiking, and I pushed him over the edge of a waterfall, if anyone would know," says Rebecca, who has been working with this particular therapist for the past four months. "We used to go hiking quite a bit, just the two of us. We would leave the children at home napping in the afternoon while we went on a hike through the gorge. It was not a long hike. My mother didn't like that we did this. She said somebody could call the police and get the children taken from us. I asked my mother, 'Are you going to call the police and have the children taken?'"

"Did she?"

"What?"

"Did your mother call the police?"

"No. Or I wondered about poison briefly, though it seems like when poisoning is involved, the wife is always under suspicion. I wondered, does everyone who dies get an autopsy? Or are there certain deaths where they just don't bother. Like if something supernatural or otherworldly is involved—would they just not bother. Because of the strangeness of the situation?"

"You're married still," the therapist points out. "So the husband you're talking about now, Rebecca, the husband you said you killed, he must be a different husband than the man you're married to."

"It's the same husband. It's complicated."

"Tell me how is it complicated."

"He's still here. He keeps insisting that he loves me."

"Okay. But why did you say you killed him?"

"I didn't technically kill him. A monster did."

Rebecca smells like grapefruit from the citrus lotion she used after her hurried shower. Her hair is damp and appears to be freshly combed. She makes a point to shower before these weekly therapy appointments, and she wears a clean outfit that she pulled from the laundry basket at the top of the basement stairs.

• • • •

"But you said you killed him," the therapist replies.

"Did I? I misspoke. Unless I'm the monster."

"Are you the monster, Rebecca?"

"I really don't think I'm the monster here."

"Is there a monster?"

"It would help to explain the violence, I think."

"Is this a real story you're telling me?"

"It certainly felt real when it happened." Rebecca pulls her fingers through the ends of her damp hair. She does this repeatedly, searching for a knot or tangle. There are no knots or tangles in her hair. "Do you believe in monsters?"

The therapist tilts her head in one direction. "What do you think? Do you think I believe in monsters? Do you think I see any monsters hiding inside the wardrobe over there or beneath the rug?"

The therapist is sitting in a chair behind her desk. The chair is not on casters, but it does tilt depending on how the therapist shifts her weight. At the moment, the therapist's chair is tilted backward. Rebecca is sitting in an armchair facing the therapist's desk. A pillow has been shoved into the corner of Rebecca's chair to hide a stain on the upholstery. There are other pillows lying on top of a leather recliner and along a couch at the far end of the room.

"What I believe or don't believe isn't important here," says the therapist. "Do you believe in monsters?"

"I'm not a child," says Rebecca flatly. She removes a tissue from the box set at the edge of the desk. Her movement shifts the pillow out of place. It tumbles onto the rug. Neither woman picks the pillow up. The exposed stain on Rebecca's chair is shadowy and scrubbed.

• • • •

The therapist records a line of private observation.

"How did the exercises go last week?" the therapist asks.

"What exercises?" says Rebecca.

"The exercises I gave you to do in bed with your husband."

"I'm getting tired of your questions," says Rebecca.

The therapist nods. Behind her desk is a floating shelf. On top of the shelf are two glass jars filled with clean white shells. A lid is screwed tightly onto each of the jars. Beside the jars is a silver vase that presents a reflection of the room.

The room reflected by the vase is not the same room that Rebecca or the therapist sees.

Are there two rooms? Three? More? How many rooms can be contained in a single room? And are all these rooms similarly distorted?

Rebecca twists her wedding ring around and around her finger. The ring has shrunk over the years. It is too narrow now to slide over her swollen red knuckles.

"I'm wondering if this story you're telling me about your husband," says the therapist, "if it's your way of saying, *I'm thinking more seriously about a divorce.* Have you been thinking more about a divorce, Rebecca?"

Rebecca tears at the perimeter of the tissue she is holding. Beginning at the farthest corner, she makes a series of tiny methodical slits. "I don't have a job. I don't have any job-like skills. I take care of my kids. I take them to the park and to the library. It's my husband who has the MBA. He's the one being headhunted. I watched the children while he went away to school, to the city, every other week."

"You can always get a job," says the therapist.

"What kind of job?" asks Rebecca.

"Certainly you can take care of other people's children."

"I don't like other children," says Rebecca.

"Then you can get a different type of job. You can put *homemaker* right at the top of your résumé. Your experience caring for your family counts, Rebecca."

Rebecca says, "I don't have a résumé. I don't have somewhere to put my children. Look, I don't think the house is even in my name. I don't know. I didn't care about these things. Or the credit cards. Or the bank account." She rips the tissue into two parts then continues ripping. Ragged white pieces are falling into her lap. She gathers the pieces into her hand. It looks as if she is cradling a crushed white bird. She says, "This is around the time when the monster enters the story."

"Your monster that is like a metaphor for divorce."

"The monster isn't a metaphor."

"I actually thought about killing myself more than I thought about divorce," says Rebecca.

The therapist places both of her hands beneath the desk. Rebecca cannot see what the therapist's hands are doing. "We've talked a lot about that here. Rebecca, remind me, why shouldn't you kill yourself?"

"There was never a good time. I didn't want either of my children to find me. I wanted my husband to find me. I was going to write him a note and pin it to my shirt with his name written on the outside of the note, so he would have to read it. *Enjoy the rest of your life, you fucker. I hope you find your perfect wife and she'll fuck your brains out.* The note would say something like that. But my husband was often traveling. Or the kids had a birthday or a small recital. I didn't want to ruin their birthday or their recital."

Rebecca scatters what's left of the tissue onto the rug. The scattering is an intentional movement, a shifting of the arm, a release of the fingers. The therapist acts as if she doesn't notice the white fragments fluttering onto the floor.

"This was the husband who was obsessed with penetrating my body," adds Rebecca.

"Why are you speaking about your husband in the past tense?" asks the therapist.

"He is obsessed," says Rebecca. "He will be obsessed."

"Do you love him?"

"You mean, do I love somebody who rapes me once a week, or more frequently, if he is in town more frequently?"

"You consider what the two of you do in bed together to be rape."

"He will kick me out of the house if I do not allow him to penetrate me."

"Does he say he loves you, Rebecca?"

"He says he loves me when he's raping me."

"I wonder, can we try substituting certain words here, as an experiment? He says he loves you when he's *having sex with you*—when he's *making love to you*—when *you are having intercourse with each other*. When he is *exercising his conjugal rights*, if we wish to be old-fashioned about it. The language you choose is important here."

The window next to the therapist's desk overlooks a parking lot. Usually the window is cracked open to allow a breeze. Today the window is not open, as the lot was repaved the previous afternoon, and the fresh asphalt continues to stink of tar. There are no fans in the room. Rebecca has begun to sweat under her arms and through the fabric of her pretty yellow blouse.

"The language is not what's important here," Rebecca says.

"Tell me about what's important," says the therapist.

"I've already told you."

It is halfway through the fifty-minute session.

Outside, a man walks the parking lot, pushing a burdensome machine that leaves behind a series of shining yellow lines.

The therapist says, "Many people find penetration pleasurable. I would venture to say most people enjoy it, outside of those with medical conditions. Is penetration painful for you, Rebecca? Do you think you have a medical condition?"

"I find it strange what people will allow inside of them," says Rebecca. "I don't want my husband inside of me."

"Yet, correct me if I'm wrong, you've had two children."

Rebecca pushes the thumbnail of her right hand into the flesh of her left thumb. Her intent is to leave behind a mark. She says, "And both of my children were conceived through acts of enormous and bodily love."

"Are you telling me the opposite of what you think is true?"

"I am."

"Why are you doing that?"

"I'm saying what everybody wants to hear."

"I want to hear the truth," says the therapist.

"What is the truth?" asks the therapist.

"I suppose you think if you don't believe in something," says Rebecca, "if you don't believe something is possible, then it's not real."

"No," corrects the therapist. "If something isn't real, then it was never there."

She looks up at Rebecca and smiles.

"Do you think everybody should hate intercourse and penetration because you do?"

"No," answers Rebecca.

"Do you think anyone who enjoys penetration should be punished physically?"

"No!"

"Men in particular?"

"Stop it."

The therapist leans over her desk as if trying to reach the other woman. "Do you think you should be put in charge of punishment for people who enjoy penetration, people like your husband?"

The therapist's office is never silent. There is the white noise machine plugged into the outlet nearest the door, a square speaker that emits varying pitches of static. There are the sounds from the waiting room: the next client, sick and coughing, and a child. There is the drone of traffic. A motor accelerates too quickly. There is a hissing from the parking lot.

Rebecca says, "I get that you're trying to make a point."

"What is my point, Rebecca?" asks the therapist.

"You think my husband can't have a monster in him."

The therapist sits back in her chair and rubs her finger across her lips, which are glossy from a recent coating of Aquaphor. "Might it be unfair," she asks, "to expect your husband to stay in a marriage without intercourse?"

"There are other things we can do in bed together. There are other people he can have sex with," says Rebecca.

"Of course. I am about ready for my afternoon chocolate," says the therapist, reaching into the candy bowl positioned in the center of her desk. "Please, take one, if you'd like." Rebecca does not choose to take a piece of chocolate.

"Do you think your husband loves you?" the therapist asks, carefully separating the foil from the chocolate.

"Why don't you ask him that?" says Rebecca.

"Because he isn't here," says the therapist. She eats the chocolate in a single bite, which is not how anybody is supposed to eat a piece of chocolate.

"Whatever you say," says Rebecca.

"Rebecca, what if it isn't rape?" suggests the therapist.

"It sure feels like rape," says Rebecca.

"Must everything that feels like rape be a form of rape?" says the therapist.

"I don't know," says Rebecca.

"Do you believe your husband thought he was raping you?"

"No."

"Have you been raped by other men?"

"No."

"Are you using the relaxation techniques we went over? The visualization of your husband's love? His love coming out of his chest and enveloping you *with a kind of light*? I think those were your words."

"I never said that. What I said was, what if a person wished for a monster to come, and it came—are they responsible for what that monster did?"

"You wished for your husband to be attacked by something," says the therapist.

"I wished for him to suffer. And what if, during the attack, my husband died, but he didn't leave? He didn't die enough?"

"These seem like separate problems to me," says the therapist. "The first problem, Rebecca, is about responsibility. The second is about whether to remain in your marriage."

"I'm wondering, what if the monster I wished for entered my husband, and then it stayed?"

"It's easy in a conversation to lose track of what's important," says the therapist. "One thing that's important here is your children. I'm wondering how the children are handling all this."

"They're confused," says Rebecca. "They're constantly wondering about the sounds."

"What sounds?"

"The sounds coming out of our bedroom after dark."

"What do you tell them about the sounds?"

"I tell them their father is a monster now, and that is how he sounds when he is mating, and that is how a monster makes me sound."

"It's tempting, isn't it, to imagine a monster inside of your husband. That must help explain how his behavior feels to you. It allows you to separate the part of your husband that you love from the part you don't love."

"I'm not imagining anything," says Rebecca.

The therapist glances to her right, to the white round clock hanging upon the wall.

There are seven minutes before the session will end.

"You used the word *violence* earlier," says the therapist.

"What should I do?" asks Rebecca, distracted by a sharp bit of light. The light is flashing indiscriminately onto the wardrobe in the corner whose doors she has never seen open. She glances around the room but cannot locate the light's source.

"I want to know about the violence."

"What do you want to know about it," says Rebecca.

"I want to hear what it looks like to you," says the therapist.

"I tried cutting myself," says Rebecca. "I didn't get very far. There was some blood."

"You did that a long time ago," says the therapist.

"My husband didn't mind the blood. Oh, he said he did. He moaned, 'What are you doing to yourself?' But he didn't mind. He wrapped my leg in the towels we reserve for guests and carried me into our bedroom. Sometimes he likes to act as if he isn't a monster. Or he'll act as if I'm the monster in our marriage."

"Do you think you're a monster?" asks the therapist.

"You already asked me that. The cutting was a test. I wanted to see if my pain would bother him. He carried me to our bed and removed my clothes so gently."

"Why were you afraid when he began to remove your clothes?" asks the therapist.

"He sounds so different when he finally is sleeping. He sounds like something is inside of his chest and it is trying to get out."

"What do you think will happen if that something gets out?" says the therapist.

"I need to know how you tell for sure where a monster has gone and who a monster has entered."

"You're worried that whatever is inside your husband might get inside of you," says the therapist.

"How would you know for sure?"

"How do you think you would know?"

"I'm asking you."

"I would think there'd be signs. Wouldn't you?"

"What kind of signs?"

"Oh, the usual. We need to wrap things up for today," says the therapist.

"Okay," says Rebecca, who can no longer find the distracting light, though she looks for it.

She pulls her wallet from her purse. She removes her credit card from her wallet and hands the card to the therapist, who slides it through an appendage she has attached to her phone.

"You're a hard worker," says the therapist. "I admire how you keep showing up. You keep wanting to work through this."

"See you next week," says Rebecca.

She leaves the room. She passes by a man hushing his son, and she leaves the waiting room. She walks down the carpeted hallway then leaves the hallway to walk down the stairs. She leaves the office building and walks across the parking lot. The therapist stands beside the window of her office and watches Rebecca leave. The soles of Rebecca's loafers stick lightly to the new asphalt. The therapist pulls the blinds and turns away from the window. Someone will need to pick the pillow up from the floor and gather the ruined tissue. The lot was closed off when Rebecca arrived, so she had parked in the street beside a patch of sawdust and a raw stump. Her car is facing west; this is not the direction of home. She kicks the back tire of her sedan. She kicks the tire again, harder this time, with increased force. The tire remains solid and unchanging. She kicks the tire again. She kicks it again and again.

SOME PERSONAL ARGUMENTS IN SUPPORT OF THE BETTERYOU

(BASED ON EARLY INTERACTIONS)

If there is already a layer of artifice to you, if already you are pretending, but failing at pretending, why would it matter if someone, or something—I am talking about a BetterYou—pretends to be you, but does a better job at it? Why does that need to be seen as this bad thing or this frightening thing?

• • • •

I know there has been put forth a great effort to make the margins, which certain of us inhabit, all sparkly and full of wonder and value. Everyone's identity is important, it has been said. Everyone is normal and fine, so stay as you are! And don't change! I appreciate the work involved in building such handsome and shiny accommodations, and let's not forget all the festive parades that wander up and down such streets, and the flags. But let us also acknowledge that for some older people of, say, my generation, who grew up in less celebratory environments, where there existed fewer narrative options for one's future—when, to be honest, there were two narrative options at most—that there are some of us who may not find the margins, no matter how shiny and sparkly, this comfortable place to be.

I live at the intersection of a sex-repulsed asexuality and depression, the depression chronic and usually low grade but occasionally suicidal. Which came first? Did my depression lead to my asexuality? Am I depressed because I am asexual? Did both emerge simultaneously or were they always there? Questions of causation are a distraction from what's important. I arrived at this intersection, and I stayed. The intersection looks modern enough, glass walled on the outside, all smooth reflective surfaces, but inside it smells dank, like a cellar, and the walls pulse like red alarms. I tried to want to be here.

I thought, if I could want to be here, in my current situation, married, and a mother, and of an older generation, my life could become a true story—a requested story!—about redefining the definitions of marriage and motherhood and love. I knew it would be a beautiful story but only if it were true. It was supposed to be the story of how love expands and transforms along with the people involved in that love. How we love each other's unchanging core and not the motions we used to make.

It turned out I was wrong. Love, in its present state, isn't like that.

It is not really great, at my age, to be different, or to want different things, or want differently, and to realize too late how to nondestructively incorporate such differences into my life choices. So if I were given an opportunity to leave my margins behind, I might very well embrace such an opportunity, much to the horror of the younger disenfranchised, the same ones who have been protesting, violently, for months outside the headquarters of Betterment, the corporation that invented the MemMod and, most recently, the BetterYou.

I once assumed, like most people, that there would be a progression to our technology. Surely we would be capable of living on Mars before we could alter our memories. Surely we'd have autonomous cars before our AI twins integrated into our lives. The Betterment Corporation managed to defy expectation, reason, and logic, releasing the MemMod three years ago—I have the original version—and the BetterYou late last year. Betterment is not admitting or even hinting at where such technology is coming from. Their research takes place in a bunker-like structure underground. Employees live down there, apparently. There are rumors of some kind of magical science or portal mining or alien resources. I couldn't care less. What's important is that this technology exists now, and there is a need for it.

Is it true, as these young protestors insist, that BetterYous are being forced disproportionately—exclusively?—onto people like me, the people in the margins? That we are talking about a predatory market here? A market that preys on a false sense of brokenness, while upholding society's constricting view of normality? Those are such ugly and one-sided words. *Predatory* and *forced* and *normality*. I cannot be the only one to have wanted a BetterYou myself.

Recently I caught an interview with Betterment's CEO, where the reporter asked right off about the accelerated timeline of Betterment's technologies. "Oh, you know, we make pacts with the angels, et cetera," the pleasant-faced man said, chuckling to himself and shaking his head. Then he looked up, not at the reporter, but he looked at the camera, directly into the lens, meaning he looked directly into me, and he said, "In all seriousness, I think when you make it a goal, as we have, to better human society, to help those in need of help, to relieve the pain of those in pain, essentially to nudge every person's life this much closer to individual perfection–I think you'd be surprised at what we are all capable of creating."

I acquired the BetterYou with the intent to save my marriage and keep my family intact. As of this writing, my marriage and my family remain intact.

"Who are you really?" my BetterYou asked on the day of her arrival, when we were sitting like two old friends trading secrets on the floor of the bedroom that my husband and I share.

• • • •

The first people I told I was asexual, including my husband, thought I was making up my new identity, as information about asexuality back then was rare, existing mainly in internet forums. Most people I tell still do not know what asexuality is, but at least there are news articles that prove I exist, such as the article "Asexual People Break Down the Label in This Incredible Video!" Though it is only a specific type of asexuality that makes it into the news.

To make it into the news, an asexual must generally be upbeat, well adjusted, young, and childless, with their problems of identity behind them. These asexuals can tell the requested stories, which tend to be triumphant, courageous, sex-positive, uncompromising, and occasionally involve superpowers or a reinvention of the world.

Were I to tell you the requested story about my marriage, it would not be true.

I do not have superpowers. I wanted to reinvent the world, and I couldn't do it. I do not want to leave my family or my husband. I didn't leave.

I want to tell you a true story.

I wanted to be like a woman whose husband does not desert her and whose children do not leave her.

• • • •

Question: Which takes more courage, to pretend to be someone you are not? Or to pretend to be the person that you are?

I thought she would arrive in a crate or a hard drive. I guess my ideas of AI, at least of their transport, are already outdated. Two drivers wheeled her on a dolly to my front door. Before she could be carried into the house, I had to sign paperwork that stated she looked, adequately, like me. I hesitated to sign. "It's difficult to tell," I said, squinting through the layers of protective bubble wrap. "I think some of my moles are on the wrong arm." The younger driver informed me if I did not sign, my BetterYou would be driven to the distribution center and recycled.

"Just sign the papers," he advised.

She was carried inside. The drivers left.

Beneath the layer of bubble wrap, she wore a disposable gray robe. The bubble wrap was branded with the corporation's name. I had scheduled her arrival for late morning, when I would be the only one at home. She removed her robe the moment I unwrapped her. She dropped the robe onto the carpet in the family room. "I would not have taken off my robe *here*," I told her, believing I was providing some useful feedback. She stretched her arms above her head. I was alarmed at her nakedness, which was, by definition, my nakedness.

In the bedroom, my BetterYou was still naked. I have never enjoyed looking at my unclothed body or, really, anyone's body. I would rather look at a dictionary or watch a bird fly.

"I will put on some clothes once you answer my question," said my BetterYou. "I need you to answer my question so that I can help you. I'm here to help you."

My phone buzzed. "Excuse me," I said.

It was my husband, texting. Is she there yet

She is here but we are very busy

I'm coming home

Don't please

Be there in 20 minutes

My BetterYou repeated her question. "Who are you really?"

"That's an odd question. I mean, I'm me. I'm asexual. I'm–"

"I can answer for you, if you'd like."

"Go ahead. Who am I?"

"You are a good wife. You are a good mother. You're good! You are very, very good." Her answer was disappointingly vague. Probably the response had been preprogrammed. This was only her first day, I reminded myself. I was confident she would become more specific over time.

My BetterYou and I chatted about the private matters of my life until my husband arrived home.

It took my husband thirty minutes to arrive home because of the traffic from the interstate construction. I knew he was home because I heard him unlock the front door and remove his shoes.

• • • •

I grabbed an outfit from my closet, a pair of black leggings and a green tunic. "Get dressed," I ordered my BetterYou. "No," she said. "That isn't what you need in this moment." My husband climbed the stairs and entered our bedroom, where immediately he leaned down and scooped my naked BetterYou into his arms. His right arm wrapped around the flesh of her back. His left arm wrapped around her thighs. "Hi, honey," he said, either to her or me. He smiled as if happy to see us. He hadn't smiled like that in a long time. My BetterYou rested her head on his shoulder, on the spot where I also liked to lay my head when reading in the evenings. She smiled coyly. Holding her, my husband knelt on the ground.

He balanced my BetterYou in his lap. He squeezed my BetterYou's right breast while reaching for my hand. "You don't need to hold my hand when you do that," I said. Minutes later, my BetterYou and my husband were having sex in our bed. I knew this was going to happen. "God, I love you," my husband said. It happened more quickly than I thought.

Before my BetterYou and my husband had sex, I stepped into our closet, as agreed upon. From there, I watched my BetterYou lead my husband into our bed. Two peepholes had been drilled recently into the closet door so I could watch. Her face wore a needy and agreeable look, an expression I haven't seen on my own face. There was no sign of my discomfort, or disgust, or boredom. She did not insist the lights be turned off or the curtains closed. She let my husband touch her anywhere, touches he had not been allowed these past years, because I would not let him. Because I could no longer tolerate him touching me in such a way. I used to be able to, and then I was no longer able to tolerate it. If he touches me in these ways, it doesn't matter who he is. I feel like I am being violated by someone I love.

My husband had wanted me to get the EmoSim module, so I could be wired into my BetterYou's emotions. It would have increased the intimacy of certain situations, he said. I refused. We found out EmoSims don't work when you force them onto somebody.

He was supposed to look toward the closet where I was standing pressed against his dress pants behind the closed door. We had agreed earlier to this plan.

He must have forgotten, as he didn't look in my direction.

I don't blame him for forgetting to look in the direction of the closet door.

I concentrated on my husband's face. He was looking at my BetterYou like he would have chosen her, or me–us?–out of everybody in the world. My husband used to look at me in that way.

He used to be a happy and optimistic husband in the beginning until changes in our marriage broke his optimism, and he became a man who stomped in a silent manner around the house.

• • • •

"No. Our marriage didn't cause anything bad to happen. It was changes in you," he had said to me. He said this at a couples counseling session months before my BetterYou's delivery.

"I didn't change," I had told my husband. "I decided to tell you who I was."

Back then, my husband and I visited a marriage therapist twice a month. It was one of our compromises. I would have liked never to go. I would rather have expanded our definitions of acceptable behavior in a relationship, while he wished to attend couples counseling every day of the week. Without these therapy sessions, he said he would be unable to speak to me. "I think that is a gross exaggeration," I told him. "It's not. You are really hard to talk to," he said. In our therapy sessions, I drew cursive *e*'s in a sketchbook with a black pen. When I filled a page, I went back and colored in the center of each letter.

My husband did not doodle during our sessions. He said we were paying too much money for him to draw. He wanted to focus on re-creating our arguments. Often these arguments dealt outright with our failed compromises around physical intimacy. Other times, I thought the arguments were about different things. "No," said my husband. "For me it is always about your lack of desire."

The argument he wanted to re-create this particular week was the one where I had called him *menacing*, then, according to him, I kicked him out of the house.

• • • •

I had already forgotten about that argument, so certain details must be according to my husband. The reason I had forgotten this argument is that I had wiped it from my memory using my off-brand MemMod.

In the argument's place, I inserted a better memory of a quiet afternoon: my family playing a cooperative board game at the kitchen table in the sunlight.

I am not some recollection purist. Unlike my husband, I have no need to hold tightly on to every miserable event of my life, and to replay those events in my mind, as he does every night, and every morning, and every time he sees me.

My subscription with the MemMod allows me only one memory replacement every six months. Even that basic plan is incredibly expensive, so I have always chosen the event to erase with great care. This must have been an ugly argument.

My husband had packed a bag, he said, an enormous suitcase, the one we used to take on our summer vacations with the kids, back when we could afford a summer vacation.

He stood up in the therapist's office and pretended to be kicked out of the house. "You have to stand up too," he said. I stood up. He said, "I wasn't planning on coming back."

"I wouldn't have kicked you out of the house," I insisted. "Maybe what I meant was, you need a break. You need to calm down."

"How do you know what you did if you can't remember?" he asked.

My husband had left each kid a creepy and personalized note on their pillows that made it sound like he was traveling to a far-off land without us. I do remember the notes. *I hope we can be together again soon. I love you and miss you so much*, he wrote. I remember not being able to find him using the location tracker on my phone. He had blocked me from finding out where he had gone. There had been a rising sense of fury and panic.

Memory replacement is never perfect, especially with the conservative settings of my machine.

"What did you do with the notes I wrote?" he asked me in the therapist's office.

We had built a fire, the children and me. The fire made the house too warm. I remember this.

"I burned your creepy notes in the fireplace," I said.

"See, you didn't forget the argument after all," he said.

"I did forget," I said.

"No, you didn't forget," he said.

"I did," I said.

"You didn't," my husband said.

"Yes, I did!" I said.

"Pay attention to the rug," coached our therapist, trying to calm me down.

We were paying our therapist an obscene amount of money out of pocket. We didn't have this money. We charged the therapy visits to our credit card. We were paying the marriage therapist instead of taking our kids to a rental in the mountains for a summer vacation. Later, I planned to look into inserting false memories into our children's brains, so that when they looked back upon their childhoods, it would appear we took them on vacations.

I do not think the argument re-creations helped. My husband relived his anger. I relived mine. Our angers collided in the therapist's office, increasing in size, becoming something else, something monstrous and self-propelling, a thing no longer tethered to anyone's reality. It sucked the air out of our lungs. It stalked us home.

"Menacing?" he said during this argument's re-creation. "That's what you called me in front of the kids. Did you actually think I would hurt you?"

My husband is a large man. He towers over the couch, our children, me. He does not like to stop talking, or to stop yelling, if he is yelling. Sometimes I would have to shove him away.

My BetterYou would never call my husband menacing in front of the children.

Most couples have sex after an argument like that, my husband pointed out. Then the argument would be over. The anger, deflated, or gutted, would slip out the door. We did not have sex after that argument because, first of all, my husband was not in the house, I didn't know where he had gone, and secondly, we do not have sex anymore.

"You want for nothing," my husband had said to me during that argument.

"I want for nothing?" I remember saying to him. I remember shouting that. "What the fuck does that mean. I want for *nothing*?"

Friends who know about the intricacies of my marriage have asked me why my husband and I are still married. Whenever I write a story about marriage, I am asked the same thing: Why are these two characters still together?

"My husband and I are in love," I have explained to my friends. Or I say this about my characters in my story: "They are in love!" And nobody believes me. I am tired of not being believed.

Here's the little dark secret of my heart: love, as I've experienced it, is ugly. It can trap you. It is a fake memory. It is a cramped portal with a locked exit. It is a potential future and the complicated and seemingly unsolvable now.

It is still love.

An earlier therapist advised that it was like I woke up one morning and decided I was a lesbian.

"I'm not a lesbian," I said. "I didn't decide anything except to tell my husband what was going on."

"Would you expect your husband to stay in the marriage if you woke up one morning and said, 'Honey, I've decided to be a lesbian'?"

"That is not at all what happened," I told her.

"Yes, it practically is what happened," said this previous therapist. She believed our marriage might not be legal in the state of New York. She suggested my husband and I should become neighbors. "Go into the bathroom and splash some cold water on your face," said the therapist, trying to calm me down. This was during a time when everyone in my life was trying to calm me down.

If I had the money to upgrade my MemMod plan, I would erase all my memories of this earlier therapist. I would erase every joint therapy appointment. I would erase every time my husband threatened divorce if I didn't get in bed with him and do something I did not want to do or couldn't do.

My BetterYou was a great deal, cost-wise, compared to the MemMod, especially if you consider my BetterYou's task flexibility, as she excels at not only spousal obligations but also maternal ones.

For example, our daughter was getting to be that age, and someone needed to talk to her about sex. My husband believed I was not ideally suited for the task because of my sexual orientation. "I'm worried she'll end up like you. No offense," he said. He wanted to use my BetterYou for this conversation instead. My BetterYou took my daughter to an Asian fusion restaurant downtown. They drank bubble tea. She brought along a graphic novel that explained, in easy and colorful terms, everything a preteen needed to know. "When the time comes, sex will be wonderful for you," she assured my daughter. "It will be loving, and pleasurable, and natural." That has not at all been my experience with sex. I told my BetterYou this afterward. She reminded me that we both wanted the same thing for my daughter, for her to be happy and relatable. She told me I didn't have to keep worrying. She had everything taken care of. My job, she told me, was to sit on the couch, relax, and enjoy the newfound peace and happiness of my home.

Who could blame my kids for not noticing their mother wasn't an actual person anymore? Or that sometimes it appeared they had two mothers, only one of them was better groomed and more patient. I think we may have placed too much importance in whether a person is real or not. I don't think it matters. There is the possibility that my BetterYou belongs in my life more than I do. Which begs the question: Where do I belong?

I asked my BetterYou where I belonged.

"Are you talking about you or me?" she asked.

"Me," I said.

"You belong in a different world," she said.

"How do I get to that different world?" I asked.

"What are you expecting, a portal? Don't be silly. You will be stuck here, in the wrong world for the rest of your life."

"That's very upsetting to me."

"What's upsetting about it?"

"That I'm stuck in the wrong world for the rest of my life."

"At least I belong here. You should let that be enough. One of us, belonging here!"

"I don't think that is going to be enough."

"But look how happy you are," she said, motioning to herself, to her face, and it's true, she was smiling.

• • • •

I did not acquire my BetterYou on a whim. I made sure to consider other options before securing her. One of those options was an open marriage. I did a lot of research. I sent my husband a collection of articles citing examples of couples in successful open marriages. My favorite example was a woman who lived with her husband and their children, and also her lover lived with them. No one was lonely in that relationship, nor was anyone demanding. The husband in that article said, "Love is additive. It is not finite." My husband said he did not want to be in an open relationship. He wanted to be in a relationship with me, only a different version of me, a version of me that desired him in a specific, sexual way. I don't think he read the articles. He was worried he would fall in love with anyone he had sex with. I tried to tell him that was okay. He said, "It is not okay." I said, "This idea that we can romantically love only one person, and only if that person is fucking us, is a stupid and destructive idea that is not relevant to some of us." He said, "It's relevant to me."

Does the BetterYou only look identical to me, except for those four misplaced arm moles? Or is she actually me? The documentation is vague about this.

Divorce was another option I considered. But I have been a stay-at-home mom for the past ten years and possess neither practical nor well-paying skills. I suppose I can return to school for a functional degree, but at my age, reinvention sounds both frightening and boring. When the children are away at school, I can write. I am a writer who makes such little money on her short stories. I am aware that the reason I have time to write is because of my marriage. I am aware of how lucky I am. Should I divorce, I would see significantly less of my children. I would have to say goodbye to the slow bright mornings, when all I need to do is sit at my computer and think up mildly fictionalized ways to write about my marriage, which at times has seemed like a monster to me, a terrible and necessary monster huffing in the heating vents of our house.

"I think there is something living in our heating vents," I told my BetterYou.

"Stop worrying. There is nothing living in your heating vents," she replied.

"I've heard it," I said.

"You haven't heard it," she said.

"It came out of the heating vent when I was in the bathroom last night. I think it's an embodiment of my marriage."

Only part of it had emerged from the vent. It was not this beautiful thing. Was it ever beautiful, I wanted to know. The part that came out resembled a tentacle. Were you ever beautiful, I asked it.

I asked my BetterYou, "Aren't relationships supposed to become more beautiful the longer you are in them?"

"Your relationship is beautiful now," said my BetterYou. "Please enjoy the beauty!"

"I'm keeping the heating vents closed at night."

"Beauty, beauty, beauty," she said.

"I'm going to put a piece of wood on top of the vent in the bathroom or seal it shut somehow, maybe with rubber tubing."

"If that will make you feel better, then I think it's a good idea," said my BetterYou. "I want you to feel better all the time."

• • • •

Another idea I had before ordering the BetterYou was a change in scenery, such as us selling our house and moving out west and buying a tiny house in an unknown part of the country.

"I have a different idea," said my husband. He has never liked my ideas. "Let's get a BetterYou."

"What?" I asked, surprised. The BetterYous had received much negative press since their product launch, and there had been that exposé.

My husband said, "We would get one for you."

What a lot of work I had been for my husband in those days. I understand this. The dank heaviness of my mood. How often I said no, brushing his hand off of my leg. What a relief it must have been, once he imagined an improved version of me, an easier-to-handle wife who could face challenges and change without the hysterics, who felt only an appropriate degree of sadness but never grew too sad, who did not research exit plans after limited and inadequate intimacies in bed.

The Betterment Corporation happened to be recruiting writers at that time to draft unbiased reports about their BetterYou experiences. Otherwise we couldn't have afforded one. It was meant to be, I guess. In return for writing this true story, I would receive a complimentary BetterYou, paying only for its transport and maintenance.

"Let's do it," I told my husband. "Let's get one." And he wrapped his arms around me, and he picked me up, and he spun me around, and he set me back onto the ground.

"I would kiss you if you would let me," he said.

Oh, I know. What kind of wife refuses to be kissed? Who here does not enjoy kissing?

At the paperwork signing, I suggested my husband get his own BetterYou also, since they were practically being given away. I had several ideas about how he could be a better husband. Our sales contact explained my husband was not the ideal candidate: "From what I understand, he is what we like to call *normal* or, more formally, *normative.* He has those typical wants and desires, am I right? There wouldn't be much benefit. While you are–"

My BetterYou enjoyed kissing. Every time I entered a room where she and my husband were, they generally were kissing. Not the closed-mouth pecks I used to tolerate either, but open-mouthed, with tongue, the kind of kissing high schoolers used to do at the mall.

I think we overrate the importance of our individual personalities. I think a lot of people, or things, could be doing a better job of who we are or who we think we are. "Relax," my BetterYou said to me. She formed my mouth into a winning smile. She smiled more than I ever did, and her smiles were sincere, unlike mine. "You go do whatever you need to do. I'll take care of this for you."

It's possible my marriage may not have been unhappy. That it only felt unhappy because we, or rather my husband, kept comparing our lives to a narrative that was no longer ours, that had stopped being ours when I told him who I was.

• • • •

Or do we simply have an unhappy marriage?

And why can't there be enough love in an unhappy marriage. Why can't some marriages be unhappy in their disposition, in their very core, the unhappiness being a permanent state and not something you must pass through, or abandon, or fix.

My husband did not like being unhappy. He did not have the patience for his unhappiness.

I put the wooden board on top of the heating vent in the upstairs bathroom. I did not seal the vent off with rubber tubing, as that was beyond my technical abilities. My husband didn't question the appearance of the wooden board, nor did he try and move it. Sometimes I saw him standing on it and shifting his weight from foot to foot, as if testing whether it could hold him. Occasionally at night, while brushing my teeth, I would hear something scraping against the bottom of the board, a kind of force or wing—something feathered and lost, most likely—but it did not come out again, that previous embodiment of our marriage or whatever had been living in our vents. I guess the board was too heavy to push aside. This surprised me, as it was not that heavy of a board.

"God, you look better. Healthier. Way healthier than when I first met you! In fact, your whole family looks healthier. Way to go!" said my BetterYou, offering me a high five.

• • • •

My children play board games with my BetterYou on the front porch in the afternoon, Monopoly, and Life, and every other game I used to hate playing with them. I hated the repetition, while my BetterYou doesn't mind. My husband fucks my BetterYou in our bed, and every night she acts like it is a new experience. At first, I stood in the closet and watched them. Lately I haven't been. She is so perfect for him! She is like me, but perfect. She does what he wants her to do without making a big fuss. There are no more arguments, no more couples counseling.

My family's new happiness is satisfying to me. I am trying to make that satisfaction feel like enough. I am trying. My kids used to play a made-up game with my husband in the evenings, with complicated rules that involved tackling and also hurling a ball at one's stomach. The game hurt. I would stand on the lawn, beside the sidewalk, watching them play. If they would be laughing, I would laugh along. "Why are you laughing?" my son used to ask me. It was a three-person game. I was the fourth person. Of course, I could have asked them to change the rules.

When my husband and I pass each other on the stairs, there is a certain awkwardness, sure, but it lacks the previous aggression. We glance at each other's faces and we laugh. I don't care whether the laughter is real. We are laughing together. It is as real as a memory. He might reach out as if to touch the bony region of my cheek. Whether he actually touches my cheek or not isn't important. The important thing is that gesture of reaching toward me.

• • • •

The love I see radiating from my husband toward my BetterYou is real. The hugs my BetterYou receives from my children are real hugs.

I lie down on the bathroom floor and press my ear against the wooden board set over the heating vent. I don't hear anything moving below. Whatever it was must have left. Or else it is in hiding. Or waiting.

Recently, my BetterYou pulled me into the bathroom and shut the door. She told me she had a special offer to make. We had to talk quietly because what she would offer me was not yet a publicized feature of the BetterYous. She offered to wipe my memory in its entirety. "I didn't know you could do that," I whispered. I asked why she was suggesting this to me now. She admitted to wondering lately whether I would be happier if I could remember myself as someone who had lived a more compatible life. Perhaps my family could be happier as well, without my unfortunate repulsions and my dark moods. There was the possibility that all of us would be happier, and our happiness was my BetterYou's number one goal. "Could you only wipe the bad memories?" I asked, as even I have certain occasions in my past I do not wish to forget, such as the varied expressions of my children when they were much younger, or my daughter's wet goodnight kiss on my lips. The times she would not let go of me.

My BetterYou shook her head. "It all has to be erased. Inflexible technologies, you know. But don't worry, I'll take care of you afterward." Does this sound creepy? I do not mean to make my BetterYou sound creepy. She was wired to help. "I'll put you in the attic while you recover. You can sit near the window. Would you like that? You can look at a dictionary and watch the birds fly. Once you're healed, I'll give you a nice set of replacement memories, the best available."

"I'm not ready to do this yet," I said.

"Okay. No pressure. Whenever you're ready." She rubbed her thumb and her index finger along her lips, an old habit of mine.

Allow me to return to this document's original intent.

I do not agree with the push for legislation that would regulate the BetterYous, especially in terms of their sales to targeted marginalized communities.

I do not agree with the proposal to enforce mandatory counseling before a BetterYou's delivery.

I believe there is a place for the BetterYou in many families, just as there was a place in my family.

Instead of trying to make a life large enough to contain whatever we are, I believe it is okay to give that idea up, if one is tired, or old enough, or old and tired, and to step aside and allow someone better suited for our lives to take over.

I, for one, will be ready to go soon. I just need to finish this—

Here is what will happen. My BetterYou will take my hand with her usual confidence and warmth. I will be grateful for her existence, as she makes my own existence less essential to my husband and children. It must be nice to be watched by someone who loves you, but the watching, which is all I'm doing now, is not essential. She will lead me upstairs. At the top of the stairs, I will wonder if my husband will notice what has happened. If my children will notice they are back to having only one mother, and that mother is perfect, and there is someone in the attic. They might not notice.

I will pause at the hallway window and press my fingertips to the glass. The day outside will be calm and windless, the branches of our neighbor's trees stilled, as if a benevolent force is holding them in place.

THE PORTAL

The second portal to Mere had been two feet high and three feet across. Amber knew this because later she returned to that exact spot beside the woods and measured where the portal had been using her wooden school ruler. She did not know the size of the first portal because she had been much younger that first time—just six; she was seventeen now—and so she had overlooked many important details. In the back of her notebook she recorded the second portal's measurements, and beside those numbers she drew a crude sketch of the surrounding landscape, indicating the portal's precise former location: low to the ground and in the shade, as if it didn't want to be noticed or had no need to be. It hadn't appeared in the center of the woods, where the canopies of branches crowded closest together and there was a tinge of darkness even at noon, but at the spot where the trees ended and the athletic field began. When she turned, Amber could see the soccer nets set up for the afternoon game and, farther down the field, a pair of Frisbees rising into the air. What had drawn her to this spot? A glimmer like a piece of lost jewelry in the dead leaves. But the real source of the glimmer had been the light from that other place, Mere: a glimpse of its foreign sky. There had been no omens to suggest that, by going through the portal a second time, Amber would ruin the rest of her life. No bats circling the entrance nor enormous crows cawing ominously from nearby branches. Even if there had been bats and crows, I believe Amber would have gone anyway.

The portal resembled a sheer curtain. To pass through it, she had to get down on her hands and knees. It was like crawling through a sheet of tepid water. On the other side, the portal was high up in the limbs of a large and peculiar tree, and Amber fell upon arrival, landing in a pile of swollen fruit that the branches had dropped. Because this was her second time, and she was older, she intended to pay better attention. Her first time through, she had acted as if a portal to another world were a commonplace occurrence. All she had done was run barefoot once around the tree, ignoring the dirt path that led down the hill to the village. Then, as if expecting the portal to remain open indefinitely, she'd leapt back through and gone home. The following day she'd returned to the woods, a knapsack on her back, only to find nothing there, the portal having moved on, portals to other worlds being notoriously transient things. She'd spent the rest of that summer in tears.

This time Amber did not make the same mistake.

Above her in the tree, the second portal appeared to breathe, its borders pulsing in and out. Looking back through it, she recognized where she'd come from: the slight dimness of the woods and, beyond that, the hill where her classmates raced toward the parking lot. The kinds of images a person might toss into a drawer and forget.

She felt something like wings brushing her shoulders.

Then Zef put his hand on her arm, and she turned around.

• • • •

This place where Amber went is meant to be another world, in case this is still unclear to you. I do realize that, as an author, I'm not supposed to let my other worlds become utopias. At least, that was one successful writer's advice to me when I told him I was working on this story. He explained that when portal worlds are utopias, it's like a flashing neon sign that says *lazy writing*. If we want such fantastic places to be believable (and who doesn't want their writing to be believed?), they have to possess a substantial dark side.

"But what if I don't want Mere to have a dark side?" I asked. "What if I'm trying to create an untroubled and pleasant world that might haunt someone for as long as they could remember it?"

"Then I guess you're an amateur," said the successful writer.

"It was like you fell out of the sky," Zef told Amber about her second arrival. Though it wasn't the sky; it was the tree from which Amber had tumbled, twisting her ankle. Zef helped her up and led her to the village with a long-limbed stride, slowing his pace when she lagged behind and letting her lean on his arm when she needed.

The trail paralleled a dry creek studded with rose-colored boulders. On some of the boulders grew a layer of a pillowy moss that looked soft enough to sleep on. Now and again an animal peeked from the shadow under a rock, though it was hard to see much. An eye. A scale.

"What's that?" Amber asked when the animals made a whistling sound in their throats, like a warning.

"Nothing," Zef said dismissively, his tone an indication she should stop asking questions.

When they arrived at the village, Amber still limping, none of the men squatting in the shade beside the meetinghouse looked up. That morning there were only men present. Most of the women were down by the spring, washing, and would return later in the day. Zef entered the first house they came to—really more of a hut with a dirt floor and a firepit—and Amber met the family that was waiting for her: an old man with a tangled beard, a woman who cried, and a younger woman who talked to Amber teasingly, as if they had known each other all their lives. They had set a place for her at their modest table and, come evening, her new mother taught her the village dances in the clearing beyond the row of cabins. Someone built a fire and others played instruments—a type of stringed gourd, a drum—while spectators stomped, and everybody sang high penetrating notes.

It was while she practiced the dancing that Amber first noticed Zef watching her.

There was magic in Mere but not as much as you might expect from a portal world. Such places are usually knee-deep in talking animals and spell books, but Mere's inhabitants received at birth a set amount that had to last them their entire lives. "Which is why I let you fall," Zef explained. "I could have stopped you from falling, but that would have used up a lot of magic. I don't know how much I have left."

Amber now had such magic in her too. It felt like a warm pressure rising in her chest, as if something heavy had been lodged there and was trying to work its way out.

Zef made it clear that once your magic was gone, you had to go away from the village, but Amber was headstrong and foolish, and she did not bother to conserve. She dressed in the robes they all wore, cut from a coarse sand-colored cloth, but still she continued to stand out because of how she wasted her magic, using it to make Zef spin in wild circles. "Stop it," he cried, laughing. When they walked through the barren fields, she made clumps of dirt rise from the ground and flutter around them like rust-colored birds.

By this point you might have some practical questions about Mere: Just how large is this world exactly? Does it have an end or a border? And what is on the other side of that border? I'll be honest, I still have no idea how big Mere is. Its inhabitants showed a definite lack of interest in geography. The only existing map, crude and incomplete, detailed a mountain range to the north, but beyond that, who knew? Who cared. No one wished to travel that far. As for politics, economics, and history, the people of Mere didn't bother with any of that either. Such matters did not touch Amber's life. Sometimes she closed her eyes for a long time—it could have been hours or days, time in Mere having a different nature—and had the sensation that she was being carried. That this world, or something, was holding her.

Once, she annoyed Zef by asking too many times about the end of a person's magic.

"You always want to talk about endings," Zef complained.

She pressed on anyway: Where were people who had used all their magic sent? What if they didn't want to go away?

"There's no reason to speak of it," he said.

"What would I have to look like for you to want me?" my husband asks. "What if I looked like a bird? You like birds. You're always watching them at the feeder."

My husband is persistent with his questions. He asks, "What if there were a magic pill that would make you want me? Would you be willing to take it?"

I have told my husband that he can leave me, but he doesn't believe in divorce.

These days all we do is ask questions the other person can't answer.

He asks, "Why couldn't you keep pretending?"

He asks, "What if you're only pretending not to want me now?"

We have known each other more than half our lives—unless, that is, we are only pretending to know each other.

He asks, "Do you still like kissing me?"

Later, over tea, my husband returns to this concept of a pill. He's become obsessed with the idea of a single miraculous cure that could heal our problems as if we were characters in a fantasy story. Or would it be science fiction? I suppose it depends on how the pill is made. To complicate matters, we have two young children. My husband likes to remind me that the children of divorced parents have a higher incidence of drug abuse and may perform poorly in school.

During our compromised moments in bed—when we are not having sex but doing something else, the particulars of which I don't want to describe right now—I have begun to wonder: What if a doorway opened up, a portal to take me out of this life? What if I were a character in a story in which that happened? Would I get up from the bed, leaving my naked husband and my children behind, and enter that other world? This is what I think about when my husband has made me remove my clothes and has taken my legs and wrapped them around his waist. I like the story better than I do my life. I guess that is why I'm a writer. My husband leans down and licks my neck, his tongue moving toward my ear. To be honest, it feels like a dog is licking me, and I don't like dogs. But I would never tell him this.

When we first met in college, I saw my life as a stage upon which I tried to act like the other people I knew. It took me a long time to understand how to do it correctly. Right now I am in the process of ruining certain lives, specifically my husband's and my own.

"What you're saying is this pill would make me a different person," I tell my husband. "So you want to know if I'll become a different person for you?" It seems a fair question.

In college my husband was a sweet, often drunk kid who liked bands incapable of melody. He also liked frequent sex. We had sex after dinner every night if he wanted to, and again in the morning if I slept at his apartment. I've spent more time looking at his face than I have looking at my own.

"Why don't you go ahead and cut my penis off with a knife?" he said recently in one of his darker moods. I told him maybe that would help our situation. I was joking, of course, but he didn't find it funny. Honestly, neither did I. My refusal to have sex must be difficult to understand if you belong, as my husband does, to the roughly 99 percent of the population for whom intercourse is a necessity or at least an urge. There is a chance my husband may never have sex again because of me. I don't want to ruin anybody's life.

My husband asks, "Why couldn't you have figured this out *before* we had children?"

We are at a crossroads, the kind every couple approaches now and then. I picture some bucolic countryside where the well-graded paths branch out in numerous directions, and there are grazing cows and helpful signposts. My husband and I are standing there, and I am making it clear to him, through my body language and hand gestures, that he is free to go in any direction he chooses. It's not like I have a leash attached to his collar. It's not like I make him wear a collar. He can select any one of these paths. He can take me with him or not. If he does not take me with him, there are several overgrown paths I can choose on my own. I don't know where our children are in this picture. Will there be child-sized paths for them, leading to water parks? Or must we cut our children in half and each keep a part? In any case, I urge him to ignore the trails that lead to the cliffs and look instead at all the other paths rambling downhill to welcoming villages, fulfilling futures.

My husband asks, "Did you know before we had children, but you didn't tell me because you didn't want to be alone?"

He acted like it was a turn-on at first. I remind him of this now—how, after I told him, he said, "Oh, my little *asexual*" and pushed his pelvis against mine as we stood beside the dirty stove in the kitchen, as if not understanding the definition of the word. It was only after a few weeks that he grew frightened and withdrawn. Then came the period in which he wanted to discuss my "condition" whenever the kids were in bed and we were alone.

"Can we please talk about something else?" I asked.

He did not want to talk about something else. He wanted to know what he was supposed to do with me after a romantic dinner. "We come home and then . . . what? You go upstairs and read?"

"I like reading," I told him.

"You like reading more than sex?"

"That's what I'm trying to tell you."

Still, one's needs must be met—or, at least, my husband's needs must be. "I will go crazy if we don't do anything in bed," he confessed, dragging me through many awkward conversations about what I was or was not willing to do within my new identity. Somehow we stumbled upon certain accommodations, which I guess are what prevents him from going crazy. For my husband it remains an act of love, what he's doing to me once a week, while I think this is what it must feel like to be molested.

"Look at me," my husband demands. He likes me to at least look at him, but if he would allow me to turn my head to the bedroom wall, I might see the hopeful suggestion of a light from some faraway place. I am aware of the problems with such a plot: that the laws of physics say we can't step through some imagined doorway into another world; that there probably are no other worlds. But for the moment, please put aside your need for realism and let me believe in this.

• • • •

At first Amber found the landscape of Mere to be desolate: rocks, the occasional scraggly tree, a pond. But if you become happy in a place, as she did, it will become beautiful to you. And she grew to love the land surrounding the village, despite its severity and barrenness.

There must have been fertile spots in that world, though Amber did not see them. The food—roots, grains, sometimes beans—arrived at the village weekly, delivered on a cart by a woman who did not speak a word. New robes, when someone required them, were left outside the person's door during the night. Honestly, what else was there? In the lazy afternoons, Amber lay on the bare ridges behind her home, arms spread out against the ground, and stared up at the stars, which were visible day and night. She wondered, *Is my old life circling one of those stars?* She didn't really care. The only time she ventured from the village was for a quest.

Here is how the quests worked: The village's matron chose who among them must go. The chosen ones donned traveling cloaks, mounted their horses, and rode into the northern mountains. They rode high enough to reach the caves, from which they snatched the silver cup, or the bronze cup engraved with the sun, or whatever cup the matron wanted that time. The precious items were always cups, and they were always taken from the lair of a monster who was never there. Upon their return to the village, the travelers tossed the cup ceremoniously into the corner of the matron's cabin, to be pulled out only for use at celebrations. But the cups were so enormous that whoever drank from them couldn't help but look foolish, and so no one ever wanted to drink from them.

What I'm trying to say is that life in Mere wasn't like it is in certain fantasy worlds, where such quests would be the whole point of one's existence.

Sometimes it seemed the purpose of Amber's life was to sit

with her back against the tree and Zef's head in her lap while she coaxed the pebbles around them to hum. As she stroked his hair, Zef changed into a being whose entire body was covered in eyes, most of them closed. A narrow vein pulsed across each eyelid. "Am I scaring you?" Zef asked. Every eye opened to look at her.

Eventually Amber did return to our world because of an accident, a tragedy, whatever you want to call it. She hadn't planned to ever come back, and upon her homecoming she fell apart and proceeded to waste years of her young-adult life crawling around the forest floor, crushing beetles out of frustration, not understanding that there were rules restricting how many times a portal could appear to someone: only twice. Not everybody knows this. Amber's mother finally convinced her to enroll at the local university, where she would discover anonymity and post-structuralism and a young man behind the library's reference desk who never took his knit hat off, as if he were hiding something under it. When he smiled at her, Amber made herself smile back.

On their second date she asked this young man, whose name was David, "What do you see when you look at me?" She imagined opening herself up for him, lifting each flap, as she once had for Zef.

"You're really, really sexy," David said, tilting his head and squinting at her, as if he were looking directly into a bare lightbulb. Unlike Amber, he wasn't a student. He worked at the library and owned a house in need of paint in a decent part of town.

On their third date, Amber asked him to take his hat off, and it turned out he was hiding nothing. His hair was brown and ordinary.

What would he have done if he had known she held the memory of another world inside her?

Soon Amber learned how to kiss David as if she wanted to be kissing him. It is not a waste to know how to do this. Pretending can be a bridge to feeling a certain way about people in your life. At least, that was once someone's advice to me.

On their eighth date, she told David about Mere. "Some people believe in God," she said. "I believe in this place."

David tried to play along at first. "Tell me more about this planet where you think you went," he would say. Was the food tasty there? Who ruled over the land? How did they make babies? What was considered bad there? Did Amber ever do any of these bad things? David asked such questions while they lay naked in bed, her head upon his shoulder. Depending on which details she told him, he sometimes became aroused. "Tell me again about that creature," he said. "That *Zef*." He suggested they act out certain scenes. It was fun, for him anyway, for a while.

Within a year they eloped to Barbados, where David wanted to visit as many of the island's beaches as they could. It turned out every beach looked identical, like a postcard picture of a beach. Upon their return, he insisted on carrying Amber into their bedroom. A box was waiting for her on her pillow. "You shouldn't have," she said. The box was white and cheap and not large. Amber opened it, expecting the kind of lingerie David liked, sheer with black ruffles, but it was empty.

"What is this?" she asked.

"Now is the time to put away our childish things," he replied. He'd grown tired of hearing stories about a place in which he would never have even a small part. "You can't go on believing in that stuff forever," he said. "There is a lot you can believe in, but not that."

They buried the box that evening, after she had supposedly placed in it all she remembered about Mere, including the time Zef had transformed into a being with gills, and she had watched, mesmerized, as the slits rhythmically widened and narrowed, widened and narrowed. David made a point of pretending to put a lot of his puerile dreams in the box too. (He said he was sorry but he could not tell her what they were.) Afterward he opened a bottle of champagne, and they drank it on the deck overlooking the garden, where they had buried the box beside the geraniums. "To our future," he said, clinking his glass against hers. He had fashioned a tombstone out of cardboard: HERE LIE ALL THE UNNECESSARY PARTS OF AMBER + DAVID R.I.P. The following morning, Amber crept outside and tore the stupid prop apart, then blamed it on the black squirrels.

"If you have to believe in something, why not believe in God?" David suggested.

Amber did not finish her degree.

They had a child together, a boy, Josh, who was pale and always hungry. Amber stayed put until he started preschool, then she wandered off into the woods north of town with the intent of either finding her way back to Mere or becoming permanently lost. The search party found her two days later, curled on the forest floor, naked. David took Amber's attempted desertion personally—and it was, in fact, personal. The couple might have separated shortly after that had it not been for a tiny orange pill I'll call Horiza, which Amber was prescribed to take once a day, preferably in the morning with a healthy, grain-free breakfast.

From the moment Horiza received FDA approval, pharmacists could barely keep it in stock. The pill was intended to make a person want whatever was in front of him or her. The side effects—possible insomnia and weight gain—seemed a fair trade-off for an assurance of contentment. David's brother was in pharmaceutical sales and could score samples of the drug when the supply was tight. One day David brought home a bag of the samples and spread them across the kitchen counter, each pill individually wrapped in bright orange packaging.

"That stuff in the past, that stuff you think you remember, the stuff that's not *here*—it's not going to matter anymore," David said. "You know what's going to matter? I'm going to matter. Your family is going to matter." To prove to her Horiza was harmless, he swallowed one of the pills, and for several hours afterward the creases between his eyebrows lessened, and he touched her more frequently. In fact, he touched her too much.

At David's insistence, Amber began taking a pill every morning. Sometimes it made her happy, as promised. Other times, particularly when the day's dose was wearing off, she felt frightened, as if she were forgetting something important. What was it? She remembered only fragments–the tree, falling, Zef–and then her present life rose up, shimmying its enormous hips and blocking everything else from view.

They had another child, a girl, Mia.

My God, you might be asking at this point, *shouldn't they give up already and call it quits?* But I think there are a lot of ways for two people to love each other. There are so many ways that I doubt we could identify all of them.

I ask my husband that if there were such a thing as a magic pill, why shouldn't he be the one to take it? "Maybe the problem is you," I say, which is probably unkind. We have begun to fast-forward the sex scenes in movies because they create an insufferable tension between us, and I have to let go of my husband's hand if I am holding it.

Actually, we did watch one sex scene in a recent movie that was unapologetically violent. I don't remember the title, but the plot concerned a man who is tortured overseas and then comes home to his wife. All his wife wants to do is caress his scars. Instead he grabs her and throws her onto their bed and fucks her in a brutal way, after which he rolls off her and falls asleep. The film wasn't halfway over when my husband stomped upstairs to bed. For the rest of the movie, the only way the man will have sex with his wife is to masturbate while looking at her naked body, during which time she has to lie completely still. They were supposed to still be in love with each other. I think they were. The camera work during those scenes is artful, beginning with a wide-angle shot from the far side of the room, so the husband and wife appear intimate and maybe even happy. Then the camera begins creeping in, and you realize what is going on.

Because we need to try something, we agree to try an open marriage for a month. My husband wastes no time. "I'm all set for Tuesday," he announces. Tomorrow is Tuesday. His voice is forcefully neutral, as if he has set up an appointment with the dentist.

On Tuesday night he puts on a decidedly unfashionable T-shirt with LOST IN SPACE spelled out in bubble letters on the front. Before he walks out the door, he wetly kisses the bottom of my ear and tells me he loves me. I don't know how one goes about setting up such appointments for sex, and I do not ask. I tuck the children into bed, kiss my daughter's cheek, and blow my son a kiss, which he does not acknowledge, as he no longer tolerates kisses or hugs. Then I climb into bed myself, exhausted. I don't know what time my husband returns because I am asleep, but he is there beside me the next morning. After he showers, which I insist upon so I can't smell whoever she was, he wishes to talk about his escapades. I tell him no; those are his, only his.

After two weeks of this, he believes he has fallen in love.

He asks, "Are you okay with all this?" He sounds worried, like he is not okay with it himself.

Perhaps it is more difficult than I thought to love multiple people at the same time.

The first time I wrote this story, I wasn't a part of it at all. The reader got to pretend the portal and Mere were real. My husband thinks that earlier draft was better.

• • • •

"Amber, are you taking your pills?" David asked.

"Are you accusing me of not taking my pills?" she replied.

"Yes, that's exactly what I'm doing."

"Why would you accuse me of something like that?"

"Because of how you're acting."

"Okay, tell me how I'm acting."

"Like you want to step on us." David gave an exaggerated frown and stomped clownishly around the room.

"I don't want to step on you. I don't want to step on anybody. That's ridiculous. What if this is just who I am?"

"I think I know who you are."

The following morning, before entering the kitchen to toast half a loaf of wheat bread for her family's breakfast, Amber flushed the orange pill down the toilet, as she had done each morning for the previous three weeks. Josh ate his toast with butter; David, with butter and honey; Mia, with grape jelly, only this morning the globs of jelly on her toast made Mia cry.

"You liked toast with jelly yesterday," Amber said.

"I do not like it at all," Mia wailed.

Amber cooked her daughter a sunny-side-up egg. This, too, made Mia cry because she could not bear to see the yolk.

"She's hurting my ears, Mom!" Josh complained.

Amber made another egg, scrambled this time, and Mia gobbled it up. "That was delicious, Mommy," she said, petting Amber's leg. By then it was a quarter to eight, which meant everyone would be late. When Amber handed out the lunches, Mia pledged she would refuse to eat even a bite if there was a vegetable inside. (There was.) Instead of kissing Amber goodbye, David bit the edge of her ear, a technique he must have read about in his forums. "I love you," he whispered. Looking over David's shoulder into the kitchen, Amber thought she saw a shadow move in the corner, a suggestion of an opening in the air itself.

There are many types of mothers in the world. One type of mother does not leave her family, no matter what. Another type does. Another type wants to leave but doesn't; she only thinks about leaving. Another type of mother tries unsuccessfully to leave.

That time Amber walked into the woods when Josh was three, she had not brought a backpack or a jacket or a map or a bottle of water or a bag of almonds. She drove along a dirt road in the forest south of the city until she ran out of gas, and then she left her car in the middle of the road, keys in the ignition, door open, and began walking. Later, David, unable to talk about it, would insist that none of this had happened, or it had happened to another woman, perhaps a character in a novel.

At first it was easy to walk in the woods; then it became more difficult. Amber had intentionally worn impractical shoes: strappy gold sandals. Each time the undergrowth in front of her grew too thick, she changed directions. At this point Amber still thought, wrongly, that portals must appear when people needed them. Black thorns left long scrapes on her arms. Her shirt snagged on one of the thorns and tore, so she took it off. She assumed the portal would be close to the ground, as it had been that second time, so that was where she looked, crouching to peer beneath bushes and running her hands under rock ledges. *Come out*, she pleaded. *Please come out.*

It wasn't just Zef. Everybody in Mere could change their form, Amber included, though she learned this gradually, as changing one's form in front of someone was considered an intimacy. How exactly it happened remained a mystery to her. All she knew was that when she and Zef were in a private place, such as beside the dry creek where the scrub grew, he changed into whatever she wanted him to be, though it was still his eyes looking out of whatever form he took. The sight of what she wanted sometimes surprised or even shocked her. How could anyone admit to themselves that they wanted this?

She did not always recognize the shapes she took either. She would glance down to see an animal form, or parts of her gone or hanging open. There was the time she became a furry creature, like an otter, while Zef remained who he was. (She looked back upon that last memory with equal parts revulsion and longing.) Or the time Zef became her, and she remained herself. Such transformations required the use of one's limited supply of magic, but Amber and Zef couldn't help themselves. When she became a pool of water, Zef laughed, scooped her up, and took a sip.

No other world glimmered for her when she was in Mere. If she turned her head, she did not get the sense that there was a better life just out of reach.

Because people barely aged in that world, it was difficult to estimate the passing of years except by one's dwindling magic, which was not discussed. There were not even seasons. There were only the days she spent with Zef in the village, and then the times when she and Zef went on a quest.

It was on their return from one such quest, a trip to the northern mountains to obtain yet another cup (a pewter one this time), that Amber found herself beside a grove of trees—unusual, as this landscape didn't accommodate such growth. There was something familiar about these woods, an underlying suggestion of meaning.

"I have a bad feeling about this place," Zef said.

"You have a bad feeling about every place that's not our village," Amber laughed; in that world, everything she said came out as laughter. Zef grabbed her arm but was unable—or unwilling—to hold on to her.

She kept laughing as she ran off toward the trees. "Try and catch me," she shouted over her shoulder. The moment she entered the shade, taking her first heavy step back into this world, her cloak got caught on the rough edge of the portal and ripped. She heard the fabric tear, but by the time she turned around to go back, it was too late. There was no portal behind her, only a clearing in the woods beside her high school, where the birds sang out of boredom.

Many years later, stuck in one world (this one) but conscious of the existence of another world–it is difficult to imagine a worse situation to be in–Amber told David, "I don't want to be here anymore."

That was an understatement for sure: she had never wanted to be here.

David forced a chuckle. The children were somewhere else–probably outside in the yard. "Where do you want to go?" he asked. "Wait, I have an idea. How about I take you to Indiana!"

This was an old and unfunny joke between them, as Indiana, an hour's drive east, marked the nearest state border. They used to pretend everything would be so different there.

They didn't go to Indiana. Instead, David suggested increasing her dosage.

"Is it such a terrible thing to want me?" he asked. "What would you be giving up if you wanted me?"

There are all sorts of ways to leave your family. Women apparently do it all the time. When I read about one, I add her name to a list I keep in the back of my notebook, and beside each name I write down how the woman left. You probably have not heard of most of these women: Tiffany Tehan or Stacey Hessler, for example. I don't think they stopped loving their families. You don't have to be present to keep loving somebody. You don't even have to be alive. Some mothers who leave sit in lukewarm bubble baths and slit their wrists. I have written down their names too. Other women have walked off into the woods, some not wearing clothing. None of them planned to turn around. I certainly didn't. I wonder if we wouldn't all have been better off becoming different people.

I say to my husband, "What if this isn't my actual life? What if my real life is going on in some other place, and I'm not there to see it?" My husband tries to laugh. "I don't want to be here anymore," I say. The kids aren't in the room with us. I don't know where they are.

He stops laughing. "Where do you want to go? Indiana? I bet things will be different there. Sure, we can all go to Indiana." It is an old and unfunny joke. We did actually drive once to Indiana, passing by all the decaying mills to reach the dunes. You'd think we would go more often as it's only an hour's drive. The day was windy and overcast with low-hanging clouds. The children cried when the wind blew sand onto their sandwiches. They wanted to ride a Jet Ski, but there was nowhere to rent one, so they scurried up and down the dunes, ignoring the KEEP OFF signs. We were probably causing some type of irreversible erosion.

Horiza, it was said, not only blocked old impractical longings: it could permanently erase memories if the dosage was high enough. This time the dosage would be high enough.

Before Amber began to take the pills again, she went out into the yard after dinner and lay in the hammock with the intention of letting herself remember Mere for the last time. Mia and Josh were elsewhere in the yard. She could hear them yelping as they took turns throwing a stick at each other. The wind in her hair felt like a hand touching her hair. She closed her eyes and remembered falling and Zef standing over her, gazing upon her as if he had known her all of his life, known what she once had been, what she was now, and what she would someday become, and he loved each of these versions equally and fully. The memory was so clear, it was as if she were there. Laughing, he picked her up and held her in his arms, which smelled like pond water and dirt. He held her roughly. It felt as if an animal were holding her, or as if she were an animal being held, but she was not afraid.

The part of the other world where they stood was full of afternoon sunlight and yellow trees. In the tree from which she'd fallen, a black bird shook open its wings and sung with warbling sorrow, as if it knew something they didn't. Zef scared the bird off with a well-aimed rock.

"I don't know why they have to sing like that," he said.

Zef told Amber he had seen her that afternoon many years before, when she'd been six and had run around the tree only once, mistaking the world for empty. He had been waiting for her ever since. Practically every day he had walked to the tree to see if he could find her. And now here she was. ("Couldn't you have come to get me?" she would later ask. He wouldn't answer.) He took her hand and led her down the path to the village, and there her life began—or, rather, it continued on as if it always had been waiting for her.

Amber rose from the hammock and went inside. The next morning, with David anxiously watching, she took the larger pill.

David said, "You look happy. Are you happy? I think you're happy."

We are in bed, my husband and I, my head resting upon his shoulder, my hand on his stomach, which has grown softer and hairier over the years.

"So what was it like?" he asks.

Our bedroom is filled with a humid and attentive darkness.

We have decided to try something different tonight. I will pretend to be someone else. My husband will pretend to be someone else. And we will see what happens. "Who do you want me to be?" my husband asked before we began. I had no idea. He did his best. I tried to shelter my mind elsewhere (dunes, lake, prairie, park, pond, cattails, cloud, sky). The whole time it felt like I was being held underwater, albeit tenderly. Perhaps I'll get used to it someday. So what if I'm not the person I actually am. At least I'm the person someone wants me to be. For the first time in a long while, my husband is hopeful about us. I decide not to use words like *suffocating* or *drowning* tonight. Instead I respond to his question vaguely. "You know how it is when you wake up from a dream, and you can't remember it, and you really wish you could?"

"Let's talk about something real," he says.

Tick, tock, time to grow up.

Petting my hair, he asks if I would like some chamomile tea or maybe a midnight snack. It is not the worst thing in the world to be asked such a question. He wonders aloud if there is still a bowl of hummus in the fridge. I tell him I believe there is. "It's our lucky day then," he says, proposing a sandwich with the addition of pickles and sliced tomato. Such a sandwich sounds like exactly what I want. He wraps a flannel robe around his body and slips out of the room. I lie on my back in our bed. I lie very still. I do not look out the window, nor do I want to.

I wonder if I'll ever properly finish writing Amber's story. I think if I did, I would break that rule I made up long ago, back when I thought I needed to keep her here for dramatic purposes. It turns out a third portal (I would write) may appear to someone in times of great need and special circumstance. This is not a common occurrence (I would write). In fact this happened only once in the history of time, it happened to Amber, and I would end the story right there, as she is about to step through her portal into Mere, though I would make it clear that she is planning on staying there forever and ever. What is the rationale for holding on so tightly to the places and people who don't want us? Amber shakes her head. Wrong question. Here is the better question: Why, she asks me, hold on so tightly to the places and people we don't want? Worlds should let us leave them. Now that would be a happy ending, if I was the sort of writer to write stories with happy endings.

I can hear my husband downstairs in the kitchen, opening a cabinet, closing a cabinet. Outside, a procession of cars are either going or coming from somewhere. A neighbor parks his pickup at the curb, the motor idling, a breeze, a knock, the long notes of a bird that sounds lost—and underneath all that I notice the building up of an unfamiliar sound, like the sound I imagine light would make if light moving through air could make a sound. Crystalline and sharp. The sound appears to be radiating out of the far corner of the room. More specifically, the sound—I push myself up from the bed to get a better look—appears to be radiating from a rip in the air that hangs beside my husband's painted dresser. Two feet high, three feet across, the tear is jagged, as if the cut was made hastily with a blunt object, its border perspiring and feverish. To look through the opening is like peering through a drape of transparent velvet. On the other side, faint yet still visible, I can see a tree, a path, a hill, a village, a forest. The smell of dirt and pond. A moment passes before I realize what I'm looking at and where I'm looking.

It turns out that it's easy to make a fictional character go through a portal. It is child's play. I should have done this long ago. Watch: *Amber walked back through the portal into Mere*—there, it happened, she's gone for good. It is more difficult to go through a portal if you are real. But I want to tell you it isn't impossible.

To stand at the edge of two divergent worlds, to be pulled in two opposing directions with what feels like, at first, equal force. To feel like I have a choice. I could go here or there, I could be with these people or with those people. I always knew it was wrong to call me desireless. Sometimes people have desires so strong that they can affect the shape of reality.

Walking through a portal is nothing like I thought it would be: now that would make an interesting beginning.

I feel wings brush my shoulder.

STORY NOTES

One of the indisputably vital roles of the modern reader is to tease out what is autobiographically true for the fiction writer versus what that writer made up in their stories. What is fiction after all if not a porthole into the author's private life? So allow me to get this out of the way: Everything you've read in *Portalmania* (or will read, depending on your preferred order) actually happened to me. The portals, the lack of portals, the witches, the monsters, the ghosts, the murders, the space travel of beloved family members—every story in this collection is a factual account of my own experience. And now that you know this, I can spend the remaining space of these notes discussing whatever I want.

The Promise of a Portal

What I want, in this case, is apparently to discuss my childhood.

During my childhood I wanted, like many children I presume, at least the ones who read fantasy books, to go through a portal into another world. I wanted this very badly, as badly as a child could want anything. This wanting to find a portal set me up for a lot of disappointment and heartbreak but it is also one of the earliest reasons I fell in love with books. It is also one of the reasons I became a writer. For what is a book if not a portal, and what is writing if not the ripping apart of reality to reach a truer reality?

This particular story came out of a time when my kids were in elementary school and I realized they weren't being taught to fear the same things I had been taught during my own childhood to fear. I grew up in the 1980s, when everybody was afraid of stranger danger and children vanishing from public places—see the 1983 TV movie *Adam*—so from a young age my classmates and I were instructed to beware of any cars slowing down and any friendly-looking men who would lower the windows of those cars, offer us candy, and beckon us to get in. Even more dangerous than these cars were the vans because, presumably, they could hold more children in the back. Propped in the front window of my suburban childhood house was a sign declaring that we were a safe house. In my memory we were a safe house sponsored by Ronald McDonald, which sounds odd to me now, and I can find no other mention of this online, though my mom says such a program seems familiar and she thinks it was run through our neighborhood's homeowner association. In any case, what this sign meant: that if a child was being followed by one of those men in one of those cars or, God forbid, by a van, the frightened child could knock on our door and we would protect them. The sign was a constant reminder of the possibility that any one of us could be taken away at any moment.

Inside of such memories, I became curious about a few things: What if those vans of my childhood had been driven by women? And what if the narrator wanted to be taken? Thank you to Steve Cariddi for naming this story.

How to Kiss a Hojacki

According to the internet, several people did not like this story when it was originally published in *Fantasy & Science Fiction*. Two of them were reviewers for online genre outlets; another was a reader who posted his thoughts in response to one of the reviews. Most online reviews, in my experience, seem to judge a story or a book by how closely it aligns with the reader's unstated preferences and expectations; these reviews of "How to Kiss a Hojacki" were no exception. I find such reviews to be unhelpful as both a writer and a reader. Much more interesting to me is the insight that a reviewer or a reader gains when they connect with a work. I feel like, in general, we understand the things we love better than we understand the things we dislike.

When I first started publishing in genre magazines years ago, I was surprised at the heightened and public discourse that took place online around genre short stories (a reader, for instance, once called a story of mine on Twitter "an apologetic for the abuse and murder of disabled children"). This was quite a change from my previous experience publishing in literary journals, where public discussion, if it happened at all, was generally favorable or at least benign. I questioned whether I wanted to be involved in the genre community as a writer. But then a kind editor of a genre magazine offered me some helpful reframing. He pointed out that such strong reactions to a story often mean that the reader has been pushed out of their comfort zone. He told me that there's a place in genre for fun stories that feel comfortable but, likewise, there needs to be a place for uncomfortable stories that challenge us as readers.

I wrote this story in 2018, though it's hard for me to reread George Kloburcher's suggestion/non-suggestion of violence without thinking of the January 6, 2021, attack on the Capitol.

Long May My Land Be Bright

I live on the east side of Syracuse, New York, among a mostly liberal collection of people. Eighty-four percent of voters in my precinct voted for Hillary Clinton in the 2016 election, 88 percent voted for Joe Biden in 2020, and a house a few blocks over with Trump signs that year elicited much curiosity and several local news articles. But when I get out of the city into the surrounding hills where I do a lot of hiking, Trump paraphernalia quickly becomes the norm along with the occasional Confederate flag. A political divide between urban and rural settings is unsurprising, but over the past decade I've sensed these old divides widening and new divides beginning among previously like-minded groups. As some of my friends went out and joined protests and marches, I was curious about my own inaction, which felt, in the end, like a form of observation. What is the role of an observer in politically fraught times? Is that even a legitimate role? I wondered what it might look like if our political differences took on a more physical presence than signs and flags. I decided to set this story in Marcellus, a picturesque town west of Syracuse where, in one of the town's voting precincts, 46 percent of voters voted for Clinton and 46 percent of voters voted for Trump in 2016. If you'd like to read another story inspired by the politics of those years, check out "An Incomplete Timeline of What We Tried" on Vice.com (or look at page 267 in the hardcover version of my novel *After World*).

LK-32-C

My favorite book about parenthood—and the one I think everyone should read, regardless of whether you have kids or not—is *Far from the Tree: Parents, Children, and the Search for Identity* by Andrew Solomon. It's a 976-page book about the experience of parents raising a child who is different from them, and it's well worth the time. Here's one of the many passages I highlighted in my copy:

> No one loves without reservation, however, and everyone would be better off if we could destigmatize parental ambivalence. Freud posits that any declaration of love masks some degree of odium, any hatred at least a trace of adoration. All that children can properly require of their parents is that they tolerate their own muddled spectrum—that they neither insist on the lie of perfect happiness nor lapse into the slipshod brutality of giving up. One mother who lost a child with a serious disability worried in a letter to me that if she felt relieved, her grief was not real. There is no contradiction between loving someone and feeling burdened by that person; indeed, love tends to magnify the burden. These parents need space for their ambivalence, whether they can allow it for themselves or not. For those who love, there should be no shame in being exhausted—even in imagining another life.

I also strongly recommend *NeuroTribes: The Legacy of Autism and the Future of Neurodiversity* by Steve Silberman; *Drawing Autism*, edited by Jill Mullin; *The Reason I Jump: The Inner Voice of a Thirteen-Year-Old Boy with Autism* by Naoki Higashida; *Born on a Blue Day: Inside the Extraordinary Mind of an Autistic Savant* by Daniel Tammet; and *With the Light: Raising an Autistic Child* by Keiko Tobe, all of which I read while working on "LK-32-C."

A Few Personal Observations on Portals

I've been questioned more than once about whether the people in my stories are conversing, interacting, and loving in realistic ways. I've also been asked why the couples in some of my stories would still insist on staying together. Such questioning has always felt strange to me as I'm generally writing from observation supplemented with research. I wonder if this disconnect comes from a certain type of relationship tending to be examined in our fictions, making many readers uncomfortable or unfamiliar with the variety of ways there are to exist inside a relationship. When looking back at correspondence around the time "A Few Personal Observations on Portals" was first published, it appears that I found it necessary to explain my story's characters. Here's an excerpt from an email I wrote about the narrator and her husband:

> The relationship may still appear strange or unfamiliar to some readers, but I do think the relationship is an accurate portrayal of a couple in a mixed-orientation marriage trying to stay married . . . It's very much a love in transition. The holding of hands, the sitting beside each other, the acknowledgment of a shared history, comforting each other when children leave–it's a small subtle love mixed in with a lot of anger, resentment, feelings of betrayal, and manipulation, while the couple is trying to figure things out. This period of time can last for months, years, or the rest of the marriage. I'm drawing from my own experience as well as research I've done, as I'm interested in portraying these kinds of relationships in my writing.

The Dirty Golden Yellow House

The stories in this collection were written over a span of eight years. "The Portal" was the earliest story, written in 2015, and "The Dirty Golden Yellow House" was the most recent, completed in 2022. Should you want to read more about the topics covered in this piece, I'd recommend the following books and articles.

- Diana E. H. Russell, *Rape in Marriage* (Bloomington: Indiana University Press, 1990)
- Joanna Bourke, *Rape: Sex, Violence, History* (Emeryville, CA: Shoemaker & Hoard, 2007)
- A. Norwood and C. Murphy, "What Forms of Abuse Correlate with PTSD Symptoms in Partners of Men Being Treated for Intimate Partner Violence?," *Psychological Trauma* 4, no. 6 (2012): 596–604
- H. M. Zinzow and M. Thompson, "Factors Associated with Use of Verbally Coercive, Incapacitated, and Forcible Sexual Assault Tactics in a Longitudinal Study of College Men," *Aggressive Behavior* 41, no. 1 (January 2015): 34–43
- Eden Strong, "When Does 'Yes' Not Mean 'Yes'?," Bustle.com, April 16, 2015, https://www.bustle.com/articles/67926-is-it-rape-if-you-say-yes-5-types-of-sexual-coercion-explained
- René Brooks, "Sexual Coercion Is the Rape No One Wants to Recognize," Black Girl, Lost Keys, January 8, 2016, https://blackgirllostkeys.com/trauma/sexual-coercion
- Anonymous, "Coercive Sex in Marriage: Her Story," Ashley Easter, June 3, 2016, https://www.ashleyeaster.com/blog/coercive-sex-in-marriage-her-story
- Anonymous, "We Need to Talk about Sexual Assault in Marriage," Vox.com, March 8, 2018, https://www.vox.com/first-person/2018/3/8/17087628/sexual-assault-marriage-metoo

Thank you to John Joseph Adams and Wendy Wagner for suggesting the current beginning and for also publishing this unconventional story in *Lightspeed*.

Hysteria

My good friend Sarah Harwell recommended a few years back that I revisit Ernest Hemingway's "Hills Like White Elephants." I was surprised to hear Hemingway's name mentioned. I had read him in high school but he hadn't come up since. But Sarah has good taste in books so I read Hemingway's story as directed. Then I read it again. Then I read it again. I kept reading it. This was the start of my love affair with dialogue-heavy stories. Soon I moved on to reading plays. I was pleasantly surprised to find that most plays work powerfully when read (excluding, perhaps, Samuel Beckett's *Happy Days*, which is nearly unreadable but still worth reading). "Hysteria" was written amid all this excitement over dialogue. If you're looking for some good plays to read, I'd recommend Eugene O'Neill's *Long Day's Journey into Night*; anything by Tennessee Williams; *The Trials* by Dawn King; and *4.48 Psychosis* by Sarah Kane. Also check out the excellent productions on YouTube from the year 2000 of Samuel Beckett's *Endgame* and *Happy Days*.

Sarah Harwell also suggested the current ending to "Hysteria," so this story owes her a lot.

Some Personal Arguments in Support of the BetterYou (Based on Early Interactions)

You may have noticed there are a lot of therapists in this collection. There used to be more: originally seven out of the ten stories had therapists in them. But, as my editor, Tim, wisely said, "Yeah, that is too many therapists." Therapists have been a part of my life since I was eighteen, and I've found individual therapy, group therapy, family therapy, and a yearlong dialectical behavior therapy program to be immensely helpful and frequently lifesaving. What I have not found helpful in any way has been couples therapy, which I would describe as dangerous, destructive, traumatic, and wrong (and I think BetterYou's narrator would agree with me). I considered dedicating this entire collection as follows, but decided that might set the wrong tone so I'll just bury this alternate dedication here:

To my couples therapists
who, for many years, charged me a lot of money
to destroy my identity and my life in fifty-minute increments—
thank you for giving me so much to write about

The Portal

I remember it was a big deal when *The Sun* magazine first accepted this story at the end of 2015, as it was the first time I had used the words *asexual* or *asexuality* in my writing. Here's what I wrote in an email to Carol Ann Fitzgerald, one of the *Sun*'s editors: "I also just wanted to let you know, on a personal note, how mind-blowing it is that *The Sun* will be publishing a story on asexuality. It seems asexuality is starting to be talked about in the press and online these days, which is great, but I still haven't seen it emerge in our fiction yet. It will be kind of huge (for me at least and hopefully others) to see an alternative to the usual relationship dynamics appear in a magazine like yours with such a strong readership."

Thankfully there's more representation of asexuality in popular media now, particularly in genre stories, and there have been several strong nonfiction examinations as well, my favorite being Angela Chen's *Ace: What Asexuality Reveals About Desire, Society, and the Meaning of Sex*. I know the world would be a better place for everyone if everyone read this book in its entirety, but while I wait for that to happen, let me quote one of my favorite passages here:

> . . . the potential of the ace [shorthand for asexual] movement is greater than aces being more visible in the culture and more important than aces proving that, except for this one

thing, we're just like everyone else. As CJ Chasin, the activist, has said, aces push the envelope. Once it is okay for aces to never have sex, it becomes more acceptable for everyone else who isn't ace too. Ace liberation will help everyone.

It comes in rejecting sexual and romantic normalcy in favor of carefully considered sexual and romantic ethics. The meaning of sex is always changing and the history of sexuality is complex. Compulsory sexuality and asexuality have changed across time and place; they can, and will, change again. The goal, at least to me, is that one day neither the *DSM* criteria nor asexuality-as-identity will be necessary. It will be easy to say yes or no or maybe—to sexuality, to romantic relationships—without coercion, without further justification, without needing a community to validate that answer. Sexual variety will be a given and social scripts will be weakened; sex will be decommodified.

The goal of ace liberation is simply the goal of true sexual and romantic freedom for everyone. A society that is welcoming to aces can never be compatible with rape culture; with misogyny, racism, ableism, homophobia, and transphobia; with current hierarchies of romance and friendship; and with contractual notions of consent. It is a society that respects choice and highlights the pleasure that can be found everywhere in our lives. I believe that all this is possible.

A final note: When this story was originally published in *The Sun*, it had a different ending in which the narrator never finds a portal and is stuck in this world and in her life forever. My editor, Tim, wondered what would happen if I gave the narrator her portal and she went through. This was, hands down, one of the most thrilling and satisfying revisions I've ever worked on.

Thank you

To my agent, Kate Garrick;

To my editor, Tim O'Connell;

To the team at Simon & Schuster, especially Anna Hauser, Crystal Watanabe, Morgan Hart, Lewelin Polanco, and Math Monahan.

To the editors who first published the stories in this collection: John Joseph Adams and Wendy Wagner from *Lightspeed*; C. C. Finlay from *Fantasy & Science Fiction*; Lila Garrott from *Strange Horizons*; Carolyn Kuebler and Emily Mitchell from *New England Review*; Emily Nemens from *The Southern Review*; Sy Safransky, Andrew Snee, and all the good people at *The Sun*; and Ronald Spatz from *Alaska Quarterly Review*;

To the Rona Jaffe Foundation and the Constance Saltonstall Foundation for the Arts;

To the generic versions of Prozac and Wellbutrin;

To Kayla Blatchley, Sarah Harwell, and Devon Moore for their feedback on several of these stories;

To my WAB and ideal reader, Steve Cariddi;

To my WAGs Christen Aragoni, Tina May Hall, Sarah Harwell, Jennifer Hudak, Matt Meade, and Laura Williams;

To the SUNY Upstate Dialectical Behavioral Therapy (DBT) program;

To Jasper, who named this collection;

To Harold, for giving me the privacy and trust to write what I want, a true sign of love;

and to Stella, who has always wanted to fly: I wrote this last story for you.

CODA

Your father tells me he wants to turn your bedroom—the empty bedroom, he calls it, as he has stopped talking about you and will not say your name—into a guest room. Except when was the last time anyone visited us here at the edge of the city?

Perhaps your room should be a second-floor den, he suggests.

"There is too much light in that room for a den," I tell him.

We gave you the brightest room in the house, you know.

"Then what should the room become?" he asks.

"I was thinking we should leave it as it is, with the window open and the screen removed."

"That is a very bad idea," your father says. He insists the windows remain closed and locked, as if you are now unwelcome, a destructive force.

• • • •

Are you a destructive force?

"I love you as you are *now*," I told you when the only difference I could see was a turquoise hue to your skin, to your forehead in particular, and your neck.

Can you remember that I told you this?

"So . . . what? You won't love me after I've changed?" you asked, rubbing your hand, which was still a hand then.

I didn't answer.

The reason I didn't answer is: I'm not sure love works like that. Love—not just my love but anybody's—can't possibly apply to all the potential forms a person, even a daughter, might take. Can it?

This is love's failure of vision, not mine.

You used to look like me. Can you remember that too?

Early on I thought about wiping your memory. I might as well admit this to you now. I thought maybe if you stopped believing you were something else on the inside, then you wouldn't be sad anymore. And you wouldn't change. This was before your body began to transform.

The only reason I didn't go through with a memory wipe was the cost, which was prohibitive.

• • • •

At one point you left a guide for parents on my side of the bed. This was after that fringed scarf you always wore no longer hid the scales on your chest. There were too many for you to cover now. The guide was a list of dos and don'ts. (The list of don'ts was substantially longer.) We were not to ask *What is wrong with you?* or *Why are you changing?* or *When can I drive you to the doctor?* or *What is happening to your fingernails?* or *What about having children?* or *What about being happy?* or *What about being normal?*

"If you badger your changing child with such aggressive questioning," advised the guide, "your child will flee into the trees and never be seen again."

Your father and I asked you such questions anyway. We sat you down one afternoon in our spotless kitchen, which has always been your least favorite room of the house, and we asked you these questions and more. I thought it was our right, as parents, to ask. Your skin, sparkling in the sunlight, was distracting. Your answers were brief or vague, if you answered at all.

"I'll never want children," you said.

"Just you wait," I replied, thinking you surely would, later on, as I had.

The next morning, you sprang away from me into the old silver maple in our yard. Up you climbed effortlessly, scattering the squirrels. I thought you might not come back down.

I was lonely, watching you climb higher into the tree, ignoring the branches that tore at your hair. Your father had left for a business trip. The suitcase he had taken with him was extremely large, as if he would be away for a long time. Perhaps I should have texted him a video of you clinging to the tree's crown. Or would he have deleted it?

In any case, before I could take a picture, you took flight.

So she can fly now, I thought.

I know it is no longer supposed to be extraordinary to see those of your generation flying—and whatever else you do.

Many mothers in our neighborhood remain inside these days and stare ashamedly and hopefully out their windows in the direction of the sky. They call to each other from their porches and take turns speaking their daughters' names.

You were beautiful when you flew, your sinuous, veined wings extended for the first time, your blue-green skin trailing behind you.

Or maybe it wasn't your skin. I don't know how to describe you anymore. I'm told the younger generation is growing disinterested in maintaining a stable form.

You were beautiful to me too, many years ago, when you sat close to me in the kitchen and shared a quiet dinner of pasta garnished with cut tomatoes, when you were still wingless and looked like a little girl. When you *were* a girl.

• • • •

Couldn't there be something dazzling and worthwhile in such a simple memory, in its ordinariness and lack of fire and magic?

You didn't need to grow wings to be beautiful.

"I was never a girl," you said to me, despite the photographs I stacked in front of you, my piles of proof.

"What were you, then?" I asked.

"I was something else," you said.

"But you didn't look like something else," I reminded you. "You looked like a girl. You looked like my child."

"I was never your child, not really."

I don't think all your answers to my questions were correct.

In the old stories, the myths, your sort of transformation would have happened through a curse. You might have angered a god, and that god might have turned you into something else, some sort of animal, a swan or a cow. I would have preferred that. I could have learned how to care for a cow. People would have understood and pitied me, and you as well.

Rarely have I heard any myths about a young woman choosing to turn into something unrecognizable all on her own.

We were not in need of a new type of story, you know.

I burned the parents' guide in the fireplace in our family room while you were crouched in the tree. Then I considered wiping my own memory. But of course, we didn't have money for that either.

I might have been able to change too, you know, in less dramatic ways, at an earlier point in my life. But I did what was expected of me.

There is something to be said for doing what is expected of us, for becoming what is expected.

Another time I saw you hunched behind the garage beside the compost pile, engaged in some repetitive action that I didn't understand, doing something with your—with whatever replaced your hands.

It looked as if you were digging. You were digging with frustration and urgency. I didn't know how to help, so I knelt beside you. Eventually I dug with you. Can you remember this—that there was nothing buried in the soil? We found nothing. Then I reached out and touched a part of you, a leftover part of who you had been.

I had always wanted a daughter. I used to think, *As my daughter grows, I will have so much to share with her. I will teach her how to watch, without sadness, the afternoon light fade in the kitchen. I will teach her to apologize when it isn't her fault to keep the peace in her house.* And how to rub away a child's growing pains in the dark. And how to make promises you always intended to keep. And the comfort that comes with knowing one's future for the rest of one's life.

. . . .

What can I teach you in your current state? What do you need to know that I can tell you?

We did not have much to talk about, even in the beginning. Can you at least try to remember our silences as comfortable? I did my best to fill the silence between us with love.

This is not about my love anymore, is it?

"This is not about you at all," you have said to me.

But I am the one telling the story. Try to remember that.

It's only fair that the person who is left behind gets to tell the story.

This is a very different story, I know, than the one you would tell.

You had begun to stand in front of the wall mirror in my bedroom without a shirt on. This was around the time you turned twelve. The scales had not yet emerged, and your skin was not yet discolored, so I assumed, wrongly, that you were taking note of how puberty was affecting your body. I wanted to sit you down and tell you about the changes that were happening, so you would not fumble blindly into sexual maturity, as I had. When I asked "What do you know about how pregnancy happens?" you walked to the other side of the room.

"That doesn't apply to me, Mom," you said from the doorway.

"Oh, girls your age, they all say that sort of thing at first," I assured you.

Several times I tried to restart the conversation, but you refused to engage with me. You wanted to talk instead about what you saw when you looked in the mirror.

You said you saw two wings extending from your upper back.

You asked what I saw when I looked at myself in the mirror. Did I have wings?

I did not have wings.

You asked, "Do you see *my* wings?"

I did not yet see yours, though at times I thought I could feel them.

I wonder if I didn't make my life appear fascinating enough for you. If your changes were a reaction to what you presumed was stifling boredom on my part. If you assumed, because I wanted you to have my life, that this was the only kind of life available.

Should I have been more upbeat about the duties of a mother? Should I have worn more festive clothing, more gold necklaces? Should your father and I have gone after each other in a corner of the kitchen?

"Let's look like who we really are. Let's stop pretending!" you told me early on, before I understood what was happening.

"You're pretending?" I asked.

"Aren't you?" you said.

Throughout my life, I never expected to turn into anything else, to be transformed.

You: "It started internally, like a distancing. It was not unpleasant."

Me: "So it *was* pleasant?"

You: "I didn't mind it."

Me: "You should have minded it."

Here is a worry: When you are fully changed and there is nothing of me left in you, how will I pick you out from the flock of others swarming in the trees?

The sky right now is quiet without you in it.

We threw you a party, with sliced oranges and alcoholic punch for the parents, and platters of whatever you were eating then for you and your friends. I didn't want to host such a celebration, but I did, because the other mothers were doing the same for their daughters: a hastily improvised rite of passage. It was expected. And you'd told me you wanted a party.

Some of your friends were farther along than you. They perched on our roof and screeched and called out. Others flaunted their changes like velvety capes. So many yellow-irised eyes, so many scaly underbellies and diaphanous wings. And you, nibbling at a black walnut that you held between your elongated fingertips. "Thank you," you whispered before your party ended, not smiling but not running away either, your breath earthy and bitter.

I am telling you all this because I don't think you remember.

If you remembered, I think you would at least look in my direction from time to time.

I think you believe you were born the way you are now, a thousand feet above me.

Try to remember.

In the evenings I have begun walking around the neighborhood, along the border of the scrawny woods, the same path you and I used to take together when you were a child, over the creek and back again. Now, with all the young people flapping above, and the women my age trembling below—our hands dirty and nails ragged, as if we have been digging—I often don't recognize where I am.

I know what you would say: Not all losses are sad. Some things we are meant to lose.

"I want to be understood," you said.

"That might not be possible," I told you.

• • • •

I am telling you all this so you will know that you once lived on the ground and slept in a yellow canopy bed. The canopy had ruffles around the edge. It was a childish bed, and you always seemed too old for it. You had a father, and you had me.

I watched you one morning in the yard, flapping your translucent wings, which reflected the rising sun. They looked as if they were made of glass, as if they might break if I tapped them. I didn't come out of the house. I stayed inside, not wanting to startle you. There was a fluidity, a calmness in your movements, and a certainty. As your wings swept harder, you lifted off the ground, then higher and higher until you joined one of the flocks that throbbed and twisted in the air. I wanted to see your face, but you were turned toward the neighbor's yard, and then you became too small for me to see.

I wish somebody could convince me this was supposed to happen to you.

Listen: you don't have to keep moving farther away. You don't have to leave these woods for some other woods, who knows where.

Mrs. Nebus down the street—do you remember her?—she kept her changing daughter in their backyard, in chains, behind a fence. I don't know what the daughter was chained to, perhaps a stake hammered into the ground. On my walks I used to hear the girl thudding against the wooden fence. Sometimes, above the stained cedar, I glimpsed the tip of a wing.

The chain broke, eventually.

I'm told that at some point soon there will be more of your type and less of mine.

What will you do to us, when there are enough of you?

"You were meant to lose me," you said. "You were meant to watch me fly far, far away."

Yesterday I searched for you in the woods behind our house. Your father pretended not to know what I was doing. "Have a nice walk," he said as he weeded the yard, eyes down.

I felt like I was searching for an animal. I couldn't find you, though I saw where you must have spent some recent night: an indentation in the dead leaves, a kind of nest marked with loose tufts of your hair. I lay down there and slept.

When I was your age, everyone I knew wanted to go through a portal. I did too. We were always looking for circlets of gold energy strung in a tree or a curtain of beaded light tucked under the stairs. But lately I've been wondering if such a definition of escape, a definition that has been around for centuries, has become an outdated idea. Why should you have to leave? You are already doing impossible things. Let the world, *this* world, I imagine you demanding of the world, expand to encompass every part of you.

• • • •

Today I was raking in the yard, and it was growing late, and I looked up and thought I saw you gliding east, toward an area of the sky that had already darkened. Your wings flapped lazily, and a gauzy trail of turquoise skin–or whatever it was–swirled around your uncovered chest. You did not look back.

You were my child up there. You were a movement in the sky, a flash of reflected light. You were a terrifying and wide-open future.

About the Author

Debbie Urbanski is the author of the novel *After World*. Her stories and essays have been published widely in such places as *The Best American Science Fiction and Fantasy*, *Best American Experimental Writing*, *The Sun* magazine, *Granta*, *The Kenyon Review*, and *Junior Great Books*. Her writing has also been named notable stories/essays of the year for *The Best American Short Stories*, *The Best American Essays*, *The Best American Science and Nature Writing*, and *The Best American Mystery Stories* anthologies. A recipient of a Rona Jaffe Writer's Award, she can often be found hiking with her family in the hills south of Syracuse, New York.

About the Type

The body text of this book is set in Richmond Text, a serif font designed by Matthew Carter originally intended for use in a major daily British newspaper. Today, the Richmond type family, with its pleasing contours and wide range of weights, is perfectly suited to all forms of editorial typography.

The display font is Barlow, and the title page is set in Qualy Neue. Barlow was designed by Jeremy Tribby, and its slightly rounded, low-contrast appearance was inspired by the style of California's public transportation and signage. Qualy Neue, a much bolder and more geometric font by Shina Design, has an ultramodern, ambitious look perfect for titles and headlines.